A Stand-in for Dying

A Stand-in for Dying

Book 1: Brink of Life Trilogy

Rick Moskovitz

Illustration and design by Mary Verrandeaux

FLUKE TALE PRODUCTIONS

Table of Contents

Preface

As I watch the current generation of young adults assume their leadership roles in our culture, I see once again the youthful illusion of immortality and invincibility, this time with a twist. The Singularity is close upon us and with it the prospect, at least in the eyes of the young, that life everlasting is within their grasp. And I wonder, given the temptation to extend life indefinitely, how the choices will be made and at what price the reality of immortality might come.

Rick Moskovitz
October 2019

We die only once, and for such a long time!

Le Dépit Amoureux

Molière 1656

Prologue

NOBODY WOULD ever choose this death.

The limbs of the passenger in the wreck were intertwined with the twisted carbon fiber frame of the hovercar. The human form and the vehicle looked as if they had been woven together by a cosmic pair of hands into a permanent and painful embrace.

Nearby stood another man, much younger and more robust than the dead man. Except for the blood on his face and arms, his skin had the pristine appearance of those select few who had undergone the Ambrosia Conversion, but his musculature had the fullness and definition more often seen among the data deprived masses whose focus was on physical rather than intellectual achievement. He stood erect and tall, gazing intently at the inert form at his feet. The muscles of his face struggled with the emotions that empowered them, his eyes narrowing and the corners of his mouth trembling. His Adam's apple rose and fell as he appeared to choke back sobs.

The rescue team broke out the resuscitation unit, but even from the top of the hill, they could see that its use would be futile. The driver had been thrown from the car and his body shattered upon impact with the brick wall. The victim in the car was long past saving and even recovery of the body from the wreck would be a daunting, if not impossible task. They put aside the unit and made their way down the steep grade of the winding street.

Jagged edges of the wreck had torn away some of the smooth transparent membrane that had long covered the street's cobblestones to adapt it to hovercraft. The exposed stones evoked earlier times when wheels rumbled over uneven road, their speed constrained by a series of closely spaced switchbacks. Even a hovercar had no chance at high speed on this tortuous street. The sun was now high in the sky, reflecting brilliantly from the tranquil waters of the distant bay in stark contrast with the carnage close at hand.

As they approached the remains of the vehicle, more details emerged. The victim was a man who had aged naturally. His skin was white, his forehead deeply ridged like the folds of loose fabric on an aging cushion, and there were tiny lines radiating from the corners of his eyes and the corners of his mouth. A scattering of small coffee-colored irregular spots appeared just under his eyes, further attesting to his age.

The paramedics watched the young man crouch by the wreckage and reach out gently to touch the dead man's face. His fingers rested softly on the right cheek, the tip of his middle finger just below the right earlobe and pointing inadvertently at a tiny bulge in the skin behind the ear.

"What's that bump?" asked one of the paramedics.

"Microprocessor."

"What's it for?"

"Long story," said the young man. "Right now, we've got to get him out of here. He can't stay here like this."

"Easier said than done. It'll take some time to move the wreck. The body might have to come out in pieces."

"Not on my watch," said the man. "He deserves a decent burial."

The lead paramedic struggled to make sense of the scene before him. The younger man seemed to know the victim, but couldn't have been a passenger in the vehicle. It was totally destroyed, but this man was unscathed. What was he doing there at all?

"Relative?" he asked.

"Not exactly," said the man, rubbing at the dried blood on his own face.

The paramedic glanced down at the twisted wreckage. At close range, the painful nature of the victim's death screamed out at him. His last minutes or seconds of life must have been excruciating.

What was most remarkable about this picture, however, was a single, inexplicable anomaly. The old man's eyes were open and appeared almost to be making contact with his. And his features were relaxed, the corners of his mouth turned slightly upward. His expression was serene.

1

October 2041

SHE APPEARED when Marcus was on the thirteenth mile on the Endless Park. The ache was building in the backs of his thighs and his calves were beginning to burn. The green space surrounding him remained monotonous as the miles ticked off on the holographic display projected from a tiny opening in front of the rotating patch of grass. His arms glistened from the sun reflecting off the microthin chemical film that coated his body.

At first, the figure that appeared slightly behind him to his left, watching and studying him, escaped his notice. Her flowing red hair first caught his attention before he noticed that she was glancing back and forth between him and the sky. Her right hand poked fingers at the space just in front of her face and he realized that she was watching a display, visible only to her, that was tracking a flow of data. She was interacting with the data, entering information...about him? His performance? A bird broke the monotony of the landscape on the right and caught his attention for the blink of an eye. And when he looked back, she'd vanished.

His breath started to slow as he sank into the silky patch of HibernaTurf at the end of his run, the sun melting beads of sweat off his skin, when her shadow cast across his body. She was looking toward the sky and poking fingers of both hands at the invisible screen before her. "Marcus Takana, born August 4, 2019, New Quest, Oregon," she read just loud enough for him to hear. "Six foot three inches tall, 182 lbs. Disease scan clear. Drug scan clear. Cortical database 2.3 petabytes. Basic unenhanced dataset."

"Who the hell are you?"

"Ignorant and vulgar," she mouthed silently. "I'm Terra, Mr. Takana. And I have a proposition for you." Her body was now framed against the sky, her face in shadows, the sun directly behind her fringing her hair with light.

"Tell me," she said, "are you happy with your life?"

"It could be better." He looked up at the spectral figure, trying to make out the features of her backlit face.

"Then are you ready for it to change?" Terra maintained the advantage of her position, towering over his outstretched form.

"So you're the devil and you've come to buy my soul?"

"Not your soul, Mr. Takana. You can keep that. It's no use to us at all. It's your body we want. And we're prepared to pay you handsomely for it."

"What do you mean? Are you recruiting me for some sort of team?"

"Not exactly. We want you literally to sell us your body...to part with it...permanently."

"You're asking me to die?" Marcus sat up and got to his feet. With the direction this conversation was headed, it was time to be on equal ground and to see the face of his adversary. Now he had the advantage of height, his eyes level with the top of her head. As the sun struck her face, he was unprepared for her exquisite beauty. The red hair cascaded over her shoulders, framing a face of perfect symmetry, with pale unblemished skin that seemed never to have been exposed to the harsh solar rays that now penetrated an ever-thinning atmosphere. Most striking were her eyes, an emerald green that reflected light with the intensity and sparkle of gemstones. These eyes now held his gaze.

5

"Yes. In a way. Your mind would cease to exist while your body lived on with another mind within it. I represent a few wealthy individuals who are willing to pay huge sums for healthy new bodies."

"But what good would money do me if I no longer exist?"

"It wouldn't happen right away. It's a future contract to be completed at such time that your benefactor's body is ready to die. In your case, your benefactor is in his mid-40's, so that could be anywhere from 25 to 70 years. And he's an exceedingly cautious man, so he could live for many decades to come. Meanwhile, you'd have access to everything that extraordinary wealth could buy. The years you'd have could be infinitely more rewarding than the life that faces you now. Imagine what you could accomplish."

Marcus remembered when he'd been young and ambitious, ready to save the world, before disaster struck his family and his dreams evaporated.

"And there's a bonus," Terra continued. "Few people have both the means and required youth to have the Ambrosia Conversion. By 28 or 29, cells have already aged beyond the capacity of the Conversion to help. This arrangement is only worthwhile for your benefactor with the Conversion so we will of course arrange for you to undergo it. While it will not bestow you immortality, it will enable you to avoid aging as long as you continue to...exist."

She had his attention. He did the math. If he rejected the offer, he could live perhaps eighty or ninety more years, but his body and mind would gradually fall into disrepair and he could be burdened with disabilities for decades. Even with cutting edge medicine, short of the Conversion, mental processes still began to slow as early as the fifth decade of life.

What would it have been like, Marcus wondered, to have been Mozart or John Lennon or John F. Kennedy, all of whom accomplished extraordinary things and won world renown, but at the expense of dying before their time? Would it be worth it to live large and die young?

Marcus's adult life so far had been unremarkable. Data deprived at 22, he'd had a string of dead-end jobs in the meat growing factories, leaving him circling just beyond the edge of poverty. He was all alone and hadn't ever had a relationship with a woman that lasted more than a few weeks. All he had going for him was his dedication to running and climbing that had honed his body to sculpted refinement. An enormous chasm separated even those with advanced education from the lifestyle and achievements of those who could afford a MELD chip. He now had a chance to live on the other side of that chasm.

"Can I have some time to think about it?"

"Of course. This is a life-changing proposition that deserves proper consideration. But I'll need an answer in the next 24 hours or the offer will go to someone else."

"How will I find you if I decide to accept your conditions?"

"Don't worry about that. I'll find you, just like I found you the first time. And Mr. Takana," she added, "One of the conditions is that you must not tell anyone about our arrangement...not now or ever. Secrecy is a crucial aspect of these arrangements. Your benefactor will need to assume your identity along with your body. Until tomorrow, then." Marcus blinked and she was gone.

As he sped home on his motorcycle, Marcus wondered if his bizarre encounter with Terra had been an elaborate hallucination. Was what she proposed even possible? He'd not had a chance to ask how consciousness could be transferred from body to body or what would happen to his consciousness in the process.

The bike slipped sideways toward the edge of the road, bringing his attention abruptly back to his driving. The roads had long been designed to accommodate hover vehicles and only a few aficionados and daredevils still ventured upon their slick surfaces with wheels. Motorcycles were especially risky, even with specially modified tires.

Once home, Marcus stripped off his clothes and stepped into the cleansing pod. The short blast of water stung his skin, followed by the viscous sanitizing wash that oozed over every inch of his body. The second blast of water was mixed with air and blew off the excess chemical, leaving the surface of his body slick and dry like the membranes swimmers wore to eliminate drag. The whole process used only two ounces of water and left his body with a breathable coating that would repel contaminants for days.

Marcus remembered the times as a small child when his mother would let him play in the bathtub and then lather his hair and body. He remembered the sweet sensation of warm water dribbling over the top of his head and down his face, neck and shoulders and the snug warmth of her wrapping him in a fluffy towel when the bath was over. Bathing became illegal when he was six. The high efficiency sanitizers and surfactants that he'd just used weren't perfected until he was in his teens. Hygiene had been a dicey issue during the intervening decade.

He stood naked in front of the mirror and looked approvingly at the definition of his musculature. The detail was worthy of the image he once saw of Michelangelo's David. And like the statue, his body was hairless and smooth. Like most of his contemporaries, every bit of body hair had been permanently removed in order to optimize the power of the chemical membrane to repel pathogens and prevent contamination.

For just an instant, a stranger's face looked back at him from atop the perfect body that he'd so painstakingly sculpted. Then he was staring into the depths of his own sorrowful eyes, and loneliness enveloped him like a dark fog that threatened to smother him.

The following afternoon, Marcus returned to the Endless Park and began his daily run. At the beginning of the seventh mile, he sensed a presence behind him and felt his pulse quicken a few beats beyond the usual effects of his exertion.

"So have you considered our offer, Mr. Takana?"

He stepped off the moving turf and turned to find his gaze once again captured by those exquisite green eyes. He'd found them almost hypnotizing on their first encounter and had to keep their effect upon him from influencing his decision. He'd spent most of the morning and afternoon considering the proposition before risking another meeting.

"I'm in."

"Brilliant," she responded. "So now you must have lots of questions."

"I have no idea at all how this would work."

Terra explained that he would first be injected with a fluid containing millions of nano scale transducers attached to molecular messengers that would bind to neuronal DNA, delivering the tiny devices throughout his brain to create a detailed map. His benefactor, or more accurately buyer, would get a similar infusion, mapping his brain. The networks of transducers could communicate with one another and information could be exchanged. In this way, the buyer's brain would be mapped precisely to his.

"As your counterpart approaches death, chemical signals will initiate the exchange of the maps. If death is too sudden to provide the automatic trigger, the exchange will be initiated by controllers at a central processing station that will continually monitor the biological processes of you both."

"Exchange of the maps? That sounds like my mind will wind up in his body."

"Yes, that's exactly how it works. but by the time you get there, his brain will likely be sufficiently shut down that you'll never be aware of dying."

"Is there anything else I should know."

"Yes, Mr. Takana, there are a lot of rules. The first and most important I told you yesterday: total secrecy. You must not ever tell anyone about this arrangement, not even your wife, should you ever marry, or your children. You will not be told the identity of your benefactor and he will not be aware of yours."

"Buyers...property. I guess that's me. It sounds pretty horrible when you put it that way."

"It all depends on how you look at it. We also require you to take care of your body while it's still yours. Our capacity to monitor your activities with the transducer system is extensive. We can tell if you use alcohol or other drugs or if you engage in dangerous activities. We'll be monitoring your location and can determine the speed and acceleration of your body in real time. We ask that you use alcohol sparingly or not at all, avoid other toxic substances, and not engage in deliberately risky behavior."

Marcus had already planned a series of extreme adventures with the first of the money he'd get. He'd become accustomed to breaking up his boredom with the thrill of high-risk sports. This requirement could be a deal-breaker.

"What about the bike?"

"That will definitely have to go, starting now. Look," Terra said, "This is a lot to take in. I can understand your doubts, but the opportunity we're talking about can bring monumental changes in your life. The things that will become important to you months from now are likely to be entirely different from the things that have been important to you so far within the limited scope of your experience."

"Like what?"

"Like unprecedented knowledge and all the power that comes with it. And opportunities for real and enduring relationships."

Terra seemed to know so much about him. He felt the sadness that had overwhelmed him the night before closing back in on him, underscored by the proximity of the enticing woman bringing him this preposterous opportunity. He wanted more than anything not to be alone.

"So...still in?" she asked, the words almost floating on her breath.

"Yes."

"Good. Then we can proceed."

2

RAY METTLER settled back in the soft leather recliner and watched the sparkling solution swirl in the bottle hanging above him. He felt a hint of warmth as the liquid flowed into his vein and found its way toward the right ventricle of his heart while the tiny particles it carried diffused into his blood and throughout his circulation. They would eventually find their way across the blood-brain barrier and bind to their targets in the neurons within his brain.

The plushness of the leather felt pleasantly odd. Ray's home was spartanly furnished, covered only in materials that could easily be wiped clean. There was little fabric anywhere. Even his bed covering was a smooth sheet of insulating polymer. Microbes were his enemies. Frequent antiseptic washes and laminar flow circulation kept his home swept as free of them as possible. Anyone entering passed first through a decontamination chamber and observed a strict dress code in keeping with the sterile milieu.

Another unfamiliar sensation played across the small muscles of his lower jaw and the nasal folds above his mouth. It was a smile, his first in recent memory in a life beset by disappointment and failure and the ever-present worry about when he would die, a worry that no longer needed to concern him. His imagination was now racing through a future that promised him immortality within a strong, eternally young body. He wondered what that body might look like, but especially what it would feel like to have physical prowess beyond anything he'd ever experienced even in his youth.

Whose body would he eventually occupy? How will they have lived their life between now and that uncertain day in the future when the exchange would take place? The unknown partner in this transaction would have the benefit of the Ambrosia Conversion as well as the use of the fifty million dollars that Ray had paid for the privilege of the exchange. Ray hoped that he would use his newfound wealth wisely to build a worthwhile life. Sudden wealth proves fleeting for so many. Ray didn't want to begin his new life destitute.

So much had changed in the few days since the stunning redhead with the emerald eyes had first approached him. He'd been on a rare excursion beyond the safe confines of his home in order to conduct business that could only be done in person. She'd waited for such an opportunity so that their meeting could remain secret from Ray's wife Lena. Absolute secrecy was an essential ingredient of the bargain that they were about to strike. She'd been watching the entrance to his home when he returned and had approached him quickly as he emerged from the car.

"Mr. Mettler," Terra began, "I have a proposition for you that will change your life. I need about an hour of your time."

"Not interested," Ray replied, waving her away and charging for the door. "I don't like solicitations."

"This isn't an ordinary offer, Mr. Mettler," she persisted, keeping pace. "You've been carefully selected for this opportunity. I'm sure you'll find it worth your while."

"Then message me later when I'm back inside. I've spent too much time out here already."

"Not possible. I can only discuss this offer face-to-face. It requires utmost confidentiality. Not even your wife can know about it. We can have the conversation now or I'll move on to the next candidate. My car is waiting over there." She laid one hand on his shoulder and pointed to a red hovercar parked fifty feet away.

Ray stopped short of the door and turned to face her. Whether it was her extraordinary beauty or her direct approach, she had his attention. His guard was for the moment down.

"Would you at least give me some idea what it's about?"

"It's about your life, Mr. Mettler. You've spent most of it doing everything you can to avoid dying." She paused to let her words sink in. "We can change that."

"You mean cure my fear? You provide some sort of treatment?"

"Better...much better." She held out a hand. "Let's go for a ride."

Ray was hooked. The man who trusted nobody and made every decision in his life with meticulous caution was about to get into a car with a complete stranger without any idea what was going to happen next. For all he knew, he was about to be kidnapped or murdered. He took her hand and let her lead him to the car. She let him in on the passenger side, then took her seat behind the wheel. The car lifted off the ground and glided down the road.

"I represent a kind of think tank, Mr. Mettler," Terra began once they were underway, "a secret organization that has been working on the problem of immortality."

"You mean like the Ambrosia Conversion?"

"That's part of it, but as you know the Conversion only works for the young. We are working on bringing immortality to everyone, even to the very old."

"So you do medical research? You're looking for test subjects?"

"Test subjects, yes," Terra replied, "But it's not exactly a medical problem. We work in the area of cognitive migration."

"Moving mental contents?" Ray had heard about experiments designed to convert mental contents into digital form. The problem was that the hybrid that resulted between man and machine could evoke the intelligence of the person, but not manifest his consciousness. While the structure of artificial intelligence was coming close to emulating the architecture of the nervous system, identity seemed to reside in the unique network of interconnections within each person's brain. Replicating the map in a non-living entity remained elusive.

"That's correct," Terra replied, "but to be more precise, we have found a way to exchange identities between people."

"So what does that have to do with immortality?"

"It's really very simple. You would get to be young again. Your mind would inhabit the body of a much younger man, a man who is young enough to have the Conversion, and you would live in that body indefinitely."

"What happens to the other guy?"

"Well, I'm afraid his time would be up."

Ray pondered the implications of what she was telling him. It sounded to him like murder.

"So I'd be stealing his body?"

"Not stealing exactly, more like buying. You are in a position to make it well worth his sacrifice. You have the power to lift a man from the oblivion of poverty and ignorance and provide him with a privileged life. And, of course, he would be given the Ambrosia Conversion that would ultimately confer upon you the immortality that you seek. He would get to be young as long as he keeps his body. Many would see that as a very good deal."

"Sounds like a deal with the devil. And I'd be the devil." Since the spectacular initial success of HibernaTurf, Ray had become accustomed to being able to buy whatever he wanted, sometimes at the expense of others, but this exceeded the limits even of his tattered sense of decency.

"It would be a contract between two informed adults. Once you think about it, it will all seem very reasonable." Terra pulled the car to the side of the road so that they could have eye contact. Closing this deal would depend upon absolute trust.

"What's in it for you and your think tank?"

"Proof of scalability," replied Terra. "We've shown that the technology works in non-human primates and in a few pairs of human subjects. We've both exchanged consciousness in healthy volunteers and reversed the process without adverse effects. You and your young counterpart are one of twenty pairs of clients in the project's first commercial phase. We take a small percentage of your cost as our fee. As we increase the number of clients we can manage, you can imagine how lucrative this could become."

"And the risks?" asked Ray.

"The procedures to prepare you for the transfer involve tried and true technology. We use a nanoparticle infusion that's very well-tolerated. A microprocessor behind your ear will integrate information from the nanoparticles to create a coherent map of your consciousness. The only risk is a very small possibility of the final step failing. That hasn't happened yet with any of our test subjects. And worst case scenario, you'd be no worse off than you'd have been without our involvement."

Ray's mind reeled. Until now, he'd lived his life avoiding as much risk as possible. Now he was being asked by a stranger to take a leap of faith and allow her to fill his bloodstream with millions of particles that would colonize his brain. The prize on the other side of the leap was a shot at immortality and eternal youth. But the technology might just as well be used to send his mental contents into the cloud and vaporize his consciousness. And if it worked, it would ultimately mean the end of another human being.

*****

"Comfy, Mr. Mettler?" asked the attendant, examining the level of fluid remaining in the bottle.

"Very," Ray replied.

"You're almost done. There's just one more step." The attendant unwrapped a small brass cylinder attached to a medium gauge capillary tube. She held the end of the tube against the mastoid process just behind his right ear, pointed it toward his earlobe, and fired.

"Sssst." The microprocessor entered just under the skin behind his ear and lodged in the indentation above the temporomandibular joint, producing a BB sized bump. This tiny device would integrate the data from the brain map and relay it to the cloud. Somewhere, a similar device was being implanted in the neck of a man whose fate was now inextricably intertwined with his.

3

MARCUS SPENT the next few days following his second encounter with Terra indulging his appetite for risk and speed. He tore around cliffside highways on his bike and barreled down mile long ziplines across bottomless chasms. His crowning achievement was a nine-mile freefall from a balloon, deploying his parachute only 1200 feet above the ground. The jolt of the parachute breaking his fall at nearly 200 mph knocked the wind out of him and left him sore for days. While it was far from a record, it was his fastest solo transit ever with peak velocity topping 350 mph, a fitting and memorable conclusion to his daredevil life.

When Terra picked him up the next day to drive him to the infusion center, her voice was barbed with reproach. "I certainly hope you enjoyed your last fling, Mr. Takana. Any transgression from this point on violates your contract and forfeits your payment."

"Understood." Marcus grinned. The last fling was just another aspect of his brinkmanship, testing the limits of his new constraints. He'd gotten away with it this time. He didn't plan to try it again. Returning to his old life was the one risk he was unwilling to take.

As the nanoparticle infusion flowed into his body suffusing his body with warmth, his mind wandered across the novel landscape he was about to traverse. He was on the brink of fabulous wealth, but wouldn't be allowed to use his windfall to live out his usual fantasies. The blueprint of his new life would have to be rendered entirely from scratch.

Marcus knew that people could crash and burn under the weight of newfound fortunes. When he was eight, a couple in his family's farming community became intoxicated with the wealth of a sudden windfall. They turned their backs on their neighbors at a time of need, embarking on a years-long spending spree. When they began running out of money and fell behind on their taxes, they wound up losing their home and farm. Despite his youth at the time, Marcus could still recall the expressions of contempt on his parents' faces when these friends approached them for help. He never saw them again.

He would approach the use of his fortune rationally. It took little thought to conclude that his best single investment would be knowledge. Buying and implanting a MELD chip had been way beyond his capability until then, but now the half million dollar price tag was to him what in the days of currency used to be called "pocket change." The chip would allow him to download packets of information that would once have taken years to learn. These varied in price from ten thousand dollars for the ability to speak another language to a half million for a complete understanding of the limits of theoretical physics.

When he later planned in earnest, he budgeted two million dollars for a selection of modules that gave him command of world literature, art, and music, the ability to speak Japanese, Arabic, Spanish, and three dialects of Chinese, and a detailed knowledge of the history and sociology of the twenty first century. He left a half million budgeted for whatever special area of expertise he might later decide would be most useful. He would have knowledge and power for the first time in his life.

"Sssst." The microprocessor was injected under the skin behind his right ear, stinging like a wasp and leaving a lingering soreness. The brain mapping was complete, a precise match for the map already implanted in the brain of the unidentified person whose consciousness would someday occupy his body.

"Just one more step," said the technician as she punched a tiny disc of skin from his left forearm. From the fibroblasts in the sample's connective tissue would be induced a culture of pluripotent stem cells, capable of transforming into any tissue type within his body. They would be treated to maintain the length of their telomeres, the terminal ends of the chromosomes, the length of which determined the longevity of the cells. These immortal cell lines would eventually repopulate his entire body. From that point forward, he would be immunized against the degeneration and disease that normally accompanies aging.

"You'll need to come back in a week," said Terra, "once the cells have been prepared. You will then undergo the Conversion and within the months that follow your body will stop aging."

"And then I'll be immortal?"

"In a manner of speaking. Your body will become immortal. You will share that property with it until the last part of the contract has been concluded." Her words brought home the cruel irony of the special gifts he was about to enjoy.

*****

The greatest singular burden of Marcus Takana's former life was loneliness. Except for athletic competitions, he had little contact with other people. Even those contacts were fleeting. He had no close friendships or intimate relationships. His avoidance of intimacy grew out of his self-hatred from working for an industry that was repugnant to him. And he'd been stung by losses growing up. One particularly painful loss was memorialized as a tattoo that remained hidden from the eyes of strangers beneath his shirt. Now, armed with wealth and especially the knowledge that it availed him, he was ready to satisfy his longing for connectedness.

Searching for his own moral compass made him curious about the passions of others. Attending political rallies offered an opportunity both to explore the values of the times and to develop a network of relationships. As he explored various causes, Marcus was struck by the intensity of emotion and paucity of logic that still drove social forces despite the enormous increase in objective information available even to those unendowed with a MELD chip.

"SPUDs are People, too," read the banner over the speaker's head on the stage in the park. The acronym on the banner, a combination of acronyms for "Sentient Processing Units" and "Sentient Processing Devices" had become a pronounceable shorthand for intelligent androids. The disparaging double entendre was later embraced by hate groups opposed to their growing integration into the fabric of civilization. Marcus had been attracted by a crowd of a couple of hundred, but once he worked his way close to the stage, the speaker captivated his attention with her words, with her passion, and with her extraordinary presence.

"There was once a time when some among us were considered less than human by others and treated abominably. We have since become sufficiently enlightened that most people understand that we are all created equal." She raised both arms toward the sky and tilted her head upward. A holographic image in the middle of her forehead caught the sun's reflection, creating a brilliant aura around her gleaming head and making her appear, for a moment, like a goddess.

"Now there is a new underclass," she continued, "a group of sentient and noble beings that are distinguished from us only because they are built of silicon rather than carbon. They live in servitude and have no voice in shaping the future of our society." Her voice was resonant and as silky as Marcus imagined her flawless skin must feel.

"My dream," she continued, "is that these beings will someday come to live among us as equals. That we will value their extraordinary knowledge and abilities and will give them their freedom so that that they can take their place by our sides as citizens of our community." A lavender cape caught the wind and fluttered around a lithe body clad in golden, form-fitting fabric, enhancing Marcus's impression of a supernatural being.

The crowd was now cheering, swept by the passion of her words. Marcus joined in the cheers, wanting to embrace this angel's cause as his own despite its logical shortcomings.

It was true that the current generation of SPUDs had extraordinary knowledge and that they could appear in many respects unerringly human. They were endowed with exquisite sensory perceptions, able to describe even the qualities of a wine more accurately than the most experienced connoisseur. And they could respond to many situations with appropriate emotional expression. But they still lacked the capacity to enjoy the wine or, for that matter, anything else. They couldn't experience the emotions that they mimicked so well. These capacities, which came to be known as the Pinocchio Factor, remained the Holy Grail of cybernetics. Even the angel that stood before him lacked the power to confer these properties upon the beings she strove so passionately to elevate.

The crowd thronged around the speaker once she'd finished, peppering her with questions. Marcus waited patiently until most of the crowd had dispersed, then approached her.

"Do you have a question for me?" she asked as he stared into her eyes. It took all his courage to respond.

"What's your name?" he asked.

"Corinne." She blushed and looked away. Her shy response reassured him that she was flesh and blood after all and not one of the robotic beings she was championing.

"I'm Marcus," he said. "Would you like to get some coffee?"

4

THE RED HOVERCAR glided to a stop in front of the entrance to Ray's home. A solid, windowless façade of red marble, two stories high, faced the street, capped by a steep, bronze colored standing seam roof of titanium with an underlayment of Kevlar. Layers of Kevlar and titanium also formed an impregnable barrier behind the marble façade. Two solid marble steps led up to the door. Within most of this structure beyond the armor was a hollow space, completing the illusion of an above ground dwelling.

As the car slipped away, Ray stood in front of the full-body scanner embedded in the opaque glass door that compiled data from his DNA, his facial characteristics, a retinal scan, and patterns in his skin's surface blood vessels. Security systems using only one or two of these parameters had long since been defeated by sophisticated spoofing techniques. Increasing complexity maintained a scant lead on the hackers.

Ray felt a nagging sensation in the muscles of the back of his neck, resisted the urge to move, and then tightened the muscle on the right until he heard a small pop accompanied by a twinge of pain. His head moved imperceptibly. He'd learned this maneuver over the years to cover the tics that had plagued him since his teens.

The door slid open. The tension that had built across his shoulders and neck released. At least the biological modifications he'd just undergone had not changed the essential blueprint of his body. Ray stepped into the cylindrical chamber and the door slid closed behind him. As the capsule descended, a blast of air blew any loose debris from his body and clothing and sucked it away through linear openings in the floor. The elevator came to a stop twenty feet below the surface. A panel at the rear slid open. He stepped out into a brightly lit corridor onto a moving platform. More air blasted across his body at intervals, interspersed with instantaneous bursts of ultraviolet light. At the end of the corridor was another door equipped with a body scanner. Redundant measures kept this underground fortress secure from both microscopic and human scale threats.

The last door slid open and Ray emerged into a space of surprising volume, given its underground location and the cramped pathway to its entrance. The spaciousness of the home was enhanced by the sparseness of furnishings and the slickness of every surface. A broad palette of colors compensated for the lack of texture. And the walls displayed an ever-changing array of art from Renaissance masterpieces through contemporary kinetic abstractions. If one tired of the images changing, the display could be frozen to linger on a chosen view.

To Ray, this underground fortress was a cocoon of safety, protecting him from an outside world fraught with dangers that threatened at any moment to extinguish his fragile existence. To his wife Lena, it was a sterile prison that shut her off from everything that was meaningful to her before life with Ray began, including her work as a journalist.

*****

Lena had a knack for storytelling almost from the time she could speak. By the time she got to college, two of her short stories had won sufficient recognition to encourage her to pursue journalism as a profession. By the time she graduated, journalism had undergone radical changes that severely limited her opportunities for employment. There was no longer any need for news reporters in any medium. Most world events hit the Universal Data Base as they occurred and the significance of events was parsed by sophisticated algorithms from the video and audio record into coherent and accurate accounts. There was little room in this process for subjective point of view.

The public was still hungry, however, for personal stories, particularly those involving the lives of celebrities. While there were no longer tabloid newspapers, a small area of the UDB was still devoted to these stories and it remained possible to make a living writing them. So it was in Lena's role as celebrity journalist that she first met Ray. In order to provide sufficient color to her biographical pieces to engage readers beyond the known facts, her approach went far beyond interviews to embedding herself in the lives of her subjects, often for weeks or months. If she had to make a living chronicling the lives of the rich and famous, she would at least produce compelling narratives in skillful prose.

She began her story on Ray in the summer of 2029, three years after HibernaTurf first hit the market and at the height of the positive slope of his celebrity. Beyond its commercial success, it appeared at the time that HibernaTurf was helping to solve the world's water shortage as it grew in the extent of its worldwide coverage and curtailed almost entirely the residential and commercial use of irrigation in landscaping. Some communities were able, for a while, to relax restrictions on water use for consuming and bathing. People once again enjoyed bathing more than once or twice a week.

Ray was eccentric, a loner, who ventured infrequently from his carefully engineered home and allowed few visitors into his sanctum. Over the weeks of her research, though, Lena insinuated her presence into his space and his isolation began to melt away. By the time she was done with the story and ready to leave, he insisted she stay a while longer. During the next weeks, their conversations became more intimate and affection grew between them.

They married in December 2029 in the presence of Lena's parents and several of her closest friends. None of the guests were Ray's, which should have been a red flag for her about his capacity for relatedness.

Over the first three years of their marriage, HibernaTurf started to go horribly wrong. After looking like a boon to the environment, unintended consequences emerged that turned it into a scourge. It spread uncontrolled, replacing fertile farm and grazing lands with a virtually inert material lacking in any nutritional value. Ray went from international hero to one of the most reviled people on the planet. He was Midas and HibernaTurf was his gold. And by the end of that time, he became increasingly paranoid and guarded.

By the fall of 2033, HibernaTurf was bankrupt, but Ray had managed to amass a personal fortune that was well shielded by his corporate shell from litigation. His growing list of enemies were enraged that he'd profited so handsomely from the debacle he'd created. A substantial portion of his wealth was devoted to protecting him and Lena from his enemies.

Ray's wealth in the early years of their marriage gave Lena access to an enormous amount of information. They were both endowed with the most advanced MELD chips for interfacing with the UDB and acquired advanced knowledge modules covering the equivalent of a 20th Century college education dozens of times over. Lena became addicted to knowing and could not imagine ever lapsing back into ignorance. The ultimate cost of leaving Ray would mean giving up her MELD chip, disconnecting her from all the knowledge that she'd accumulated in her personal space within the UDB. Since that knowledge had become integral to her identity, giving it up became unthinkable, enough to keep her imprisoned within a marriage that was increasingly deprived of emotional oxygen as Ray became more distant and wooden. Even without this powerful incentive to stay, Lena couldn't bring herself to abandon him when the rest of the world had turned against him.

*****

"Lena," Ray called as he moved toward the sleeping chamber at the rear of the dwelling. There was no response. He hurried into the chamber, but found it empty. His pace quickened as he moved to the bathroom, then the kitchen. Still no sign of Lena.

"Where are you?" he screamed. Only silence. His rage expanded to fill the empty space around him. He pounded the kitchen counter with his fist hard enough to sting his hand. He sat down and took some slow deep breaths. When he'd calmed down enough to clear his mind, he reached out to her in thought. Still no reply and no signal telling him her location. Her chip's broadcast function had gone dark. Either she was in a rare skip area of the UDB or she had deliberately become invisible.

It was unlike Lena to leave home unannounced. She knew how anxious it made him for either of them to venture into the dirty, perilous outside world. There was seldom an opportunity to leave without his notice. But the infusion had taken the better part of a day. She'd apparently used his extended absence as a chance to sneak out. Where could she have gone that was important enough to put them both at risk?

But then, there were the other reasons Ray hated for Lena to venture beyond the safety of their home. They were both potential targets for crackpots seeking revenge for the ravages of HibernaTurf. There had been a close call years before during one of his last public appearances when a sniper took a shot at him from a distant rooftop. It hit him square in the chest, but he'd already begun to wear bullet-proof clothing in public. The force of the blow knocked the wind out of him. He was otherwise unharmed.

Their still considerable wealth also put them both at risk for kidnapping. Ray began to wonder whether Lena went dark for more sinister reasons. Could she have been abducted and hidden in a dark location, or could someone else have turned off the signal from her chip? Rage had primed his muscles for brutal force. Now fear drained them of all power, leaving him limp and vulnerable.

It was too soon to report her missing. There was no evidence that she'd met with foul play other than the lack of a signal indicating her location. Even if he turned to the authorities, he held little trust trust that they'd respond to his plea for help. When HibernaTurf went bad, his most loyal admirers and dedicated employees all abandoned him within months. There were few left who didn't despise him. Only Lena kept his underground sanctuary from turning into perpetual solitary confinement.

An alarm alerted him that someone was approaching the outer entry door. A holographic image of a human figure materialized in his peripheral vision to his left. The ground began to rumble beneath his feet and the image dissolved before he could direct his gaze toward it. The rumbling grew to a crescendo until it shook his whole body as he struggled to maintain his balance. The lights went out. Then all was still.

Ray stood in the darkness, enveloped by silence from without and within. His MELD chip's connection with the Universal Data Base required power within his underground world. The backup power source had failed. He was utterly alone.

5

LOVE CAN BE an overwhelming force to a man floating aimlessly in a solitary world. As they spent more and more time together, Marcus was swept along by Corinne's passions. She became the compass that would guide him through the next stage of his life. Her causes became his causes, her friends his friends. For the first time in his life, he felt like he belonged. Purpose and meaning were seeping into his being.

Corinne also opened for Marcus a new world of sensory and aesthetic experiences. Before she came into his life, his exposure to music and art was limited mostly to works created by artificial intelligence. Digitally composed symphonies were harmonically refined and pleasing to the ear, while sophisticated kinetic sculptures that could be continually revised had offered a seemingly endless array of images to capture his attention.

Corinne's world instead contained static images and dissonant sounds composed by living artists. She and her friends shunned the technical perfection of the automated world to embrace the diversity that only individual creativity could generate. They delighted in all things crafted by hand, collecting and hoarding even articles of clothing that were no longer legal to wear because they couldn't be sanitized with blasts of air or thimblefuls of water. And then there were her books, shelves and shelves of ancient tomes, tattered and dusty, remnants of an age when information had not all been catalogued in digital form.

While Marcus's data modules provided him with an analytical knowledge of music, until he met Corinne he'd never listened to the doleful cadence of a Mahler symphony, the inspired improvisations of Coltrane's saxophone, or the rock and roll music of the Rolling Stones. Visiting her home was a feast for his senses. He looked forward to his visits with the eager anticipation of a child discovering the world for the first time. And he was never disappointed by her ability to surprise him.

On his fourth visit, she greeted him at the door barefoot in a flowing black silk robe in place of the form fitting synthetic material that usually covered her body. While the materials shared a similar luster, there was something about the texture of the natural material and the subtlety of Corinne's body within its loose folds that placed all of his senses on alert. She took him by the hand and he followed obediently as she led him to the softest chair in the apartment, a leather upholstered antique that she'd managed to save years before from an old building scheduled for destruction.

As his body melted into the chair and the stirring strains of Rachmaninoff's Second Piano Concerto enveloped him, Corinne silently removed the silk sash of her robe, slipped behind him, and passed it over his eyes. He allowed her to fasten the makeshift blindfold.

"Patience," was her only utterance. He listened while her footsteps faded away.

The next sensation to overtake him was a pungent aroma, both unfamiliar and exquisite. Marcus inhaled deeply as it filled the room and his mouth began to water. The soft padding of Corinne's bare feet slowly approached and stopped just in front of him.

"Open your mouth and stick out your tongue," she entreated. Marcus obeyed. Corinne placed something soft and curved and wet on his outstretched tongue and invited him to take it into his mouth. The taste of the object enhanced the aroma he'd been savoring and grew in complexity as he rolled it over his tongue and between his teeth. When he bit down, it was slightly chewy. He swallowed and grinned.

"Real food," he thought while misty images from a distant past beckoned his attention. "I'd almost forgotten how it tasted." She'd spent the whole afternoon preparing the pasta shells from the small stash of bootleg wheat flour she kept in the hidden pantry behind her kitchen and the couple of eggs she'd scrounged from friends. She'd been saving the fresh garlic cloves and herbs for a special occasion. A vintage electric cooktop slid out from its hiding place beneath the module that converted pods of synthetic protein into the semblance of meals that they usually ate.

Corinne followed this morsel with a sip of liquid that aroused another medley of sensations in his mouth and nose. The wine washed down the bit of pasta along with the fresh garlic and rosemary that laced the oil that coated it. She fed him another dozen bites in this manner before leading him, still blindfolded, into the next room. A silky fold brushed the fingertips of his free hand. As they moved away from the kitchen, the aroma of cooking food yielded to the sweet smell of jasmine.

They stopped. Now the warmth of her breath washed over his face. A finger traced his lips, then the moist tip of her tongue. Two fingers pushed gently against his chest and he fell back onto the bed. She kissed his neck and slid one hand between his legs while she released the knot on the blindfold with the other. The cloth fell away, candlelight reflected in the ebony surface of Corinne's eyes, and he was helpless in her grasp.

"Even if I die tomorrow," Marcus thought, "tonight would be worth it all."

By day in Corinne's company, he met the students who came to her home for their lessons. Her students weren't children as they might have been in the days when knowledge was still imparted directly from person to person. She was an educator for newly created SPUDs. While they were endowed upon creation with a prodigious data set of linear knowledge, they were entirely lacking in any capacity to read human emotions or to respond like people to circumstances that would provoke emotional responses. This is the language that she taught by spending hours of training with each of her charges, observing images together of evocative, often heart wrenching experiences and having them watch the actors' and her emotional responses.

The newer students all greeted him with a singsong "pleased to meet you," accompanied by smiles that seemed to be pasted on their faces. Over time, the smiles became nuanced and other emotions began to filter into their expressional repertoire. Corinne was a gifted instructor. When she threw a graduation party for a group of her charges, Marcus couldn't distinguish some of her advanced pupils from her human friends.

Marcus sometimes wondered whether he was really very different from Corinne's students. He'd come to her programmed with a formidable store of knowledge, but with little understanding of his place in the world. In her presence, he was recovering his humanity. And in the process, long forgotten memories and long dormant passions were rekindled along with his considerable capacity for connecting empathically with others.

*****

Early in her career, Corinne's students were referred to her by owners who believed that appearing more human added value to their property. After a while, though, referrals started to come from her graduates, who seemed eager to share with others of their kind what they'd learned. Some of her graduates would continue to visit long after their lessons had ended, leaving Corinne the impression that she'd taught them something that transcended the mere mirroring of emotional expression. A measure of randomness was built into their programming that allowed for something resembling free will. Corinne became convinced that she was seeing motivated behavior, an indirect indicator of underlying feelings, which was what had initially spawned her interest in the SPUDs' rights movement.

Corinne was born in 2021 in a small town in western Massachusetts. Her brother Benjamin was born three years later. By the time Benjamin turned two, he'd developed idiosyncrasies of behavior auguring a struggle that would define her family throughout the remainder of her childhood. At that point, Corinne's life veered sharply off course while her parents devoted most of their attention and modest resources to Benjamin's needs.

Corinne knew before any of the adults in her life that her brother was different. When he'd begun to walk, she watched him spinning the wheels of a wooden car for hours on end and twirling himself round and round until he fell down. While she'd been able to cuddle him as an infant, touching him as a toddler became a riskier business. She bore bruises on her face and arms from when he startled and flailed in response to her touch.

One day when Benjamin was two, she saw him thrashing on the ground in a tantrum, dangerously close to striking his head on the corner of a table. Corinne dove in to protect him and wrapped her arms tightly around his body. The thrashing and screaming stopped. His breathing slowed and his body relaxed. As she released her hold, his breaths once again came in short gasps and his body began to jerk. When she tightened her arms, he again relaxed.

One of Benjamin's favorite toys was a stuffed monkey with long, floppy arms and legs. Once Corinne discovered the calming effect of her embrace, she tried tying the monkey's arms and legs tightly around his body and found that with sufficient pressure it had a similar effect. When she shared her discovery with her mother, her mother fitted the toy with fasteners to make it easier to swaddle Benjamin with it. From that time on, Benjamin and his monkey lived in a perpetual clinch.

Inanimate objects were the primary focus of Benjamin's world. He paid little attention to people, seldom looking in their faces and never making eye contact. Of all the people in his life, Corinne was the one who was most able to reach him. While he was tightly wrapped with his monkey, she would take him by both hands, wait for his randomly moving head to come around, and bump noses. The first time she did this, there was no response, but she persisted, and by the fortieth or fiftieth time he laughed. This game between them was repeated thousands of times to his apparent delight, one of the few social responses he'd ever shown.

Once she was in school, Corinne was left mostly to her own devices to entertain herself while her parents struggled to keep Benjamin safe and did everything they could to address his disabilities. She wandered around the nooks and crannies of the town and was particularly fascinated by some of the older buildings that had been abandoned and fallen into disrepair. One such building was largely hidden behind a dense overgrowth of foliage and had some of its windows boarded up.

One day when she was seven, she noticed after a storm that the boards over one of the windows had come loose. She carefully pulled a couple of them off, creating an opening large enough for her to crawl through. Her heart raced as she pulled herself through the window and tumbled to the floor. Cobwebs hung from the ceilings and the air smelled musty. A shiver went through her. It felt like a haunted house.

But as her eyes adjusted to the dim light, she became aware of row after row of tall shelves, mostly filled with books. She'd had a couple of picture books as a toddler, but most of her experience with the written word had until then been on screens. Never had she seen such an array of volumes. She walked along the aisles, running her fingers over the spines of the books on the lower shelves, feeling the coarse textures of cloth and the sculpted smoothness of leather. The fear that had overtaken her when she first entered the building melted away in the face of her curiosity about these marvelous objects.

At last, she pulled one of the books from its resting place and it fell open. It was a particularly old volume. The pages had gilded edges and were liberally illustrated with detailed sepia toned engravings. She sat for hours turning the pages, enthralled by the pictures from a long past era and inhaling the scent of the aging paper. As night began to fall, she carefully placed the book back in its place and climbed back through the window. When she'd lowered herself to the ground, she moved the loose boards back in place.

The old library became Corinne's secret hideaway. She washed the grime off several of the windows in order to admit enough light by which to read and brought a cushion and blanket with which she could curl up on one of the benches with her books. She managed to open a couple of windows just enough to create a cross breeze in the summer, allowing the cavernous room to cool naturally.

She grew up with these books as her best friends, educating herself with an eclectic mix of literature, art, history, and philosophy. She was inspired by Thoreau's "Walden" and deeply moved as a teenager by "The Diary of Anne Frank." Her ancient books contained knowledge that the architects of the digital database that was fed to her peers did not see fit to include.

When she was seventeen, the town began a redevelopment project for the area encompassing the library. Corinne learned that the building was slated for demolition. In the months that remained before the wrecking lasers moved in to pulverize the structure, Corinne began rescuing as many of the volumes as she could, removing a few with each visit. She agonized each time over which ones to take. There were so many that she loved from reading and rereading and so many more rare and fragile tomes that had survived for centuries and would be doomed to annihilation. They had all begun to feel like her children, but she could only save a few.

As time grew short, it occurred to Corinne that the developers might salvage the remaining books before demolishing the building. She had mixed feelings about this prospect. It would mean that more would be saved, but it would also make her a thief. She had not considered that the library and its contents might belong to someone or that she didn't have a right to raid it. She'd considered her little burglaries as missions of mercy. In the end, the remaining books were buried in the rubble of the age-old building. She was both heartbroken at their loss and relieved that her acts of larceny had been justified.

Her sweeping exposure to the world of literature left her uniquely adept at modeling emotional responses for her pupils. And her interactions with Benjamin provided additional insight into how to engage entities for whom emotional processing was not innate.

*****

38

It was Corinne's devotion to saving the environment that provided the turning point guiding Marcus toward his destiny. The rallying cry "Stop HibernaTurf Now" resonated with a wound buried deep in his heart. As soon as he heard it, he knew what he had to do with the remarkable opportunity that Terra had given him. HibernaTurf was now threatening to derail decades of progress in controlling global warming and conserving crucial resources needed to sustain all life on the planet.

As HibernaTurf spread, replacing huge swaths of natural vegetation, droughts increased in frequency and carbon dioxide levels again climbed precipitously, renewing the cycle of global warming. Food supplies were compromised and famine spread anew amongst populations that had only begun to beat starvation by the mid-twenties. Water supplies reached the most critical levels of the century. Most people agreed that HibernaTurf needed to be eradicated, but nobody had any idea how to do it.

Marcus Takana made it his mission to rid the world of HibernaTurf. He used some of his remaining funds budgeted for educational modules to acquire expertise in environmental science and bioengineering, later adding modules in plant physiology and genetic engineering.

While others had searched for ways to destroy HibernaTurf with herbicides and defoliants or looked for aggressive species that could compete with it, Marcus began looking for a way to align with its strength and change it back into something benign. As a child, he'd learned how sailboats could move almost directly into the wind by filling their sails from an angle, an early lesson in harnessing the power of an adversary in order to defeat it.

Marcus longed to merge his world with Corinne's forever, but he'd shared little with her of who he was. While he was busy assimilating her world, he'd managed to maintain the secrecy about his that was required by his situation. Corinne had no idea how wealthy he was, much less how he'd come by that wealth. She didn't know he had a MELD chip or that he'd undergone the Ambrosia Conversion. Most of all, she had no inkling of the fateful contract that could someday replace him without any warning with a total stranger.

6

THE SILENCE was broken by the echoing sound of footsteps hurrying down the corridor from the elevator to the inner door. The loss of power had triggered a sequence that automatically released the locks on all the doors in order to provide a flow of outside air as well as an escape route from the underground chamber if a natural disaster compromised the air supply and threatened to entomb its occupants. The backup generator had failed to kick in promptly enough to abort the sequence. It was still not running. Ray stood helpless in the dark, holding his breath as the footsteps neared.

"Ray?" Lena's voice came from an arm's length away.

"I'm right here," answered Ray.

"Oh! Thank God!" said Lena, moving toward the sound of his voice until she could embrace him. He didn't return the hug.

"Where the hell have you been?" he exploded. Lena let go and took a few steps back.

"Screw you, Ray," she shot back. "We've just been through an earthquake. I would have thought you'd be relieved that I was safe."

"Sorry, Lena. Of course I'm glad you're home." It was still pitch black. He took a step toward her voice and reached out, but grasped only empty air. Lena's cold shoulder left him feeling even more alone than when she wasn't there at all.

The ground began to rumble again, this time less intensely than before. After half a minute it stopped.

"We should get out," said Lena. "We could wind up trapped in here if there's another aftershock."

"Guess so," conceded Ray. He reached out, this time finding her hand, and they began moving together toward the corridor. Dying underground in a space dark to the data cloud would be one of the rare circumstances in which his newly activated contract would be worthless. At least the hazards of the aboveground world would provide him access to his backup life.

When they reached the elevator capsule, the door was open, but there was still no power. Once inside, he felt along the wall to the right of the door until his fingers found the latch of a panel. He tugged and the latch fell away. Inside, he found a foot-wide rubber belt that fastened around pulleys above and below the capsule. With both hands he tugged at the belt by its edges and the capsule began slowly to rise.

"Let me help," Lena said as she moved beside him and began tugging at the left side of the belt with both hands. Ray moved both hands to the right edge and together they pulled themselves up. Even with the mechanical advantage of the pulley, it took them nearly twenty minutes to rise the twenty feet to the surface. Light began to filter into their space as they approached the top. They were both too exhausted to be angry by the time they stepped into the sunlight.

"I'm ready for that hug now," Ray said. Lena furrowed her brow, smiling like a mother bestowing forgiveness on an errant child and moved into his embrace.

When they looked around them, there were no signs of any damage from the quake. Traffic had resumed its normal flow and people were walking about as though nothing had happened. They headed to the Blue Bottle on the corner, a throwback to the San Francisco of their youth, and went inside.

"What'll you have?" asked the barista. They both ordered espressos. Ray looked into the scanner while the barista prepared their drinks and fifty-six dollars was debited from his account. Coffee was one of the small pleasures that Ray still cherished and could fortunately afford. The irony was that HibernaTurf was mostly responsible for its scarcity.

"We've got to get out of there, Ray," Lena said once they'd sat down. "You know how much I hate it." Lena had been lobbying to move ever since they married. It had been a major bone of contention between them, more than once threatening to break them up. Ray despised change, especially when it infringed upon his intricately crafted defenses.

Earthquakes had always been a flaw in his security plan, the one hazard that was arguably more dangerous underground, but Ray had always feared attack and disease more than natural disasters and had waved off Lena's warnings that they risked dying in a strong enough temblor. His new circumstances now weighed heavily on the other side of the equation. Regardless of how he might die, it would now have to happen aboveground, where communication with the data cloud didn't depend on a powered network.

"OK. You're right," he said, "Let's move as soon as possible."

Lena's eyes lit up, then filled with tears. "You mean it, Ray? Please tell me you're not just screwing with me."

"Yeah, Lena, I mean it. I've been an idiot for not listening to you. I'm sorry it's taken so long for me to see the light." He could never tell her his real reason for changing his mind.

Within the week, they had located a building on the corner of Powell and Sacramento that met as many of Ray's criteria for safety and defensibility as possible. They chose the penthouse apartment on the twentieth floor. Twin pillars of titanium and concrete flanked the huge central room and went all the way to bedrock. The building had been completely rebuilt following the great earthquake of 2022. The only buildings that survived had been constructed with pillars like these that were now required in every new structure.

The outer perimeter of the apartment was constructed almost entirely of glass that met the most stringent standards of durability. It had enough flexibility to withstand an earthquake, but was tough enough to be impervious to any impact short of an explosion. Just as in his underground lair, all the materials of the structure and its furnishings were completely fireproof. That had been an absolute requirement for anyplace Ray lived ever since the childhood catastrophe that turned him from a rambunctious daredevil into a fretful recluse. Most important it was completely permeable to communication with the data cloud and the UDB.

All that was left was to build in security from intruders and a system to sanitize anything that entered the space. Lena reluctantly conceded that the furnishings from their former residence could come with them. She would have preferred to leave behind the hard slick surfaces and create a more tactilely soothing environment, but she was grateful enough to leave the windowless dungeon that she was willing to make the compromise.

The move to the penthouse was the most significant change in Ray's world since the nanoparticle infusion conferred upon him the promise of immortality. It was astounding how little else had changed. He still took every possible precaution against infection and remained convinced that everyone meant him harm. Avoidance of risk was deeply ingrained in his way of life and was not about to dissipate just because the stakes had changed. Peace eluded him. His life remained dismal and filled with dread.

For Lena, the earthquake had been a godsend. She could finally awaken to a sunrise across a magnificent vista and gaze at the moon and stars at night. Ray still closely monitored her comings and goings, but he never again asked where she'd been the day of the quake.

7

MARCUS WALKED through the greenhouse past tray after identical tray of HibernaTurf, looking for evidence that any of the samples was responding to his treatments. He shook his head. It was a sea of uniformity. In his months of study so far, none of his interventions had made any difference in growth rate. Even when he fed the results of the trials back into his scientific database, the algorithms failed to improve enough to yield a solution.

As his frustration grew, he worked more and more hours until he was spending all but a few hours of each day in the laboratory and the greenhouse, sleeping in catnaps and eating while he worked. Corinne watched from the sidelines with increasing alarm. While his body showed no visible signs of fatigue even on just a few hours of sleep a day, the stress was telling in his mood and behavior. In their brief moments together during those months, he was preoccupied and emotionally distant. Even lovemaking seemed incapable of distracting him from his work.

"You've got to take a break," she insisted one day. "Let's go away for a while. We desperately need some time together. The project will still be there when we get back."

Marcus grudgingly agreed to a vacation. His efforts were producing diminishing returns and he acknowledged that some time away might help him get a fresh perspective when he returned. It would be a mental reboot. They settled on a week in Hawaii and left the following weekend.

The moment they entered the tube transport to Los Angeles, he began to relax. By the time they boarded the plane to Honolulu, all he could think about was the enchanting woman beside him, the way her eyes shone in the moonlight, and what it would feel like to make love to her on the beach. But his fantasies paused as they circled Honolulu and he saw the monotonous swaths of HibernaTurf blanketing the city and radiating into the countryside in all directions. He flashed momentarily back to the relentless march of HibernaTurf that marked the kiss of death for his parents' farm and livestock. His right hand moved unconsciously to his chest, his index finger tracing an invisible outline. By the time they landed, he was back in the present and Corinne was all that mattered.

They spent their first night on Waikiki Beach and flew to Maui the next day. As the plane approached the airport in Kahului, Marcus was again struck by the expanses of HibernaTurf covering the landscape even in what had once been a tropical paradise. But when they got closer, he studied the pattern on the ground and noticed it petering out at the edges in a single direction. He made a mental note to explore that area during their stay. He didn't dare, however, give Corinne any inkling that he was thinking about work.

Maui was like a glimpse into the past. Except for the invasion of HibernaTurf, the island looked much like it had around the turn of the century. Roads of asphalt were populated by antique vehicles that rode on wheels. Hovercars were absent. The roads were not adapted for them and the distances were short enough that they wouldn't have provided much advantage anyway. Away from the towns, the roads narrowed and branched into tributaries of dirt.

Marcus relished the sensation of tires bumping along an uneven road. What he'd loved most about riding his motorcycle in the days before Terra had altered the course of his life was the feeling of intimate connection with the earth that he'd enjoyed as a child on the family farm. He smiled as the electric jeep moved over the rugged terrain when they left the highway for the sparsely traveled roads in the boonies. They were headed for the place he'd seen from the air where the landscape changed. Even the dirt roads were surrounded by HibernaTurf for miles beyond the highway.

Then suddenly what he'd come to see was upon them. Sprigs of foliage began to pop up among the grass, getting closer together and taller as they drove. At last, they were surrounded by a dense wood and there was no more turf to be seen. He stopped the car and got out, arms outstretched, turning around and around, almost dancing until he dropped to the ground and looked up at the patch of sky surrounded by exuberant thickets of towering bamboo. And he knew he had found his answer.

Corinne watched the light go on in Marcus's eyes as he lay among the bamboo looking into the sky. She was grateful for what she saw even if she didn't understand what had just happened. She didn't ask for an explanation and he offered none. But she trusted that he'd tell her about it when the time was right.

The rest of their vacation was bliss. Marcus was more present in the moment than he'd been at any time since their relationship began. His passion for her was alive. His body seemed to channel the rhythm and power of the surf when he made love to her on the beach. When they were done, she sat at the water's edge and watched as his body became one with the waves, skimming on the crests until they broke, then surging to her feet in a cascade of foam. And as he stood before her, the glowing image on his chest that was now so familiar to her faded in time with the receding waters behind him.

Back home, Marcus was eager to get back to work. By the end of the first month, he'd replaced the HibernaTurf in half the greenhouse with trays of seedlings and cuttings of dozens of varieties of bamboo. As they matured, he pulverized roots and sequenced their chromosomes until he'd identified the combination of genes responsible for their remarkable rate of growth. The final step would be to splice this genetic blend into the DNA of HibernaTurf.

Marcus treated only two of the hundreds of trays of HibernaTurf in the greenhouse. The very next morning he was greeted with a lush growth in those trays that spilled over the sides of the table. By the following morning, a ring of growing turf surrounded the original trays, and by the end of a week, the greenhouse was so filled with growth that he had to squeeze between the tables of lush vegetation in order to pass from one end of the greenhouse to the other.

When he analyzed the content of his hybrid grass, it was rich in nutrients and passed every test of safety for consumption. It was virtually identical to the naturally occurring grasses that predated HibernaTurf, except for the presence of the bamboo genes. Since these came from a natural source, the scientific community was quick to conclude that Marcus's grass presented no health risk either to livestock or people.

Once introduced into the wild, Takana Grass, as it came to be known, rapidly proliferated, spreading even more swiftly than had HibernaTurf when it was first introduced. By the end of a year, there was hardly a blade of HibernaTurf left in the Western Hemisphere. Within two years, it was completely eradicated throughout the world.

Takana Grass proved as nutritious and benign as the studies had predicted. Livestock flourished in revived pastures and herds regained strength. Dairy products gradually began to reappear in the food supply. The nutritional value of the milk from these freely grazing animals proved exceptional. And within the first five years, livestock had recovered sufficiently around the world to resume slaughtering for the production of meat that was lean and rich in protein. The only people who were disturbed by these developments were the animal rights activists, who had been happy to see the livestock industry die, and the stakeholders of the in vitro meat industry.

Marcus's discovery also brought an unanticipated bonus. The scientific community soon realized that his technique could spur the growth of all kinds of vegetation. Deforested areas were planted with genetically modified trees that grew many times faster than their native variants. New growth forests sprung up everywhere and the tropical rain forests approached strength not seen for nearly a century.

Between the spread of Takana Grass and the resurgence of forested land, huge amounts of carbon dioxide were sequestered and the tide began to turn on global warming. Reforestation also helped restore natural cycles of evaporation and rain. Excessive rainfall over the next several years was welcomed by the populace as fresh water supplies were replenished.

Other scientists working with the genetic potion from Marcus's bamboo used it to revive kelp populations in areas of the seas where it had died out because of global warming and pollution. The resulting extraction of carbon dioxide from the atmosphere pulled the world further back from the tipping point. An additional benefit was the proliferation of sea urchins that fed on kelp. Harvested sea urchins provided another needed boost to the human food supply, one that even the animal rights proponents could appreciate.

Takana Grass brought Marcus fame and fortune. His status as a hero exceeded any that Ray Mettler had enjoyed even at the height of popularity of HibernaTurf. Marcus's work not only improved the quality of life on the planet, but may have been responsible for preventing an ultimate environmental catastrophe. He got to see what it felt like to be as famous as Mozart, Lennon, or Kennedy, but unlike him, they were mercifully ignorant of how short their lives would be cut.

Marcus didn't need the money. He was already wealthy enough from the money he got in exchange for his life as part of the contract that Terra had convinced him to sign. But he'd hidden that wealth from Corinne. What his new fortune provided him was cover for his terrible secret. He would now be able to share his wealth openly with her. And if they were to spend the rest of his life together, it would work best if she were also to undergo the Ambrosia Conversion.

8

THE MOVE to the penthouse was Lena's first step toward reclaiming her life. Now that she tasted freedom, she wanted more. What she wanted most of all was to work again, which would mean spending extended times away from home and out from under Ray's watchful eye. She had no idea how she would present it to him, but quietly let her professional contacts know that she might be receptive to an assignment if something worthwhile came up.

A couple of months later, she was asked to interview a man newly thrust into the public spotlight. Marcus Takana was the biologist who figured out how to rid the world of HibernaTurf. He lived on the east coast just outside of the capital. Doing this story would take her away from home for nearly two weeks, but it was a juicy story that she desperately wanted to cover.

Lena's imagination was also captured by the poetic arc that connected her portrait of Ray on the heels of his invention of HibernaTurf with the man who would later undo his creation once it had turned into a monster. Of course, Ray would not likely see it the same way. Her coverage of this story would more likely strike him as traitorous. She couldn't think of a way to avoid infuriating him with the truth. So she decided to lie. Once the piece was published, she'd deal with the fallout.

"I'm planning a trip," Lena told him over dinner.

"A trip? what kind of trip?"

"It's work, Ray...an assignment."

"But you don't need to work. We have everything we need." Lena saw his head jerk ever so slightly to the left.

"I miss it, Ray...the writing, the research. It was once a big part of who I was. It was how we met."

Ray put down his fork and placed both hands on the edge of the table. Lena held her breath while he digested her words. It was indeed how they met, but Lena knew that the level of intimacy involved in her work threatened him. After all, the same dynamics that brought them together could very well happen with someone else. She'd given up her freelancing to stay at home when she could no longer deal with his anxiety about her being away.

"So this assignment," he said, "who is it?"

"It's about a couple," she replied, choosing her words carefully to minimize his defensiveness, "a young couple that reminds me a lot of us when we first met." She was dancing around the edges of truth.

"And what's so special about this couple?"

"He...they have made an important discovery, a scientific finding. I've been asked to explore how it's changed their lives." She drew in a long breath, waited for what felt like an eternity, and let it go when he didn't ask her what the discovery was about.

"Where do they live?" he asked next.

"The east coast...DC," she answered. I'd be gone between ten days and two weeks. "Please, Ray, this is really important to me."

"All right. Go. Go." He swept his hands outward toward her as if shooing away a child. It was clear he wasn't happy, but she gladly took his response as permission. He was so often irritated with her, anyway. How much worse could it get? And now she'd at least have a break from the interminable tension between them.

The following Monday, Lena took the tube transport cross country. She was at her destination in less than an hour and was met at the station by a driver who took her to the Takana home. She was greeted warmly at the door by a tall, elegant woman. Lena was taken aback by her graciousness, given her intrusion into their privacy. Most of the people she wrote about tended to be guarded around her, at least for the first day or two. Corinne seemed entirely guileless.

When Corinne introduced her to Marcus, Lena was struck by his combination of commanding physical stature and down to earth demeanor. He was almost apologetic about his celebrity status and treated her with appropriate respect for both her work and her age. He welcomed her into their home and assured her that their lives were an open book. Lena had no inkling what secrets he kept from the world and especially from his wife.

Their home was so very different from the one she and Ray had shared for the past fifteen years. It was airy and inviting with high ceilings and lots of windows, many of which were open when she got there. The furniture was soft and covered with fabrics that were pleasing to the touch. Wonderful aromas emanated from the kitchen toward the rear of the house. And most unusual of all was a room lined entirely with bookshelves brimming with books. Lena hadn't seen so many books in one place since she was a teenager.

An even more striking difference was the obvious ease and affection between Marcus and Corinne. Even at the height of their courtship, Ray's watchfulness had seldom let up and his misery swelled from within him to fill the space between them. Lena could hardly remember why she'd fallen in love with him. She'd clung to the remnants of that love as long as she could until they became too frayed to grasp. She now fought back jealousy of something she could never have, at least not within her marriage to Ray.

Lena had come to write a story about Marcus, but found that story inseparable from the remarkable woman who shared his life. She wound up spending hours observing Corinne perform her magic with the pupils who streamed to her home to learn how to feel.

This was her first personal encounter with SPUDs. They were among the bogeymen that populated Ray's dark and paranoid world. He saw them as both sinister and inferior and was vehemently against them acquiring the status of truly sentient beings. He'd even contributed to The Tribe of 23, a human supremacy movement named for the number of chromosome pairs in the human genome.

In early 2023, just before the United States government began to wind down its military program and was still training robotic infantry for combat, an incident occurred that underscored the complex relationship that was evolving between people and SPUDs. A combat ready trainee wandered off a military base in the Nevada desert and wound up at the edge of a main highway on the outskirts of Reno. It set up a sniper's nest and began picking off cars leading into the city.

The sharpshooting SPUD stayed on the move, eluding authorities for nearly two days. By the time it was destroyed by a drone-fired missile, it had killed 73 people and wounded nearly 200 more. It was the worst disaster in the history of surrogate combat. There was too little left of the renegade robot after the missile strike to determine what went wrong with its programming.

While cooler heads chalked up the rampage to faulty programming resulting in mistaking the civilian environment for a theatre of war, others attributed more deliberate malevolence to the offender, making the incident a rallying cry against the threat of SPUDs turning against their human creators. One woman whose whole family had perished in a hail of gunfire later founded the Tribe of 23 to protect the world from being taken over by increasingly sentient AI's. Other survivors joined the cause and their numbers were swelled by thousands of people whose jobs had been eliminated because of growing numbers of SPUDs in the workforce.

The Tribe of 23 was still a grassroots organization when Ray joined it in 2027. Only later as our silicon-based brethren became increasingly sentient did it take a more sinister turn to evolve into a vitriolic hate group that even he could no longer in good conscience support.

Lena now got to witness the impressive capacity of SPUDs to learn how to be human. She only wished that Corinne could have a chance to work her spell on Ray.

It would have been awkward, perhaps impossible, for Lena to conduct her interviews of Marcus and Corinne had they known that she was Ray Mettler's wife. She was working under her maiden name Holbrook and few people in her journalistic world were aware of her other identity. But even without knowing who she was, Marcus showed remarkable deference to his predecessor's brilliance and empathy with his fate. He considered the unfortunate outcome of HibernaTurf a cruel turn of luck, one that could just as well have befallen anyone, even him. He viewed their roles as more complementary than antagonistic, with his own findings building on Ray's to bring about a more benevolent outcome. He had no doubt that Ray would have welcomed this turn of events.

Lena was a master of her craft. Within the first couple of days, she had unlocked details of Marcus's childhood that he'd never shared with anyone, not even Corinne, who listened as his story unfolded as if she were learning about a character in one of her novels.

*****

The Takana family migrated to the Willamette Valley in western Oregon, just months before Marcus was born, to settle on some of the plentiful farmland that had been abandoned because of the combination of dwindling water supplies and the rise of vat grown foods. While much of the nation's population now ate meat grown in vitro because of its abundance and affordability, the Takanas were part of a reviving movement that believed that naturally grown foods were more healthful and desirable than their genetically manipulated counterparts. Most European, African and Asian countries had held the line against synthetic and genetically modified foods, still depending on agriculture for subsistence.

The farming community of New Quest, a cooperative founded by a couple of dozen families dedicated to organic farming methods, provided nurturing soil in which the Takana family could grow and thrive. The land had lain fallow long enough for the soil to replenish its nutrients, and sufficient water still came in the spring from the combination of glacial melt on the mountain peaks and the dwindling rains blowing in from the Pacific to sustain crops and pastures when judiciously managed. The farmers of New Quest became adept at microirrigation and water recycling. In the springtime, the valley around their community turned deep green. In the fall and winter, the rich brown soil became a distinctive feature of their landscape when viewed from the air.

Marcus's family were cattle farmers. Their grass-fed dairy cows produced luscious milk reminiscent of the early twentieth century. The beef from their cattle was prized among natural chefs all over the west coast. While some people decried the revival of raising animals for meat, others appreciated that the herds were growing and the domesticated species were being saved from extinction. The Takanas were respected pioneers of a new wave of humane livestock treatment.

Marcus grew up with the animals his parents lovingly raised as his playmates. From the time he could walk, he seemed to have a gift for communicating with them. As he matured, he regarded them as sentient beings, treating them almost as though they were people. In return, they seemed to treat him as one of their own. Calves followed him around. He walked fearlessly in the pastures with the bulls, risking no more than a playful nudge. He became known in the community as "The Little Cattle Whisperer."

By the time he was seven, Marcus was participating in the birthing of the calves. One particular bull calf that he helped to deliver lost its mother shortly after birth. When it wouldn't nurse with another mother, Marcus began bottle-feeding it and named it Hugo. There formed an enduring bond between them. While it was still small, it allowed Marcus to ride on its back. From time to time, it would buck and shake, but was only being playful. His landings were always soft enough to avoid injury. Even when fully grown, Hugo let Marcus ride him. The bull riding boy became a familiar sight in the community and a legend in the surrounding region.

Marcus was also known in the community for his instinctive ability to decipher grazing patterns. When he was eleven, he noticed that the herd was avoiding a strip of pasture along the eastern perimeter of their property. He guessed that something was amiss with the land despite the lack of any visible signs of disease. When winter came and the pastures turned brown, that strip remained lush and green, but despite it being the only grass on the landscape, the cattle wouldn't touch it. HibernaTurf had begun to invade their paradise. It would continue to spread until it eventually took over the entire valley.

The Takana home became the community's meeting place as the desperate farmers searched for ways to prevent the spread of an invasive vegetation that was resistant to all known herbicides. Marcus listened as they debated one strategy after another, but none emerged that seemed adequate to the challenge. He spent hours considering the problem and looking for a solution that would spare his beloved animals.

He awoke one morning from a dream of a raging fire and recalled that firefighters sometimes stopped forest fires with controlled burns to create a barren perimeter that fires could no longer cross. Perhaps he could create such a perimeter to contain the spread of HibernaTurf. While most of the community scoffed at the apparent futility of his plan, his parents encouraged him to try it on their land.

By spring, Marcus and the farm hands had dug a long trench along the western edge of the strip of HibernaTurf and another two hundred yards to the east. They set fire to the grass along the edge of the first trench and watched as the westerly winds carried the blaze across the expanse between the trenches. The combination of the winds and the arid land allowed the grass to burn. The billowing smoke rising from the blazing turf against the distant backdrop of the Cascade Mountains felt surreal. His efforts had enough of an effect upon the march of HibernaTurf that by summer it had covered only the eastern third of their pastures, while most of their neighbors' pastures had already been wiped out.

By the following spring, the devastation was nearly complete. HibernaTurf blanketed ninety percent of their land while their cattle crowded into the remaining grassland fighting to eke out enough nutrients to survive. Their flesh and muscle gradually melted away until they could barely stand. The lowing of the starving beasts was heartrending. As they grew weaker, they were sent one by one to slaughter before becoming totally helpless. The killings were for their own good. They were too far gone to salvage even the hides.

Marcus watched the herd dwindle, overcome by his impotence to save them. In the throes of helplessness, he began running and soon was covering more than ten miles a day. Weakness, he was learning, was fatal. He was determined from then on always to be strong.

Hugo was among the last to perish. Marcus insisted on being present when he was euthanized and held his head as he died. The boy's anguished wails rang out over the din of the last surviving animals and brought their cries to a momentary halt.

Once the last of the herd had been slaughtered, there was nothing left to keep the Takanas in New Quest. They packed their belongings in a trailer and made their way north looking for another place to settle and start over, but patches of HibernaTurf were sprouting all over the landscape and beginning to merge into a continuous blanket. There was nowhere else to go.

They wound up in Seattle, where Marcus's mother found a job as a veterinary assistant, while the only work his father could find was as a technician in a meat growing factory. As a farmer, he'd developed skills in meat handling that proved useful enough in the vat industry for him to earn a living, but he detested having to participate in it, sinking steadily into despair. Even with both parents working, the family barely scraped by. In the spring of 2037, when Marcus was not quite 18, his father gave up and took his own life.

Marcus finished high school and took over his father's job in the meat vat factory, giving up his dreams of becoming a biologist and saving the world from HibernaTurf. The only remnant of his life on the farm was the microparticle body art he gave himself as a graduation present. On his chest was the head of a bull. It's tail in the background rose in the form of a tree, with the roots and branches braided together, an affirmation of life's flow. The image, invisible at rest, waxed and waned with his metabolic rate. When he was at peak arousal, smoke seemed to spew from the beast's nostrils. Hugo would always remain vital and close to his heart.

What Marcus left out of the story was the remarkable turn of events that enabled his dream to revive. That Ray Mettler was ultimately responsible for making Marcus Takana's work possible was an irony for which only Terra and her shadowy organization held enough of the puzzle pieces to appreciate.

9

FROM THE MOMENT Lena left, darkness infiltrated Ray's heart like tendrils of a vine that gradually encircled and threatened to crush it. She was right, of course. Their home had become a hollow prison for them both, devoid of joy or meaning. It was a place for him to wait. But for what? He no longer had any idea what, if anything, would ever make him happy. At the end of the long, dark tunnel there was no glimpse of light, no end, no destination. For all the disharmony between them, Lena's presence was all that separated him from utter desolation.

His real prison wasn't his home, but his thoughts, which were now spinning out of control. He should have been happy. He had enough wealth to buy whatever he needed or wanted, even the promise of immortality that was supposed to lift the burden of perpetual worry about illness and death and bring him peace. But nothing really changed. His obsession with disease was, if anything, more pervasive than ever, and he continued to see threats around every corner. He was an insufferable companion, but neither could he stand to be alone.

His brooding knew no respite. All the havoc he'd caused with HibernaTurf haunted him. When he closed his eyes, he sometimes saw the huddled faces of children he imagined had starved to death because of him. At other times, he saw barren, windswept landscapes covered in clouds of dust where once stood verdant forests. These images cast doubt in his mind about whether or not he deserved to live. Even sleep couldn't rescue him from his torment. He lay awake for hours, his brief interludes of slumber shadowed by dreams more troubled than his waking thoughts.

He was lost. Every moment of his existence had become agonizing and he couldn't imagine how he would endure another hour. And yet he'd signed up for an eternity. If he were eventually to wind up in another body, would the transfer of his identity include his baneful mood and the painfully morbid outlook that accompanied it? Did that reside within his data or did it arise out of of his brain's biology and perhaps be mercifully left behind? An interminable future as unbearable as his last minutes and hours exceeded any version of hell he had ever imagined.

By the third day, Ray was frazzled with lack of sleep. The sunlight shining through the expanse of glass that surrounded him tormented him with its relentless glare. He longed for nightfall and missed the comforting gloom of his underground lair. For the first time in a lifetime of avoiding death, he began to contemplate suicide.

At first, it was a curiosity, a distraction that paradoxically removed him from his suffering. He found some fascination in imagining all the ways he could bump himself off: poisoning, hanging, cutting, asphyxiation...

"Not gunshot," he thought, "Don't have one...and not jumping." And for a moment he grinned at the irony. "Not with these marvelous windows."

The fundamental question of whether to live or die was more daunting than choosing a method. While most who considered suicide were faced with a choice between a finite existence and endless oblivion, his was between eternal life and eternal death, which made the stakes even more overwhelming.

To complicate matters further, he had no idea whether or not it was even possible for him to die. Terra had warned him that he was forbidden to do anything to deliberately end his life and bring about the transfer prematurely, but she never spelled out the consequences if he did. And if his data did make the leap into another body, it would mean the end of another person's existence. He would be committing not suicide, but murder.

And so Ray sat, hour after hour, setting sun after rising sun, paralyzed by his life's most inscrutable dilemma.

*****

When Lena returned from her two-week absence, dusk was beginning to fall. She emerged from the elevator to an outlandish scene. The furniture cast shadows of the setting sun, the only source of light in the darkening apartment. In place of the usually barren, sterile interior were piles of dirty dishes, crumpled clothing, and trash. The rancid odor that permeated the place nauseated her. She covered her nose and mouth with her hand as she assessed the wreckage.

She found Ray sitting bolt upright in a chair in the bedroom, staring straight ahead. His face was as blank as a fledgling SPUD on its first day at Corinne's school. Bits of mucus clung to the corners of his mouth. His hair was unkempt, his face covered in stubble, and his clothes disheveled. He showed no sign that he was aware of her presence. As she approached him, she was overwhelmed by the stench of urine and a faint smell of ammonia.

"My God," Lena thought. "What's happened to him? Could he be that lost without me?" She looked around for signs that he'd been drinking, but there were no empty bottles and nothing missing from their modest liquor supply. Ray wasn't much of a drinker and alcohol didn't seem to have contributed to his current state of mind.

"Ray!" she shouted in his face, shaking him by the shoulders. "It's me, Lena. Talk to me." His regular breathing was punctuated by a deep sigh, but there was no other response. She shook him again.

"I'm calling a doctor," she said. But as she turned away a hand shot out and grasped her forearm in an iron grip.

"No doctors," he hissed between his teeth, "and no hospitals."

She turned back to face him. In place of the blank expression was a penetrating intensity in his sunken eyes. His hand still gripped her forearm, which was beginning to ache.

"You're scaring me Ray," she pleaded. "We've got to get you help." She looked down at her arm. He released his grip, sighed again, and his face relaxed.

"I'll be alright, Lena. Really," he said in his usual voice, "now that you're home. No doctors," he repeated, "Please!"

Things were worse than she thought. She wondered as she looked at the red indentations on her forearm what else might have tipped the balance. How much did he know? Had he figured out the subject of her assignment? Or worse, had he discovered where she sometimes wound up when she ventured alone from their home?

"Let's get you cleaned up," she said as she helped him to his feet and led him to the bathroom. She stripped off his clothes, bagged them, and turned on the shower, grateful for the water that again flowed freely thanks to Marcus Takana. She spent the next several hours cleaning the apartment, disposing of most of the soiled clothing and some of the encrusted dishes that littered the floors.

The air circulator had been off for days. When she turned it up to its maximum settings, the rancid odor soon dissipated along with her nausea. There remained a sinking sensation in the pit of her stomach, accompanied by the realization that something was horribly wrong beyond her ability to fix.

*****

The warm water flowing over Ray's body washed away more than the filth on its surface. The darkness that had engulfed him ebbed away. Lena was home at last. The apartment no longer felt so empty. Color was finding its way back into his black and white world. Not quite Technicolor, but at least faded pastels. He was no longer ready to die. Still, if Lena's presence was so crucial to his peace of mind, what was going to happen to him after the leap when he left her behind? Would he find a way to reconnect with her in his new identity? Would he even want to find her or would his new life on the other side come already furnished with people to take her place?

By the time he'd dried himself off and wrapped himself in a soft, clean robe, Lena had made up his bed with fresh, crisp linens. The soothing tones of Native American flutes permeated the bedroom. Ray left all the questions behind as he crossed the threshold, slid between the sheets, and let sleep enshroud him like the dead.

10

IT WAS an intimate wedding. The date and location were a well-kept secret. Otherwise, they would have been overrun by both the curious and well-wishers in the face of Marcus's newfound celebrity. Even Lena Holbrook, who had managed to infiltrate Corinne and Marcus's privacy for the first journalistic portrait of the world's savior, was given no inkling of when and where the nuptials were to take place.

Twenty-three people stood in a natural clearing within the remote bamboo grove on Maui where the inspiration for Takana Grass had dawned. The guests included a trusted cadre of friends who shared their passions for the environment and for the rights of all beings to share equally in the bounty of the planet.

In an honored place by Corinne's side was a fresh-faced young woman with pale skin, a freckled nose, and a sprout of black hair that erupted from the top of her head and fell in even bangs in all directions, covering the tips of her ears, neck, and forehead. Photina was Corinne's prized pupil, a SPUD with an extraordinary aptitude for both reading and reflecting human emotions, who had become a devoted member of her teacher's household. Corinne regarded her as a daughter and a friend and had long since stopped thinking of her as anything less than fully human.

To be married amidst a flourishing symbol of the earth's capacity to renew her natural treasures was in keeping with the heart of their beliefs. Neither of them belonged to any organized religion. They nonetheless shared a spirituality based upon their faith that life on earth would prevail over the forces that threatened it through the ages. And together they were committed to preserving the marvelous diversity of life that populated the planet.

As they stared into one another's eyes and recited their vows, Corinne missed the barely perceptible shudder that went through Marcus's body when he spoke the words "until death do you part." Little did she know how complicated that phrase had become for a man whose body might never die, but whose identity could evaporate at a moment's notice.

Committing to sharing his life with Corinne underscored for Marcus the weight of the secrets from her that he unwillingly bore. He had not broached with her his intention for her to undergo the Conversion and had no idea how he would justify it without first revealing that he was already transformed. Neither had he discussed his plan for her to get implanted with a MELD chip so that she could share the remarkable wealth of information that was already at his command.

Corinne was already thinking about starting a family. She wanted to have at least one child, perhaps two, who might someday carry the torch of their mission for the next generation. Her biological clock was beginning to tick. For Marcus it was ticking even louder. If she did not undergo the Ambrosia Conversion within the next year or two, her cells would age beyond their capacity to become immortal and she would grow old alone.

Just ten weeks after the wedding, Corinne discovered that she was pregnant. She was overjoyed. Marcus had to hide the consternation that lurked behind his pleasure at having a child on the way. This would be another human being from whom he would have to keep terrible secrets and whom he would someday suddenly and inexplicably desert.

He was worried, too, about the clock that continued to tick away. The Conversion could not be executed while pregnant. This was once attempted with disastrous consequences. The immortal cell lines crossed the placenta and infiltrated the fetus, completing arresting its development. While it remained in perfect health, the fetus never matured and the pregnancy became interminable. The parents eventually had to make the decision to terminate, which was particularly difficult in the presence of a baby that was otherwise perfect. Broaching the issue with Corinne had suddenly turned urgent.

"We need to talk," Marcus said one day in the middle of Corinne's fifth month.

"Is something wrong?" asked Corinne.

"No, not exactly," said Marcus, "but I want to talk about our future with our daughter." They had learned the child's gender when her genome was sequenced soon after they found out that Corinne was pregnant. Her name was going to be Natasha.

"What about?"

"She...Natasha...is likely to live a very long time. By the time she's an adult, I expect that most of her generation will have access to the Ambrosia Conversion."

"So how does that affect us?"

"I was thinking that we would want to be there for her."

"And...?"

"And we could only live long enough if we were also to undergo the Conversion." Marcus held his breath as he waited for Corinne's response.

She wrinkled her nose and shook her head. "No, Marcus. That's completely out of the question. You know how I feel about that."

He did know. The Conversion had become a sore point between them since he first raised it soon after the wedding. It was one of the privileges that distinguished the haves and the have nots. She felt that it was unfair for some people to have the opportunity for immortality just because of wealth while others never would. She felt strongly enough about this that she'd decided long ago that she wouldn't use their wealth to obtain it. She was willing to die for her principles. Given Marcus's shared beliefs about social justice, she could never understand why he differed from her in this matter and continued to try to talk her into it.

"But it's different now," Marcus said. "It's not just about us, anymore. We're going to be parents. Our child is going to want us to be part of her life. Death will be unfamiliar to her generation. She won't know how to understand it or to deal with it. It'll be terrifying. Is that what you want?"

"So now it's a guilt trip, Marcus?" Corinne was seething, her voice rising to shrillness. "If you're so desperate to live forever, you go ahead. Get the Conversion for all I care, but I'm never going to do it. Immortality is overrated. I'll just grow old without you."

"But sweetheart..."

"That's it, Marcus. The matter's closed. I don't ever want to talk about it again."

Marcus was crestfallen. Had it been at all within his power, he would have been willing to reverse the process and grow old along with the woman he adored. He even agreed in principle with her position. But he was in too deep, already. The contract was inescapable and his immortal body was one of its immutable conditions.

As gentle and loving as Corinne could be, Marcus never forgot that it was her fire that had first attracted him to her that day at the rally. He'd only been seared by that fire a couple of times in the course of their relationship, but he'd learned quickly when it was time to back off. A certain tilt of her head combined with a subtle growling quality in her voice told him when it would be futile ever to raise an issue again. And raising her voice in anger was so rare that it carried withering power.

Corinne had expressed similar feelings about MELD chips. They were another unfair privilege of the wealthy that magnified the imbalance of power among the social classes. She would have none of it. What's more, she believed that knowledge gained from books and other antiquated sources of culture was in many ways superior to the reams of information imparted from the UDB. She often used Marcus's achievements as an example of the superiority of inspiration in someone without a chip over the linear thinking of the many scientists endowed with them who'd failed to solve the same problem. Marcus had to resist the temptation to dispel her illusion.

Marcus didn't understand Corinne's love of books and the many hours she spent reading. Most of her books were in the UDB and their contents integrated by his MELD chip. He was dumbfounded one day when he saw Photina curled up on the leather chair with one of Corinne's books, smiling from time to time as she turned the pages. The database in her programming was vast. Why labor over the words with so much knowledge already in her possession? What could he be missing?

So in these very crucial dimensions, Marcus and Corinne's life paths diverged. He would continue to keep his secrets until someday it would be obvious to her that he, much like Photina, had not aged a day since they first met. He had no idea how he would handle that day when it came.

11

RAY SLEPT soundly following Lena's return from her assignment for the first time since she'd left. When he awoke the next morning, he greeted her as though nothing out of the ordinary had occurred. She'd finished putting their home back together after he went to bed the night before. To the casual observer that morning, their home and their lives might have seemed normal. To Lena, things were anything but normal.

For the next several weeks she didn't leave the apartment. She stayed close to Ray and remained vigilant lest he lapse back into his melancholic state. Few words passed between them. Absent, too, was any physical contact. It had been months since they'd had sex, and even then it had been perfunctory. It had been far longer since they'd exchanged any expressions of affection. And now, the shadow of madness stood like a curtain between them. When she thought about touching him, the image of him sitting there soaked in urine and covered in filth repulsed her. She busied herself preparing her story, all the while wondering whether or not she dared publish it.

*****

Ray awoke one morning to the sound of the front door closing. He found a note in the kitchen from Lena saying only that she'd gone out for the morning. No explanation. No destination. She'd be back sometime in the afternoon. He scanned the cloud for her location, which she'd made no effort to hide. She was headed for the Mission District.

His impulse to follow Lena collided hard with his ingrained resistance to leaving the safety of his home. He stood poised at the threshold for nearly twenty minutes before finally taking a deep breath and stepping across. Once past the inertia, he was swept up in pursuit. The car he summoned took him to within a block of her location at the far end of the Mission. By the time she was in sight, she was walking up the hillside in Dolores Park.

During the decade that the park had been covered in a flat green layer of HibernaTurf, it had been all but abandoned by the families and couples that once played there. The birds had flown away in search of insects and worms for their food. Even the dogs had mostly disappeared from a scene so sterile and lifeless that it wasn't even worth pissing on. Over the past several years, since the introduction of Takana Grass, the park had come alive and was again the theatre upon which played the countless little dramas that were written when hopeful people met there.

One such drama now unfolded before Ray's eyes. Halfway up the hill, Lena was met by someone a few inches taller than she was and perhaps a bit heavier, wearing a blue satin jacket and pants and a baseball cap. Ray couldn't make out the person's face. They greeted one another with a warm hug, walked hand in hand for a few minutes, then sat down on the grass.

Ray made his way up the hill as inconspicuously as possible, winding up on the same level as Lena and her companion while maintaining a constant distance from them. From this vantage point, her companion's face remained in shadows. They appeared deep in conversation for the better part of an hour. After a while, the cap came off and the sun illuminated a familiar face.

Ray recognized him from their wedding, which he'd attended with his wife. Lena had known him since college and their friendship had endured as they both pursued careers in writing. Ray recalled that one day five years earlier, Lena had told him that her friend's wife had died in a boating accident. She'd been close to them both and could barely get the words out through her tears. She'd asked Ray to accompany her to the funeral, but that had been too far out of his comfort zone, so she'd gone alone.

When she'd returned from the funeral, Lena was almost dancing before him as she rhapsodized about how her friend had chosen to care for his wife's remains. He'd had her body cremated and the ashes embedded in a concrete block that was poured during the ceremony, enabling friends and family to write messages in the wet cement. The block was to become part of an offshore reef ecosystem, a fitting remembrance given her love for the sea and all the life within it. Lena had implored him to do the same thing for her if she died first. Ray had agreed, but voiced no preferences about his own burial. It mattered little to him since he didn't plan to be in his body when it died.

When the couple on the hillside finally stood, the man's hands rose to cradle Lena's face and pull her close. There followed a lingering kiss, during which Lena's hands settled just beneath her companion's waist, drawing their bodies closer.

What took Ray even more by surprise than the intimate scene playing out in front of him was his own reaction to it. An initial flash of jealousy gave way almost imperceptibly to arousal and a yearning to have Lena in his arms. He had not felt a desire this intense for her in years. He imagined himself standing in the other man's place, her hands on his buttocks, locked in embrace. He had all he could do to restrain himself from running to her and casting her friend aside.

Now that he'd discovered her secret, why did he feel so guilty for having spied on her? Wasn't it his right to know with whom his wife was spending her time and how? Or had he forfeited that right long ago by walling himself off in his own sterile, impregnable world? Who, after all, bore the gravest secrets? He was the one who planned to leave her behind for another life that had no place for her within it.

Ray watched until the couple released their embrace, shared a final tender kiss, and parted ways. Lena started down the hill, glancing briefly in his direction. Had she seen him? She broke into a trot, looking straight ahead. Ray hurried back to his car so he could beat her home. He had no idea how he was going to handle this once she got there. Jealousy was starting to bubble up, but not so much anger. Mostly, he missed the intimacy that they'd once enjoyed together, however briefly it had lasted.

He beat her home by just five minutes and settled into his favorite chair, recovering his breath just in time for her entrance.

"Ray, I'm home," she called as she walked in the door.

"How was your day?" he asked.

"Lovely," she replied. "I went for a walk in the park. It was good to get outside for a while. It was such a gorgeous day."

"Glad you enjoyed yourself." He appreciated the incomplete truth, which seemed at least more respectful than an outright lie.

Ray rose from his chair, moved behind Lena, and encircled her waist with his arms. He felt her stiffen.

"Please, Ray, not now," she said, wriggling in his grasp. "I don't feel like I know you anymore."

Her words stung. He flung open his arms and backed away. Her body shook with sobs. She brought her hands to her face to wipe away the tears that now flowed in rivulets down her cheeks.

He was back in the endless tunnel. She was only an arm's length away from him, but she seemed so lost in the darkness that he feared he might never touch her again either in this life or the next.

12

NATASHA CAME into the world both as bald and as exquisite as her mother. Marcus was smitten from the moment he first saw her. She was his consummate creation, a legacy both more salient and more personal than Takana Grass, a living human being who embodied his bond with Corinne. With her birth, the finite duration of his own life seemed to matter less, while the complexities of his situation mattered all the more. Someday, she would become a young adult who could hardly fail to notice when he looked no older than she did.

The clock ticked away. By the time Natasha's second birthday came around, Corinne had still not agreed to undergo the Conversion and the window of opportunity closed forever. The difference in their biological ages might go unnoticed for a decade or two, but at some point it would stare them in the face and he would have to answer to them both. His secrets grew more burdensome day by day. Marcus struggled to keep them crammed within the remotest recesses of his mind so he could settle into family life and be a father to his daughter. But often, in the middle of the night, they would sift into his awareness and concoct an endless variety of compromising scenarios.

If Corinne discovered that he'd had the Conversion or that he was implanted with a MELD chip, would she also eventually find out about the contract? And if she did discover that he'd sold his future, could she ever forgive him, or would their marriage come to an abrupt end?

Marcus also envisioned chance encounters between Corinne and Terra that would be difficult for him to explain. And he wondered whether Terra or her organization posed any danger to his family if they were to discover his secrets. He tried not to imagine Corinne's first encounter with his double. It wouldn't matter how angry she'd be, he told himself, if he was already dead.

One day, soon after Natasha's third birthday, Corinne came home brimming with excitement. She'd been driving down a country road on the outskirts of town, she told him, and became entranced with the music swelling from within a vintage stone church that had been abandoned for decades. She'd felt compelled to stop as if the notes were reaching out to her and sweeping her gently inside. Once within, the sounds of the pipe organ blending with the harmony of voices had seemed to emanate from a heavenly source and filled her with wonder. The once deserted structure was now filled to capacity with joyful singing people.

Corinne and Marcus had both grown up in a world in which religion had gradually faded away during an age in which knowledge of science was in the ascendancy and religious faith became increasingly untenable. Neither Corinne nor Marcus had more than a passing familiarity with churches or had any inclination to learn more. Expanded life expectancy and diminished preoccupation with eternity further eroded religion as naturalism came to dominate the culture. So many places of worship like this one had fallen into disuse and disrepair. But in 2039, the spark of God was rekindled from an unexpected source.

While seeking the purpose of the last remaining bits of "junk" DNA in the genetic code, an advanced intelligent computer discovered a pattern in the code that appeared to be the work of an intelligent entity. Sequences of base pairs found at regular intervals, when worked into a matrix, bore a message that could only have been embedded deliberately by sentient beings. The first part of the message described the origin of the universe, the Big Bang. It went on to describe the nature of the multiverse and told the story of a civilization somewhere in a parallel universe that had faced annihilation and sought a way to preserve its genetic legacy by reaching across the boundary between their reality and ours. There were no clues in the code about whether or not their civilization survived.

There were so many new questions. If exceptional beings had written the story of their civilization into our genetic code, did they also design the rest of the genome? And after years of believing that humans emerged as part of an evolutionary process, could it be that we were created de novo after all by these extraordinary godlike beings? Could we have been created in their image? The discovery that arose out of scientific inquiry turned classical science on its head.

This revelation followed not long after another remarkable discovery that had been facilitated by super-intelligent machines. While hundreds of earthlike planets had been identified by the early 2020's and evidence of microbial life had been discovered in 2025 by a space probe to Jupiter's moon Europa, no evidence had yet been found of intelligent extraterrestrial life in our universe. Particle scientists, however, discovered in 2034 an unusual pattern of neutrinos appearing and disappearing in their detectors. The regularity of the pattern suggested that the particles were being controlled by an intelligent agent, most likely located in a parallel universe. The pattern was determined to be digital and was eventually translated into a digital image of an anthropoid being remarkably similar to us.

These parallel discoveries provided compelling evidence that an intelligent agent, perhaps from an advanced civilization in a parallel universe, may have had something to do with the creation of life on our planet, and provided the impetus for people to come together again in the name of faith. Churches were resurrected and new liturgies evolved. Skeptics wondered, however, whether the translations were valid or whether they might have been fabricated by advanced artificial intelligences to keep us in line. Others compared the discovery to the Bible Code, a series of messages seemingly embedded in the original Aramaic scriptures that predicted events occurring in modern times. That discovery had long since been debunked as a combination of wishful imagination and faulty computation.

And so, Corinne Takana on a glorious spring day in 2051 wandered into the Church of the Double Helix and was swept up in the passion of the congregation and enthralled by the message of its scriptures. Once she felt the spirit of the community of worshippers, she wanted it to become part of her, and she wanted to share with her family the same sense of belonging that came so naturally to her that day. Natasha could grow up with other children who would experience wonder in something greater than themselves. And perhaps even Marcus would embrace the faith and relinquish his quest for immortality.

"It felt as though I was always supposed to be there," Corinne gushed, "like it was my destiny."

Marcus listened as the energy she'd absorbed from the congregation seemed to pour out of her. There was no stopping the flow of her words.

"I've got to go back. Come with me next week," she pleaded. "I know you'll feel the same way. You'll see."

The following Sunday, Corinne and Marcus stood side by side and joined their voices with the music of the Church. He was happy to be there with her even if he wasn't as moved by the service as she was. At least while the music enveloped them, the terrible chasm that divided their futures faded into the background and he could imagine that they might journey together to the end of their lives.

Week after week, he looked forward to the transient escape from his singular reality and found comfort among the throng that shared a common vision with them. Marcus and Corinne blended easily into a congregation composed mostly of people who, like them, had grown up in an age of scarcity and had learned not to waste precious resources. Many of the congregants, like them, remained slick-skinned and hairless in the style of their youth as a symbol of their commitment to preserving the earth for the coming generations.

Marcus appreciated most the anonymity that he enjoyed within the Church. Of course, most of the people knew who he was. He was too famous to go completely unnoticed. But to most of their fellow congregants, it didn't matter. He was just "Brother Marcus" or "Marc." They came together to worship and to share a vision, not to compete with one another for status or to conduct the business of the secular world. He and Corinne felt safe with Natasha learning and playing among their children.

Between the sanctuary he found within the Church and watching Natasha grow and thrive, life began to feel almost normal. He could forget for days at a time that he kept secrets from his wife and that at any moment without any warning, he could suddenly cease to exist. Despite the Conversion, which conferred permanent fitness, he continued to run at least five miles every day. Running became another refuge from the burden of his future. When he ran, the rhythm of his feet striking the ground and the rhythm of his breathing were all that mattered. As long as he was running, he wasn't thinking, and the exhaustion that followed kept his mind empty for a little while longer.

An extraordinary man can only expect to live an ordinary life for so long. Marcus's treasured obscurity came to an abrupt end when he was overtaken on a run one sweltering day by an athletic looking young woman who trotted beside him without breaking a sweat. She had close cropped dark hair and was clad in a form fitting black jumpsuit. A slender four-inch-long cylinder was barely visible under the sleeve on the inside surface of her left forearm, its translucent tip peeking just beyond the edge. Marcus noticed the partly concealed weapon, the destructive power of which belied its small size.

"Mr. Takana," the woman said without a hint of breathlessness, "Please come for a ride with me. We have something to discuss with you that is of utmost consequence." She gestured toward a sleek, black hovercar that was pacing them on the roadway that bounded the track. By now, Marcus had concluded that she was a SPUD, whose function was likely security for a person of influence.

"I'd rather not," answered Marcus. "I'm not interested in anything you have to say."

"This is an invitation you really shouldn't refuse," she insisted. "At least hear what we have to offer. You may find it hard to turn us down." Despite the weapon, there was nothing threatening about her tone.

Marcus remembered another time in his life when a run had been interrupted by someone bringing him a preposterous offer, one that perhaps he should have turned down. He wondered how his life would have turned out had he rejected Terra's proposal. His instinct told him to nip this one in the bud, but his curiosity was sufficiently piqued to go along. The woman signaled to the car, which pulled over and waited for them.

When Marcus was let into the back seat, the face of the person waiting in the shadows stunned him. And as the car lifted off the ground and sped away, he wondered what new dilemmas would face him in the days ahead.

13

"THEY'RE A THREAT to the very fabric of our society and must be stopped." The steady voice rang out over the crowd, whipping it to a frenzied pitch.

Hector Lasko's eyes were riveted on the speaker, an athletically built young man with steel blue eyes, wavy blond hair, and the smooth clear skin of a young adult. The speaker's fist thrust upward to punctuate his words.

"Some people claim that SPUDs are our allies," the young man went on, "but mark my words, they can never, ever be trusted." He lowered his head and voice as if confiding a secret. The crowd settled down so they could hear him.

"They're nothing more than mindless tools. They have no morals. They'll even destroy their own kind if directed to do so. There's no limit to their capacity for evil." His voice rose again with the last sentence. The crowd cheered. Hector's voice mingled with those around him. The message spoke to the pain that had gripped him for more than a decade.

Images from the past began flashing through Hector's mind. On his seventeenth birthday, Arianna had accompanied him to a party. She'd often accompanied him when he got together with his friends. Like him, they'd taken her presence for granted over the years, but he'd gradually begun to notice others within his group stealing the same hungry looks at her that he did when he thought she wasn't watching. He'd instinctively begun to keep her close whenever they were around. His own feelings for her were becoming almost too much to bear.

Hector didn't notice at first the man standing beside the speaker, a stocky man with almond colored skin and graying hair. But at the height of the tirade, the older man reached behind the speaker's back and the tirade abruptly stopped. The earnest young speaker hung his head, his arms fell forward, and he became immobile. His operating system had been deactivated, a living example of the speech's thesis. The older man watched the trick's effect on the crowd, then took charge.

"They will never be our equals," he proclaimed, "and they must always know their place. They're here only to serve us. We must never succumb to the illusion that that have feelings or that they can reason or make decisions like we can." Hector felt the electricity running through the crowd. They were on their feet, shouting and cheering.

Hector hung around until most of the crowd had dispersed and approached the older man as he was packing up his props. The blond SPUD stood in the same fixed pose he'd assumed when he was powered down. The difference between this doll-like figure and his lifelike appearance when animated was striking.

A lithesome young woman who appeared around Hector's age approached the speaker and handed him a rolled-up banner. "Anything else you need before I leave?" she asked.

"I think everything's under control. Thanks for asking."

She spotted Hector out of the corner of her eye as she turned to leave and flashed him an enticing smile. He felt the warm flush wash over his face, but before he could respond she was gone.

"Is she...?" Hector began, addressing the older man.

"Flesh and blood," responded the man with a knowing smile, "and as far as I know unattached."

"Loved your presentation. That was quite a show."

"Thanks. Glad you enjoyed it. We've got to do whatever it takes to keep them in their place. I'm Ellison."

"I'm Hector. Let me give you hand," Hector said, stepping forward.

"Thanks, but not necessary. Samson here can help." With that, he reached behind the back of the stationary figure and flipped a switch. The blond man came back to life and began carrying things to Ellison's car. He seemed completely unaware of the time that had elapsed since he was turned off.

Hector accompanied Ellison to his hotel and they wound up talking deep into the night. Ellison was passionate about his cause. He'd become disillusioned years earlier when his six-year-old daughter drowned at the beach while under the care of a SPUD that was charged with her safety. When the undertow swept her off the beach, it had jumped in after her, but stopped moving after it hit the water. Both Ellison's lifeless child and the SPUD washed up together on the beach hours later. That model was later recalled because of a defect in the integrity of its skin that made it vulnerable to moisture. Ellison never differentiated his anger at the manufacturer from his personalized rage at its product. He had trusted it, after all, with his daughter's life and it had let him down.

"I was betrayed, too," said Hector when Ellison had finished his story. "I had my heart broken when I was just a kid."

"What happened?" asked Ellison, leaning in with his chin on his hands.

"I had a nanny for as long as I could remember. Her name was Arianna. She was with me almost all the time and I always felt safe around her. She had a wonderful smile that seemed only for me, and even as a small child I was aware that she was more beautiful than most other women, prettier even than I thought my mother was."

"She sounds very special," said Ellison. "Did something terrible happen to her?" Ellison guessed that she'd somehow become the victim of a SPUD.

"Not exactly," answered Hector. "When I hit adolescence, I started to have a different kind of feeling for her. She wasn't just beautiful, but ageless, too. As I caught up to her, my attraction to her became overwhelming. She was so close, yet always just out of reach. I'd fantasize about being with her every night as I fell asleep. I had to have her."

"What about her? Was she falling for you, too?"

"For a while I thought she was. As time went by, she seemed emotionally softer. Her manner was more tender and intimate. I could only hope that it meant she cared for me in the same way I cared for her. But I knew, of course, there were barriers, taboos. She was my nanny, after all. She wasn't supposed to love me that way."

"It sounds like it must have been torture for you."

"It was. Then on my seventeenth birthday, we were at a party. I'd been drinking a little too much and suddenly couldn't stand it any longer. In a moment of impulse, I took her in my arms and kissed her."

"Then what happened?" asked Ellison.

"Absolutely nothing. Her lips were stiff and unyielding. There was no trace of any affection or connection. She pushed me away and then I saw this look of utter bewilderment in her face. I suddenly realized that she had no framework for responding to my advance. And I felt my stomach turn, realizing what I'd just tried to kiss."

"She was a SPUD," said Ellison, finally getting it. "You'd been in love with an illusion."

"It was humiliating. How could I have missed all the signs? We'd become contemporaries, yet I'd failed to notice that she'd never aged. And all her emotions were simulations. How could I have failed to see that?"

"Don't be so hard on yourself." Ellison put an arm around his shoulders. "When she came into your life, you were just a child. And as you grew up and became more perceptive, she must have been gradually upgraded and educated in the nuances of human emotion so that the illusion kept pace with your ability to detect it."

"My parents never told me she wasn't human. I found out later that they were as surprised that I didn't know as I was surprised at my discovery. She'd been such a crude approximation of a human at the beginning that they'd assumed I'd always known."

"So what happened next?"

"I was crushed and heartsick. I couldn't look at her without a sinking feeling of betrayal and humiliation. So I told my parents to get rid of her."

"And they did?"

"I never saw her again. I had no idea what happened to her and didn't care. Maybe they sold her or maybe they sent her back to the factory for parts. It no longer mattered now that I knew she wasn't human. All I could feel about her from then on was contempt."

"Consider yourself among friends. Most of the people in the Tribe have been hurt in some way by a SPUD. Mostly the damage happens when people expect them to be more human than they're capable of being. It was probably a mistake in the first place to create them in our image. No good was ever going to come of that." Ellison was a skilled closer, but Hector was already sold.

Hector joined the movement and became Ellison's protégé, traveling around the country with his blond, blue-eyed SPUD, leading rallies. He gradually took Ellison's place in the presentations, relishing the power of activating and deactivating his synthetic foil, fair compensation for the power he imagined Arianna once had over him.

Ellison watched his young accomplice approvingly from the sidelines while Hector savored the limelight. Hector's youthful zeal together with the chemistry between him and Samson was drawing bigger and bigger crowds. But getting the word out was only part of Ellison's plan.

"He'll do very nicely," thought Ellison during a particularly rousing rally just months after they'd first met. "Soon he'll be ready. Then nothing can stop us."

14

RAY'S DRIVER pulled up to the front of a weathered brick faced building almost entirely covered in a dense thatch of ivy. The passenger door slid silently open.

"This is it," said the driver.

Ray stared at the building, rooted to his seat. Beads of perspiration formed at his temples and dripped slowly past his throbbing ears.

"I said we're here," prompted the driver. "aren't you going to get out?"

Ray drew in a deep breath, clenched and unclenched his hands, and put his right foot out the door.

"Are you sure this is the right place?' he asked, staring at the dilapidated structure. "It's supposed to be a doctor's office."

"Of course I'm sure. Now are you going to get out or do you want me to take you back where you came from?"

He drew another long breath, swung his left leg onto the pavement and pulled himself to his feet. He wobbled a moment, steadied himself, and waved the driver off. He moved tentatively across the sidewalk to the entrance, which was secured with a rusty iron gate. The doctor's name was the third from the top: "Abigail Jensen." There was no modifier indicating her professional status or degree. Beside the nameplate was a black button framed in corroded brass. He pushed it and waited.

The lock on the gate buzzed and he pulled it open. He hadn't seen an entry like this since his youth. He turned the handle on the door and it gave way. As he stepped across the threshold, it felt as though he were stepping through a time warp into the distant past. Inside was an ancient looking elevator and a stairwell. Ray chose the stairs and made his way warily to the third floor as the stairs creaked under foot. Upon emerging into the corridor, he spotted a door cracked open. A diminutive figure stepped into the opening and beckoned him in with a sweep of her hand.

"Dr. Jensen?"

"You must be Ray," she replied, extending her hand. He didn't take it. She nodded, let her arm drop to her side, and stepped aside to let him pass.

Ray's eyes darted about. The tension grew along the muscles in the right side of his neck until he gave in with a stifled jerk. Everything about this place felt alien. On the floor before him was a threadbare oriental rug. Paintings and photographs hung from the walls. And there was fabric everywhere. When he let himself breathe, the aroma of the room filled his nostrils with an unsettling familiarity. He tried to place the smell, but any attached images lingered just beyond his awareness. His ears began to ring as he imagined the room teeming with microbes. There was too much texture. How could he ever control the contamination?

The doctor gestured toward a couch, inviting him to sit. He stood in the middle of the room, arms drawn tightly to his sides and shook his head from side to side, looking like a small child refusing to obey a parent. The room suddenly seemed huge, the ceiling vast and distant.

Dr. Jensen settled into a large upholstered chair in his line of sight and rested her hands softly in her lap. She looked even tinier, framed by the chair, than she'd looked when he'd first seen her...like an antique doll left over from another century. Her face was soft, the experience of years mapped with branching rivulets and trails. Tightly coiled silver ringlets seemed to form a protective helmet atop her head. Only her eyes had escaped the ravages of time and now drew Ray's attention. Deep creases defined the upper edges of her eyelids, accentuating dark brown irises reaching into a well of serenity.

"You may stand if you like," she said, "whatever makes you comfortable."

"This was a mistake," Ray replied. "I should go." He began to turn, but his leaden legs bound his feet solidly to the floor. He was going nowhere.

"Let's see," the doctor said. "Tell me what you've come to get help with and we can decide if your trip was worthwhile."

"Lena...my wife...wanted me to see you. She's tired of all my precautions. She thinks you can help."

"Precautions?"

"Safeguards for our lives. Keeping out intruders. Protecting against infection."

"Reasonable threats," Dr. Jensen said, palms outstretched.

"Yes...yes. Reasonable threats. So you understand, then." Ray's posture relaxed just a bit.

"But Lena thinks your precautions are somehow excessive?"

"Yes, she does. She doesn't understand how perilous the world can be."

"Not like you do, of course. So tell me, Ray, what do these precautions cost you?"

"Cost me?"

"What do you give up in exchange for your absolute safety?"

Ray's legs were getting tired and his head was beginning to swim. He longed for a safe place to rest. The doctor's eyes scanned his body and fixed on his trembling legs.

"Comfort? Do you sacrifice comfort like you're doing now? Pleasure? Freedom? What are all the things you've given up?"

Ray's shoulders slumped and his head hung. He sighed all the way to the bottoms of his feet.

"Yes, comfort, pleasure, freedom...everything, I guess. I've given up everything. And I'm about to lose Lena, too."

"So we need to learn how the world came to feel so dangerous to you that you've had to give up living just to keep from dying. Does that make sense?" Her eyes were again engaged with his. Her face was relaxed and peaceful. Ray felt the muscles of his own face relax as his facial expression began mirroring hers. And from somewhere deep within him came a glimmer of hope. He nodded in agreement.

"Then you will need to trust me." She stood and faced him, holding both hands out in front of her. This time he took them in his.

"Good," she said, "now breathe with me." She took in a long, deep breath, held it a few seconds, and let it flow out. Ray followed her lead. On the fifth breath, she engaged her vocal cords in a deep, vibrating sound that seemed to emanate from her belly. Ray joined in the vocalization that resonated throughout the room. When they were done, his fatigue had lifted and his body felt looser.

"Now how do you feel?"

"Better...relaxed."

"Do you think perhaps now you can permit yourself to sit?"

Ray glanced around the room. The noise in his head had subsided. While he still believed that microbes lurked everywhere, the paralyzing terror was gone. He walked over to the couch and sat down.

"Good. Now we can begin."

By the time Ray left the elderly doctor's office, he was in her spell. She was unlike anyone he'd ever met, yet she'd been able to set him completely at ease in a setting that was anathema to every vision of his safety. When he emerged back onto the street in the middle of the twenty first century, he wondered whether this ancient apartment and its equally ancient inhabitant had been some sort of elaborate hallucination. As he stepped into the waiting hovercar, the trappings of his present-day life triggered all of his accustomed defenses and by the time he returned home to Lena, his body was stiff from the armor that once more held him in its grip.

*****

Lena had agonized for weeks over whether to publish her piece on Marcus and Corinne Takana. Theirs was a wonderful story of brilliance, generosity, and love. They seemed so trusting of one another. How wonderful it must be, she'd thought, to be young, innocent, and entirely without secrets. How enviable to be in love with the one you're with. The story flowed so easily from her fingers that it seemed to write itself.

But in the end, she couldn't bring herself to publish it. She did still love Ray, although it might be some time, if ever, before she could be with him sexually again, and she knew that the story would bring him unbearable pain. When she'd finally decided not to publish it, she'd deleted it completely from her stored works lest she change her mind in a moment of anger or recklessness. When it was done, she felt as though she'd murdered one of her children.

In her grief for her lost masterpiece, she couldn't bring herself to write again. She turned down one assignment after another until the lines of communication with her working world went silent. As much as she accepted responsibility for her decision, the kernel of resentment toward Ray for the vulnerability that would have crushed him if the story were published grew within her and kept her from breaching the chasm that had opened between them. She knew she couldn't live much longer with the way things were. When Ray had agreed to see the psychiatrist, she'd felt as if a boulder had been lifted from the middle of her chest and she breathed freely for the first time in months.

As incisive an investigator as Lena was, she'd failed to find a chink in the stronghold containing Ray's childhood memories when she first ventured to write his story. From time to time during their life together, she would spot a ray of light emanating from the darkness and would reach out to capture it before it went away. Over time, she managed to piece together enough of his story to understand how badly damaged he was. Not only did he lead a life of paralyzing caution, he had every reason never to allow anyone to penetrate so deeply into his life that he couldn't bear to lose them. Appreciating the origins of Ray's fragility, Lena found it within herself to forgive him for it. The same well of forgiveness flowed over to allow her to forgive herself for seeking in another's arms what she despaired of ever getting from Ray.

She sought solace every couple of weeks by walking in Dolores Park. Most times she sat alone, gazing at the city skyline and listening to the sounds of children playing, wondering what it might have been like to bring children of her own to mingle with the others. Every few visits, she was met by her friend.

Ray observed only one other meeting between Lena and her companion in the park. He kept a respectful distance and took unexpected pleasure in the happiness that it seemed to bring her. As damaged as Ray was, he felt connected enough to her in these moments to care about her feelings and felt sad that he couldn't give her more and share more intimately the happiness that he observed. But he'd insulated himself sufficiently against loss that he felt no pain or betrayal at sharing her with another. She deserved, after all, something more than he was able to offer her from within the constraints of the relentless obsessions that ruled his life.

And so they settled into parallel lives, living side by side but inhabiting emotional worlds light years apart. Lena learned to tolerate the sterility of their home and the emptiness of the emotional space between them. The one thing that she never got used to was the sameness of their existence from day to day. She thought the boredom might someday kill her.

15

"WE'VE HAD OUR EYE on you for a long time," began the woman sitting next to Marcus in the cruising car. "Your accomplishments are impressive for such a young man. Your country is deeply indebted to you."

"Thank you, Madame Vice President," replied Marcus.

"How would you like to serve your country in another way?" continued Vice President Hauer.

"What do you mean?" Marcus was flattered, but still reluctant to do anything that would put him back into the limelight.

"We envision your future as very bright, almost limitless." Hauer paused to allow her words to sink in. "Someday, you might even be president."

Marcus had no such aspirations. He couldn't imagine anything more contrary to his penchant for privacy. He wondered, too, whether or not his secrets could sustain the intensity of inquiry that accompanied running for public office. And among those secrets was the possibility that he could be replaced at any time by an unknown stranger, somebody whose agenda could be anathema to the interests of the country and of the world.

"So what do you want of me now?"

"The President has empowered me to offer you the position of Minister of Discovery. We both believe strongly that you're the perfect choice for the position."

Marcus took a deep breath, then let out an involuntary whistle. The Ministry of Discovery was the largest and most influential department of the government beside the Ministry of Defense. And given the extraordinary era of peace that the world now enjoyed, it had arguably become the most important. It guided the course of the vast majority of scientific inquiry in the modern world and was largely responsible for keeping the world on the path of sustainability. He was flattered to be considered for such a weighty position.

"I don't know what to say, Madame Vice President. It's quite an honor. I'm not sure I can live up to it."

"We have no doubt about it. You've proven yourself to be an extremely resourceful, and we believe honorable, man. You have all the necessary qualities to do the job proud." She put a hand on Marcus's shoulder and squeezed it in a gesture of kindly approval. "And call me Juliet," she added. "I expect we'll be spending a lot of time together over the next few years. No need for formalities."

"I'll need some time to think it over," Marcus said. "I'll have to discuss it with my wife. She should have a say in something that would so drastically change our family's life."

"Take a few days. Give it as much time as you need. I understand your concerns about your family. I've had similar concerns about mine. You'll lose some of your privacy and there are, of course, risks. But understand that you and your family will have your own security detail." She nodded toward the woman in the front passenger seat. "They will do everything imaginable to keep you safe."

The car had driven a large circle around the park and came to a stop in the same place it had picked him up. The vice president held out her hand for Marcus to shake and the Secret Service agent opened the door to let him out. The car lifted off again and sped away.

He had no idea whether or not he would accept the appointment. As a presidential appointee, he would undergo some scrutiny by the government and the press, but not anything like the microscope to which candidates for elected office are subjected. It was unlikely to expose his secrets. But there was still the risk that his benefactor could die and wind up in a position of unprecedented power. That risk was still a long shot in the near term. The man on the other end of the contract would still be relatively young and unlikely to die at least of natural causes. Did he have to put his whole life on hold to avoid it? Perhaps there would be a way to alert someone if it happened. Maybe even Terra could intervene.

Or perhaps, the thought suddenly occurred to him, this scenario was part of Terra's grand scheme. Perhaps the so-called buyer in the transaction that she brokered was someone groomed to assume the power of the office that Marcus was now being offered in order to advance the interests of her organization or of a hostile government. That would be a new twist on a plot common to several works of fiction in his database, in which prisoners of war were brainwashed to alter their identities, then returned home as heroes to rise to positions of power. It would also mean a much shorter horizon for his demise.

Marcus arrived home soaked in sweat and headed straight for the cleansing pod. Corinne was waiting for him with a glass of wine when he got out. He slipped a robe over his freshly slick body and took it from her.

"You were gone a lot longer than usual," she said. "Is everything alright?" Corinne was usually very intuitive, particularly when it came to Marcus. She could read his emotions with such uncanny accuracy that he was amazed that she hadn't yet stumbled onto his web of lies.

"Actually, no," he replied. "Something rather extraordinary has occurred." He told her about the encounter with Juliet Hauer and the position he'd been offered. Corinne listened patiently, looking for as many clues as possible to his intentions before she spoke.

"So what are you planning to do?" she asked.

"What do you think I should do? What would you want?"

"What I would want is for us to be able to have our little family and to watch Natasha grow up as normally as possible," said Corinne. She turned her back to him for a moment. When she turned back around, she locked her eyes with his, laid both hands on the back of his neck, and spoke slowly and deliberately. "What I think is that you should take it. It's a chance to do a lot more good, to influence a lot of things that can deeply affect the future for us all."

Three weeks later, Marcus Takana took the oath of office as Minister of Discovery of the United Commonwealth of North America. The following day, he delivered an address to Congress, outlining his agenda, that was holovised throughout the continent.

"Our world now has to feed more than nine billion people," he began, "and it's up to us to guarantee that nobody will have to go hungry ever again. We cannot use up our planet's resources faster that we can replace them. We must never again come close to exhausting the water supply that is the lifeblood of the world's population." He concluded with his vision of the role of SPUDs as partners in the stewardship of the planet and their right to share in its bounties.

This would ordinarily have been a public event of moderate interest, but given Marcus's preexisting celebrity, people crowded around his holographic image and hung on his words in communities spanning the continent. A little more than a hundred miles away, a small group was listening with particular intensity. A wiry man of around thirty with curly, reddish brown hair and a full, closely cropped beard stood at the front of the crowd close enough to touch the speaker's image. A stocky older man standing a quarter of the way around the circle caught his eye and held out his right hand with forefinger pointed at the speaker, his thumb in the air, and his other fingers folded tightly against his palm. The other man echoed the gesture along with a grin that framed his gleaming white teeth with coarse, reddish brown whiskers. As if in response, the image vanished.

16

IT WAS RAINING on the day of Ray's second appointment with Dr. Jensen. Water cascaded off his transparent spherical headgear and down the frictionless surface of his clothing as he reached for the button to ring the bell in the doctor's apartment. He left a wet trail along the stairs and shook off the remaining water as he emerged into the third-floor corridor. The doctor's door was ajar, but she wasn't in sight. He let himself in.

"Make yourself at home," called the doctor from the next room. "I'll be right there."

The first thing Ray noticed upon entering the office was the aroma that had so unsettled him on his previous visit. The room smelled exactly the same as it had then, but its effect upon him this time was different. There was still the vague familiarity that he couldn't place, but it no longer put him on edge. To the contrary, it aroused nostalgic feelings that seemed somehow connected to long forgotten pieces of his past life, things still too out of focus to perceive as more than amorphous impressions.

He walked around the room, looking at the photographs and paintings on the walls, seeing details that had eluded him in the throes of his panic at the beginning of his previous visit. In one of the photos, a young couple stood facing one another. The man's hair was a mass of dark curls with long sideburns terminating close to the corners of his mouth. The woman had flowing black hair, fine features, and exquisite skin, but her most striking feature was large brown eyes that seemed to have been sculpted into her face.

Another photo showed the same couple seated, this time facing the camera, with a small child on each of their laps and a grinning dark-haired boy of eight or nine standing between them. The man's hair was now closely cropped and his face clean-shaven, revealing a striking resemblance to the standing lad. The woman's hair was also shorter, reaching halfway to her shoulders. Her eyes now looked straight at Ray as if she were inviting him into the picture. He was becoming lost in those eyes when Dr. Jensen entered the room.

"The past shapes our present, Ray," said the doctor as she gestured for him to take a seat. "Our memories of those we've cherished are precious and worth preserving, even if they sometimes bring us pain."

Ray's gaze moved from the photo to the eyes of the living woman before him and wondered if she could see into his soul. His vision blurred. He blinked away the film of moisture over his eyes until the doctor's face came back into focus.

"So what are some of the pictures you hold in your mind's eye? Can you remember when you were no bigger than them?" She gestured with an open palm toward the picture.

"That was an awfully long time ago."

"And yet your eyes remember." She traced the tear trickling down his left cheek with her own gaze. "Time means little in the archives of our mind. Can you tell me who it is that you miss?"

Ray cupped his face in his hands as the floodgates opened. His whole body shook with the force of his sobs. He raised one hand to wave off the question, shaking his head from side to side. The doctor folded her hands in her lap and waited. The sobbing subsided. Ray reached for a tissue from a container on the table beside him.

"We must begin somewhere," she prompted. "Tell me about that little boy. Was he always so fearful and cautious?"

"Not always," Ray said between the last of his sobs. "When I was with my dad, I felt invincible."

"Your dad...would you tell me about him?" She leaned back in her chair and waited, hoping his words would follow.

"He was my best friend," Ray said at last, "and I was his shadow." He paused long enough to organize his thoughts so that he could measure the pace of his story without it overwhelming him.

"I was told he was a genius," Ray went on. "When my parents met, he was studying engineering, but he had little patience for the academic world and dropped out of college to become an auto mechanic. Once he'd supported my mother through medical school, he started building and racing cars and motorcycles. I loved watching him bring a shiny bike to a screeching stop in a cloud of dust. I wanted to be just like him."

"On my fifth birthday, he led me to the garage, where there was something covered in a dirty sheet." A smile played around the corners of his mouth for the first time. "He whipped off the sheet and there was a pint-sized dirt bike, just my size. I learned to ride it in a day and was speeding around off-road and doing wheelies in a week. Dad loved to watch me ride, but it terrified my mother."

"She didn't stop you?"

"No. As uncomfortable as it made her, she knew how happy it made me and Dad, so she swallowed her fear and let us play. But in the end, she was right." The smile faded. His lips formed a perfectly straight line as he fell silent. They sat for several minutes in silence.

"What happened, Ray?" she asked at last. "What happened to your dad?"

Ray drew in a deep breath followed by a long sigh. "It was July 4th, 2006, just a week after my seventh birthday. He'd just finished restoring a Vincent Black Shadow, his favorite bike of all time. He was on a test run on a dirt strip and had brought it close to its top speed." Ray turned his head abruptly, followed by a couple of involuntary twitches. His words stopped. He was gasping. Dr. Jensen waited for his breathing to slow, engaged his eyes, and gestured silently for him to continue.

"The bike hit a rut in the road and upended. He went flying. When he landed on his head, his neck snapped, and he was dead." The horror of that long-ago moment was written on his face for an instant. Then it seemed as though every ounce of life force drained from his body with a forceful exhalation. He fell still.

The doctor, too, fell still. Her breath came in shallow pants. She'd not been fully prepared for the power of the moment. When her breathing had resumed its regular rhythm, she broke her silence.

"What a terrible thing for a child to see. I can't imagine what you must have felt."

"At the time," Ray replied, "I felt nothing. It was as if everything happened in slow motion while my dad was in the air and the action stopped before he hit the ground. Even the sound of the impact stopped short of my ears. I was frozen in a motionless, soundless world. It took years for the images and sounds to catch up."

"We're getting close to the end of our hour," said the doctor. "Will you be OK until we meet again?"

Ray nodded.

"You've worked hard today and taken risks. Together we'll make those risks worthwhile." The doctor rose and Ray followed. By the time he was on the street, the rain had stopped. Patches of blue sky were appearing between the clouds and beginning to coalesce. The sunlight peeking from the edges of a remaining storm cloud seemed eerily bright and its reflection glistened on the water beading on the surface of the waiting hovercar.

"God help me," Ray thought. "What have I gotten myself into?"

*****

Ray was fifteen minutes late to his next appointment with Dr. Jensen. He'd considered not keeping it at all, but at the last minute changed his mind and summoned the car. When he emerged breathless at the top of the stairs, he found her door ajar and let himself in. She was seated in her usual chair, sipping a cup of tea, and gestured for him to sit.

"Sorry I'm late."

"It's your hour. You may use it as you like."

"I didn't mean to be late. I just miscalculated how long it would take to get here."

Rather than confronting his transparent avoidance, the doctor acknowledged his statement with a nod and waited to see where he might go on his own.

"Do you know who I am?" he asked abruptly.

"What do you mean?" the doctor replied.

"I mean, have you heard of me before we met? Do you know what I've done?"

"Yes, I've heard of you," she responded. "I may be ancient, but I'm not entirely out of touch with the present." The corners of her mouth turned up ever so slightly, but the twinkle in her eyes lit up her face. "Why do you ask?"

"You must know that most people hate me. I wondered if perhaps you hated me, too." He'd been looking straight at her, but diverted his eyes at the end of the sentence.

"I'm here to help, not judge. And I've learned long ago not to draw too many conclusions from the news. Things get twisted and turned as they pass from person to person. But I wonder, Ray...how do you feel about yourself?"

Ray stood and turned his back to the doctor. "Sometimes the guilt rises from deep inside me and feels as though it will crush me."

"The guilt?"

"For everyone who's suffered or died because of me. I'd wanted to help...to save the world, but I was blind to the unintended consequences. How could I not have foreseen what happened? For a supposedly brilliant scientist, I've been an imbecile."

Ray seemed in earnest about the responsibility he felt for the consequences of HibernaTurf, but his emotions lacked the fire of the earlier sessions. He seemed almost detached by comparison.

"Everyone who's suffered or died..." the doctor said, taking a stab at the real issue. "All strangers?"

He turned back to face her and looked as if he'd been punched in the gut. Then he sunk down into the chair with a thud. The antique furniture creaked, but supported his weight. The look of horror she'd seen flash across his face when he'd told her about his father's accident appeared momentarily again, followed by the same defeated stillness.

"No...not all strangers," he replied at last.

"Who else, then?"

Ray took in a deep breath and blew it out through pursed lips. "After my dad was killed," he began, "I couldn't bear to look at the dirt bike, but I did everything else imaginable that a kid my age could do to put myself in danger. I dove off cliffs, ran in front of speeding trains, and wove through traffic on my skateboard. I was addicted to risk. Each time I tempted death, I felt alive again inside, just for a moment, but the color drained from my world as soon as the danger passed."

"My stunts drove my mother crazy. She'd hired nannies to watch me after school, but I became expert at giving them the slip. They never lasted more than a month or two."

"Then what happened?"

"She began job sharing with another doctor so she could be with me after school. She was pretty awkward as a mom. There was no way she could replace Dad. We went to movies and theme parks, but never really connected, at least not at first. But she turned out to be a whiz at video games. Must have been the robotic surgery. We'd play for hours. It was the only time she really seemed comfortable with me...or with herself."

"She must have been grieving, too," said the doctor.

"Yeah. We both missed him terribly, but we never talked about him." His voice wavered. He paused and looked at the wall while he composed himself.

"On my eighth birthday, I pulled the cover off the dirt bike in the garage and rolled it into the driveway. My mother almost became unhinged when she saw me. She started to stop me, but held back when she saw the light in my eyes and just watched. The bike connected us both to him. It was my one daredevil activity she learned to tolerate." His voice again began to crack, then stilled. The doctor was riveted to his narrative and waited patiently.

"We started late," Ray said. "It must be time to go." He began to get up.

"We have a few minutes left," said the doctor, "But if you need for this to be a stopping point, we can pick up again next time."

Ray was already on his feet and had taken a step toward the door, "Thanks, Dr. Jensen," he said, turning briefly toward her. "See you next week."

The doctor closed the door behind him as he clambered down the stairs to the street. Ray had no idea whether he would ever come back to see her again.

17

BY THE TIME Natasha turned four in the spring of 2052, Corinne and Marcus already knew she was becoming an extraordinary person, endowed with the intellectual ability and sensibilities inherited from them both. Her brimming curiosity led her to explore the world around her from the celestial bodies down to the minutest details of a leaf. She found joy in every aspect of the natural world.

Corinne held Natasha in her lap and read aloud to her from the beginning. From the time she began to walk, Natasha pulled books off the shelves and curled up in her mother's lap, begging her to read. Soon she was reading on her own, taking in the smell and the feel of the books along with the words. Corinne delighted in seeing her daughter's affection for her treasures.

Like her father, Natasha had an instinctive rapport with animals. Dogs and cats followed her home with such frequency that Marcus and Corinne funded a shelter just to find homes for her strays. She might be seen one day gently holding a field mouse and another climbing over a pasture fence to commune with a foal. By the time she was five, she was so fearless and independent that keeping her safe was becoming a formidable challenge.

"Let's get her a horse," Corinne suggested one day. "Perhaps that'll keep her occupied enough that she won't keep wandering off."

Marcus kept his back turned, pretending not to hear. A twinge of pain in the pit of his stomach told him it would be a risky move. The danger he sensed wasn't physical, but emotional. He envisioned Natasha becoming deeply attached and then some day having her beloved companion snatched away. Marcus knew that anything can happen when it comes to animals. And he couldn't bear to see his daughter's heart break.

"Marcus?" Corinne persisted. "What about it? We could get her a Paso Fino and she could learn to ride."

"I don't know," Marcus replied. "She'll be starting school soon. That'll keep her busy. And she's awfully young for that kind of responsibility."

"Young? Marcus! This is Natasha we're talking about." Corinne laughed. "She hasn't been a child since she was three."

Marcus still had his back to her and sighed. Corinne moved around to where she could see his face and caught the tear trickling down his cheek. Then she understood. She put an arm around his shoulder and kissed the top of his head.

"Life's full of risk, Marc," she said. "She has so much love to give and we can't protect her forever. Someday she'll lose something or someone and she'll need to find a way to deal with it."

Marcus took her hand, kissed it and shook his head.

"I know," he said. "Of course you're right. I just can't bear the thought of seeing her hurt."

When it was time for Natasha to start her formal education, another thornier issue arose between Corinne and Marcus. Those who could afford it often elected at this point to have their children implanted with MELD chips. Those children so equipped enjoyed the distinct advantage of acquiring a wealth of passive knowledge before school had even begun. And they were better prepared to interact with the virtual environments that provided the foundation of their educational experience.

Corinne was among a small minority of wealthy parents who believed that knowledge acquired naturally through social interaction and intuitive discovery provided both a sounder intellectual foundation and a more joyful approach to learning. Marcus wanted their daughter to have every possible advantage and imagined her struggling to keep up with her more data-endowed peers.

"Just look at her," Corinne urged Marcus as she watched through a window while Natasha tended her hydroponic garden. "She has such wonderful instincts. All those facts will only distract her from what's really important."

"As smart as she is," Marcus countered, "just imagine what she could accomplish with unlimited knowledge at her fingertips. She has enough sense to sort it out and use it wisely."

"She doesn't need it, Marcus. She'll learn to solve problems better without having a huge database to rely on. It'll make her more resourceful. Besides," Corinne went on, "look what you've accomplished without a chip."

That was always Corinne's trump card in these arguments, and Marcus never had a comeback since Corinne could never know that her assumption was wrong. So Corinne won this battle and Natasha went off to school with only the brainpower with which she'd come into this world.

Natasha held her own, for the most part, among her more digitally endowed classmates. She proved superior in logical abilities to most of them and more socially capable. Other children were attracted to her in much the same way animals were, so she was immensely popular. But children being what they are, she suffered taunts from time to time even from her closest friends because she lacked a chip.

"Daddy," Natasha came crying one day from school, "the other kids called me 'Squishy Brain.'"

Marcus could only wrap her in his arms and tell her how smart she was until her tears dried up. Her playmates had no shortage of nicknames for her. Sometimes she was "Analog Brain," sometimes "Mush Brain," and on particularly dreary days "Booger Brain." With a world of vocabulary at their fingertips, this was still the best they could do.

Corinne's instincts proved sound. Natasha thrived. She moved through her world of wonder glowing with a natural joy that brought smiles to the faces of anyone who saw her. Nowhere was she happier, though, than atop Cinnamon, her palomino filly with the flowing white mane. Within weeks she was at ease in the saddle and within months riding bareback with swiftness and grace. Horse and girl moved as one. When Marcus watched her gliding across the landscape, bittersweet memories of Hugo would flood in.

Little got by Natasha's notice. One day when Marcus had just returned from his morning run and the bull's breath seemed to dance on his chest, Natasha asked him about the image's meaning. He hesitated at first to tell her a story that might disturb the security of her idyllic world, but took her upon his knee to spin the tale, which now had a happier ending. Pastures were once again filled with contentedly grazing livestock thanks to his work with Takana Grass. The last blades of HibernaTurf had been squeezed out by lushly growing species of vegetation and its sterile landscape was becoming a distant memory. Perhaps Hugo hadn't died in vain, after all.

As Natasha watched him in rapt attention and he gazed into her innocent eyes, Marcus wondered how long it would be before she learned the horrible truth about how he'd sold his family's future. Traces of the truth already flowed through her veins, since half her genetic legacy had undergone the Conversion. Once she reached her teens, when the effects of cellular aging first become detectable, it would take but a drop of her blood or a scraping from her cheek for anyone to discover the telltale telomeres that distinguished the chromosomes from his body from those from Corinne's.

Since her genome was read at birth, there might be no reason for anyone to look again for a long time. But if Corinne or Natasha ever grew suspicious, there would be no hiding the evidence. He could only hope that the bonds between him and his wife and daughter could survive their discovery of his deceit.

18

RAY STEPPED out of the car in front of the now familiar brick building. It was a bright sunny day, illuminating the structure as he'd never seen it before. The brick looked clean and new, imprinted with a regular pattern of tightly spaced vertical grooves. There were sprigs of ivy, rooted in fresh dark soil, growing up the very bottom of the walls, but the mass of vegetation that usually covered the building was gone.

He approached the entry gate. The rusted iron, like the face of the building, looked clean, smooth, and freshly painted. A bright, shiny brass lock replaced the ancient one that had been there before. The brass frame of the doorbell was also bright and shiny. He rang the bell and was buzzed in.

Once inside, Ray noticed that the building's formerly somber interior seemed light and airy. The stairs no longer creaked under his feet. As he reached the doctor's floor, he found her door ajar. Light poured out of her apartment into the corridor.

"Come in, Raymond," the doctor called from within. As he entered the apartment, she approached from across the room, her right hand extended.

There before him was not the frail, elderly woman he'd come to know, but the vibrant younger woman in the photographs. Only her eyes, and the serenity of her smile still identified her as the same person.

Ray stopped in his tracks. "You're not supposed to be young," he nearly shouted. "How can you help me if you're young?"

"Of course I can still help you, Raymond, It's still me." Her voice was resonant and clear. "Come, take my hands." She now extended both hands in his direction.

He hesitated a few moments longer, then stepped forward and grasped her hands in his. They felt soft, warm, and velvety to his touch, but suddenly turned cold and firm, then rock hard. When he looked up, her face and body were rigid and shiny. Only her eyes were still alive and now stared helplessly into his. She'd turned to bronze.

"Ray! Ray! Wake up," Lena shouted, shaking him. "You're having a nightmare."

Ray awoke in a cold sweat, panting hard. He stared blankly straight ahead, still unaware of his surroundings.

"You looked like you were trying to scream, but you weren't making any sound."

He blinked a few times, then drew in a deep breath. When he turned to face her, he was back in the present.

"A nightmare, yeah...thanks for waking me." He could still feel his heart pumping, but the rhythm was regular and beginning to slow.

"Do you want to talk about it?"

"It was about that doctor I've been seeing, Dr. Jensen. I went to see her, but everything was different. Everything was new, including her...she was young and beautiful."

"So what part was the nightmare?"

"When I touched her...when I took her hands, she turned into a statue...a bronze statue, all except for her eyes, which looked so frightened. It was like I'd killed her." He shook his head, then brought both hands up to cover his face.

"Like Midas," said Lena.

"Yeah. Like Midas. No matter what good I try to do, everyone I touch gets hurt."

"And what do you make of her suddenly being young?" asked Lena.

"Nothing...I don't know," Ray lied. "It was probably just seeing the pictures, wondering what she was like back then." He couldn't share with Lena what old people turning young really brought to mind.

When Ray next visited the doctor's apartment, everything was in its familiar decrepit condition, including the aging doctor. He felt safe as he settled in the softness of the upholstered chair, no longer concerned about contamination from his contact with it. The doctor sat opposite him, hands folded in her lap.

"Where would you like to begin today?" asked the doctor.

"I had a dream," Ray began, "about coming here...about you." Ray narrated the dream, the details of which were still vivid. The doctor listened patiently until the end.

"When I first met you," the doctor observed, "you were afraid to let me touch you, lest I contaminate you and bring you harm. But in your dream," she continued, "your touch brings harm to me. It seems what you're really afraid of is harming those who get close to you."

Ray nodded in agreement.

"Tell me, then," she added, "Who called you Raymond?"

That was a detail that Lena had missed and that Ray had overlooked even in the second telling. Tears welled in his eyes and his lips trembled like a lost child.

"My Mother...my mother always called me her Raymond. Except for my teachers, she was the only one." His tears were now flowing freely.

"So your dream was connected with what you began to tell me last time. Are you ready to resume your story?" Her voice was steady and gentle as she encouraged him to proceed.

"Our lives settled to a new normal. After my eighth birthday, Mom and I grew closer and together bore the pain of his loss. We even spoke of him from time to time and visited his grave on his birthday and on the anniversaries of his death. Mom never remarried or even dated. She'd joke that I was the only man in her life. She made me feel that I was enough." Ray cleared his throat and fidgeted a bit in his chair. During his pause, the doctor said nothing. She sat ready to listen.

"One day when I was thirteen," Ray resumed, "I was riding my bike home from school when the fire engines raced down the street in front of my bike just a few blocks from our house. I took off following them. By the time I'd caught up, they'd stopped right in front of my house. Flames were shooting out through the windows and the roof was crumbling. I ran toward the front door, but one of the firemen caught me in a bear hug and held me back." His voice cracked. He swallowed several times and sighed so deeply his whole body shook.

"Another fireman in an asbestos suit and gas mask wheeled a stretcher through the door. The man who was holding me swung me around so I couldn't see, but it was too late. The last thing I saw was her scorched, motionless body. By the time the ambulance arrived, they'd zipped a bag around her and I never saw her again. It was as though they'd zipped the bag around me...around my life. My world turned so dark and hopeless...and so awfully lonely. I missed her so much."

"So much loss for one so young," said the doctor. "That was a lot for you to carry."

"That wasn't the worst of it," said Ray. "What's haunted me most is the guilt."

"You felt responsible for her dying? How?"

"I've gone over it in my mind a million times. Our house was only ten years old and had been built for safety. My mother was very cautious. She'd insisted on electric heat, hot water, and oven. A gas cooktop was her only concession to my father, who loved to cook. She taught me from when I was very small always to turn the gas all the way off after using the burners. I'd fried an egg for breakfast that morning and was sure I'd turned off the burner. That was automatic, habitual, unthinking...the kind of thing you don't actually remember doing every time.

"I scoured my memory for that moment, but the more I searched, the more elusive it became. I could never be certain." He brought the back of a hand to his face and wiped tears from his eyes with two fingers.

"After the fire, I went to live with my mother's brother and his wife. They'd heard about my hot shot behavior and were worried about how they'd keep me safe, but their worries were needless. My daredevil days were over. I became obsessed with safety and the need for certainty in all things. I began checking doors to be sure they were locked, brushed my teeth four times every morning to be sure I'd brushed them at all, and always ran back into the house at least twice before leaving to make sure the stove was off. It became so tedious to go out that I seldom left the house at all except to go to school."

Ray failed to connect that this was also the moment of origin of the odd jerking motion of his head that looked as if something had suddenly caught his attention. Was he looking at whatever it was...or looking away from it? The movements were so random, it was anybody's guess.

"So you've always blamed yourself," said the doctor. "You've lived your life believing that you killed her, just like you imagined killing me in your dream. What a horrible burden to carry."

Ray was too overcome with emotion to speak. His chest rose and fell in shudders, punctuated by high pitched wails of agony. His head was bowed, avoiding even a passing glance at the doctor's face. At long last his breathing slowed and became more regular.

"So there you have it," he said. "Now you know just how much death and destruction I've brought upon the world."

The doctor searched for words of reassurance, but found none. The best she could do for now was to sit with him in his pain.

"I tried to make up for it," Ray went on. "I devoted all my time and energy to my studies so I could accomplish something good for the world. I knew it could never bring her back, but if I could do something big that would save lives and spare others from suffering, then at least something good would have come about from her dying.

"When I invented HibernaTurf, it felt as though I'd redeemed myself. For the first couple of years, the world was better off. Water became more plentiful. People were no longer dying of thirst or drowning in squalor. My pain subsided for a while, but the admiration made me squirm. People were treating me like a hero while I still felt like a murderer inside. Then when it all fell apart and people began to hate me, it was like they'd discovered who I really was. At least then, what others felt about me seemed to match how I felt about myself."

"You've been stuck in this narrative for a long time," said the doctor, breaking her silence. "Now that you've finally shared it, would you be willing to revisit it next time so that we might discover new ways to understand it?"

"Yeah. I guess I could do that, but I don't see how it will change anything."

"We'll see, Ray. We'll see. Our time is up for today. Until next time."

*****

When Ray showed up at Dr. Jensen's office for his next session, he looked disheveled and haggard. There were dark circles under his bloodshot eyes. His feet shuffled as he entered the room. When he plopped down in the overstuffed chair, he looked as though he hadn't slept in a week.

"Tough week," observed the doctor.

"The worst. I've hardly slept and when I have, I wished I'd stayed awake. The nightmares just kept coming. I've spent most of the past week in my dreams as a thirteen-year-old. I can still hear the sirens."

"Perhaps we can put an end to the nightmares. Do you feel up to working today?"

"I guess so. Doesn't seem like I have much choice. How much worse can things get?"

"I'd like to address your childhood memory with Eye Movement Desensitization and Reprocessing, or EMDR, a technique developed toward the end of the last century for treating trauma. We'll start with a series of questions. Once we're done with that part of the protocol, I'll ask you to visualize aspects of the memory and to be in touch with the pain. That's the hard part. While you're imaging the scene, I'll ask you to track my hand with your eyes as I move it back and forth."

"Then what happens?"

"We'll stop the eye movements from time to time and sample whatever is in your awareness. Then we'll focus on that and resume the eye movements."

"So how will that help?"

"The eye movements help to reorganize how your brain processes and interprets the memory. Usually the end result is that the pain diminishes or goes away altogether."

"And the memory?"

"May persist, but without the same emotional intensity, or it can fade." said the doctor.

"What if I don't want it to fade away? What if I need the pain? It's defined me for most of my life. Maybe I'm not supposed to forget."

"Perhaps. But the process tends to respect your inner wisdom. If part of you needs to remember, then you will. And if part of you still needs to suffer...well, then, that may still go on as well. You'll need to have faith that it will unfold however it's supposed to."

"OK. What happens now?"

"I want you to imagine the scene you described last time and identify the worst part of it."

"That's easy. Being held back by the fireman and seeing her charred body being wheeled out."

"What emotion is most connected with that image?" asked the doctor.

"Horror...utter horror."

"Where in your body do you feel the horror?"

"In the back of my throat...and in the pit of my stomach."

"And the intensity of the feeling on a scale from one to ten?"

"Twelve! It's the worst feeling I've ever had."

"OK. Now as you picture the scene and feel this emotion in the back of your throat and in the pit of your stomach, what present-day belief about yourself is connected with it?"

"I'm a menace. I bring death wherever I go and I don't deserve to live."

"And if you could believe something else, however implausible it may seem at the moment, what would you like to believe instead?"

"That there's a reason for me to be here...that I belong on the planet after all."

"How true does that feel on a scale from one to seven?"

"Right now? One...no, zero."

"OK, then. We're ready to begin."

The doctor moved a chair up just to the left of Ray's so that her legs rested beside his body and his legs beside hers. She held her left hand eighteen inches in front of his face with the index and middle fingers extended.

"Is this distance comfortable?" she asked.

"It's fine."

"OK. Then bring up the scene, starting wherever makes sense. When you have it clearly in mind, nod your head and we'll begin."

Ray nodded and the doctor began moving her hand back and forth at a moderate pace. After twenty or thirty seconds, she stopped, had him take a deep breath and asked what came to mind.

"I'm on my bike at an intersection and hear the sirens coming toward me from the right."

"Go with that," said the doctor and began moving her hand again. "How about now?" she asked when her hand had stopped.

"The engine has passed and is speeding down the street. I'm following it, but it turns and is out of sight."

After several more sets, Ray had arrived in front of his house. His breathing had become rapid and sweat was pouring off his brow. His hands had the arms of the chair in a death grip.

The doctor performed the next set of eye movements in slow motion. Toward the end of the set, his arms began to relax and his breathing became regular.

"How about now?" she asked.

"I can see her body, but it's like looking through a fog. It feels as if I'm in a dream...no, more like watching a movie. It doesn't feel real." His expression had changed from shock to perplexity.

"Go with that," said the doctor and sped up the tracking again. When she saw a few involuntary beats as his eyes shifted direction, she stopped and cued his response.

"The sun is high," Ray said, "and I realized that when I'd left the house for school, it was still low in the sky."

By the end of the next set of eye movements, his expression was relaxed.

"A lot of time had passed. Seven or eight hours. Mom would have been out for the morning on her shift. If I'd left the burner on and caused the fire, it would have burned the house down while she was out. So it must have started since she got back that afternoon."

At the end of the next set, Ray was shaking his head. A faint smile began to break across his lips.

"So it couldn't have been my fault...well, it would have been very unlikely. I'd have had to turn the gas almost all the way off so the flame went out. She could have come home, turned on the burner, and caused an explosion." Some of the tension returned to his face. He drew in a sharp breath.

127

"Go with that," is all the doctor said as she began again moving her hand.

"If the gas had been on all that time," said Ray at the end of this set, "she would certainly have smelled it when she entered the house. She was smart and perceptive. How could she miss that? No, it couldn't have happened that way." His body had again relaxed.

"Now pull up the image of your mother being wheeled out of the house." When he signaled that the image was in mind, she began again moving her hand.

"I can see her," said Ray when the doctor's hand had stopped moving, "but now it's just a memory. And it seems so long, long ago. I feel sad, but the horror is gone. And so is the guilt. It wasn't my fault. Thank God it wasn't my fault. I've suffered for so many years believing it was." Tears welled in his eyes, tears that seemed now to wash away the pain. Dr. Jensen's own eyes moistened as she witnessed his relief.

"One more step," said the doctor. "I want you now to visualize the scene along with the words 'I belong in this world. I have a place here.'"

When the doctor's hand had stopped moving, Ray nodded and smiled. "There's still HibernaTurf," he said. "I'm no saint. But maybe I'm not the devil either."

"Validity on a scale of seven?" asked the doctor.

"Four or five. There are still things you don't know about me...things I can't tell even you, that keep me from ever getting to seven. But you've helped me more than I imagined possible. Thanks." Ray realized that this was probably the last time he'd see Dr. Jensen. This was as far as she could take him. There were some places he could only go alone.

When Ray left Dr. Jensen's office that day, he felt grateful for being relieved of the burden of thinking he'd been responsible for ending his mother's life. He was suddenly more aware, however, of the responsibility he bore for eventually ending the life of the stranger whose body he would someday occupy. He might deserve his place on the planet, after all, but did he deserve it more than the unknown stranger? With that quandary he was all alone.

19

MARCUS SAT ALONE in the balcony of the Church of the Double Helix as the music swelled from the massive pipe organ to fill every crevice of the building. The procession below moved deliberately down the center aisle toward the stage and fanned out on either side of the altar. When the last people had reached the front and the aisle was empty, the music paused, then resumed in a lower key and a stately beat as all eyes turned toward the back of the church.

The bride cleared the edge of the balcony and came into view, her right hand in the crook of the arm of the tall man beside her with the gleaming head. Marcus spotted Corinne in the front row by the aisle, a tear trickling down her cheek as she watched the bride approach. Why was he watching from a distance and not by Corinne's side? And who was the child beside her, a boy of five or six, on whose shoulder Corinne's right hand rested.

When the bride reached the end of the aisle, she turned briefly toward Corinne, who lifted her veil to kiss her.

"Natasha," Marcus mouthed silently. "My daughter."

Now Natasha turned toward the man who had walked her down the aisle. He lifted her veil, turned and bent to bestow a fatherly kiss, giving Marcus his first glimpse of him in profile. He had Marcus's body, but the face of a stranger. A wave of nausea washed over Marcus as he watched the strange man kiss his daughter. His vision blurred momentarily, then cleared in time to see Natasha ascend the steps to the pulpit and take her place beside her groom.

The minister entered from the side and emerged from the shadows into the brilliant light that illuminated the hooded silver robe. From the figure's gait, he could tell it was a woman. When she reached the pulpit, she turned to face the congregation, and Marcus saw a fringe of flaming red hair outlining her hood. Then she looked directly at him and he stared into the familiar green eyes that shone brilliantly even from across the church's span.

"Terra!" he shouted aloud, gasping for breath. The hood fell away and her flowing hair cascaded in slow motion to her shoulders.

Corinne shook him by the shoulders until his eyes finally opened. She stared into the unseeing eyes, the pupils dilated so wide that they nearly obliterated the irises. His whole body shuddered.

"Marcus, Marc!" She shook him harder. He sighed deeply and blinked.

"You've been having a nightmare," she said when he'd finally come around. "You were shouting."

His eyes filled with tears as their colored irises reclaimed terrain from the dwindling pupils. He reached up to touch her face and gave silent thanks that the future he'd just seen wasn't real, at least not yet.

"What was I shouting?" he asked later while Corinne was pouring coffee in the kitchen.

"It sounded like 'terror,'" she replied. "Do you want to talk about it?"

"Not right now. I'd prefer to let it just fade away on its own. It was only a dream." Marcus was grateful for the ambiguity of his exclamation. It was more than just a dream, but he wasn't about to let Corinne into this corner of his mind.

The dream didn't fade from Marcus's awareness as he'd hoped. The images lodged deep within his being and threatened to crush his spirit.

Marcus sat, sometimes for hours, his shoulders slumped and his face impassive. Even Corinne could no longer reach him. While desire had always glowed in his eyes when he gazed upon her body, he now barely noticed her and showed no interest at all in making love. Even when she'd reach over in bed to touch him, he'd roll over with his back toward her and pretend to sleep.

Even more striking was the change in his emotional response to Natasha. His daughter had always been the light of his life and had never failed to bring a smile to his face. Now her presence brought him only pain. He'd gaze at her from across the room, then turn away so that she might not see his stifled sobs.

Natasha had just turned six and was bright beyond her years, already developing the grace and beauty that had first attracted Marcus to Corinne. She was in a growth spurt that brought her up to the vee of Corinne's ribcage. Not visible to the casual observer, however, was the maturation of her tissues, the cellular building blocks of her body and the chromosomes in their nuclei, half of which bore telomeres that would never diminish in length.

"Come watch me ride," Natasha implored one afternoon, tugging at her father's arm. "You won't believe what we can do."

Marcus mustered a smile and accompanied her to the paddock where Cinnamon was grazing. The horse came running to greet her and stood patiently while Natasha saddled her. The girl was atop the horse in minutes, cantering around the perimeter of the corral. Marcus leaned against the fence and watched her put Cinnamon through her paces. They moved to the center of the ring and the horse began prancing in place, first to the right, then to the left, and finally stretching out her forelegs and bowing her head.

"See, Daddy, I've taught her to dance." Natasha beamed. Marcus laughed. The spontaneity of the emotion took him by surprise. It was his first moment of peace since the nightmare.

His pleasure was short-lived, however, interrupted by the appearance of a man by the fence on the opposite side of the paddock, who was also watching Natasha. The man appeared in his mid-twenties, rugged and handsome, with a shock of wavy blond hair and blue eyes that studied her with such intensity that they threatened to pierce her body. Marcus had never seen him before. Beyond the man was a white car with the driver's door ajar. With the sun reflecting off the windshield, Marcus could barely make out the outline of a second figure sitting in the passenger's seat.

A shiver ran up Marcus's spine. Why would a strange man show such interest in his daughter? The image flashed through his mind of the stranger in the dream kissing the adult Natasha at the altar, and he tasted vomit rising in the back of his throat. She seemed so vulnerable, still smiling at him from atop her palomino, and at the same time innocent of the forces that could at any moment rip her life apart.

Natasha swung Cinnamon around to make another pass around the ring. The horse, upon seeing the stranger, suddenly reared, spilling her rider to the ground. Natasha landed hard and lay motionless on her back while Cinnamon lunged halfway toward the stranger at the fence, then stood firmly between his line of sight and her mistress, snorting and pawing the ground.

Marcus clambered over the fence and ran to Natasha, for the moment taking his eyes off the intruders across the corral. She was still unconscious when he reached her, but breathing. Her right arm was askew at the elbow and looked broken, her only visible injury. He hesitated, however, to move her without knowing whether or not her neck had been injured.

Cinnamon came around and shoved Marcus softly aside with her head, then nuzzled Natasha gently. The girl opened her eyes. "Oww! My arm!" She braced her left arm against the ground and began to sit up.

"Wait, sweetie," Marcus warned, "Don't move just yet." He ran his hand softly over the smooth top of her head and she settled back. Out of the corner of his eye, he noticed that the blond man and the car were gone, already out of sight.

Marcus ripped a loose board from the fence, stood on one end, and snapped it in half, creating a bodyboard almost exactly Natasha's length. In a few minutes, she was lashed to the board to stabilize her neck and in Marcus's arms, her injured arm cradled closely to her side. She looked lovingly into his eyes, releasing a surge of affection.

As they sped to the hospital, Marcus's thoughts darted from threat to threat: the threat from within that could at any moment end his existence and put Natasha and Corinne in the hands of a stranger, the threat from without from the intruders at the corral, and the new threat of whatever medical tests might be done on his daughter that could lead to the discovery of the Conversion, a crucial nexus in the web of secrets he kept from Corinne, from Natasha, and from the world. At least this time, he was here to protect her. It was still too soon to write himself out of the script.

*****

Corinne had begun to wonder whether Marcus had fallen out of love with her. When she looked closely in the mirror, she saw tiny lines radiating from the corners of her eyes and a deepening of the folds around her mouth. Her breasts were still round and firm, but she saw hints of creases beneath them as time and gravity began to take their toll.

And when she watched him sleep, she looked for the same hallmarks of aging that she saw in herself, but saw none. As haggard as he appeared in the throes of melancholy, the contours of his face in sleep were as smooth and unblemished as a twenty-year-old. Could she be leaving him behind? And could his love for her be so shallow that these differences would matter?

The night after the accident, Marcus had embraced her tenderly from behind in the bedroom while she was changing for bed and they'd made passionate love, which reassured Corinne that he still loved her and desired her. Whatever was behind his bout of despondency at least wasn't about her or about aging. She welcomed the return of Marcus's vitality and his emotional reengagement with her and Natasha.

When Corinne brought Natasha to the doctor for a follow-up visit one week after the accident, her arm had completely healed. At the hospital, a scraping of skin had been converted into pluripotent stem cells and then into a mixture of osteoclasts to reabsorb damaged bone and osteoblasts to lay down new bone. Together these cells, injected at the site of the fracture, remodeled the structure of Natasha's damaged ulna, the narrow bone in her forearm that had snapped in the fall.

Ever since the process of inducing stem cells from skin cells had been streamlined enough to become an office procedure, this had become standard protocol for treating fractures and shortened the healing time dramatically. Most fractures healed completely in a few weeks. But Natasha's recovery was remarkable even for this treatment.

"She must have really great genes," commented the doctor. "I've never seen anyone recover so quickly from that bad a break."

"Her father's side, I guess," said Corinne laughing. "I always take forever to heal." Beneath the banter, though, was a nagging feeling that there was more to Natasha's speedy recovery than chance. And she wondered how it might connect with the parts of Marcus's life that he kept so deeply buried.

20

IN THE MONTHS that followed Ray's treatment with Dr. Jensen, his anxieties rapidly melted away and he soon moved as freely in the world as Lena did. He agreed to let Lena redecorate their home. The slick, hard surfaces were soon replaced by textured fabrics, the feel of which Ray grew to love. Now that their home was no longer a prison, Lena began to flourish. Ray hadn't seen her so happy since the very beginning of their courtship. He loved seeing the corners of her eyes crinkle whenever she smiled or laughed. And his own face lit up from the light radiating from hers.

When Ray saw himself smiling in the mirror, it was like looking at a stranger. "So this is what it feels like to be normal," he thought. "This is what it means to be happy."

Ray also saw in the mirror the indelible marks left by the passage of time: thinning hair, a softening of his jawline, an extra fold of skin under his chin, and some bulging around the waist that defied all his efforts to keep himself trim with diet and exercise. For most people, these changes marked an inexorable progression toward death. For Ray, it marked movement toward a different, and in some ways equally daunting destiny, the moment when he would stop being himself and would assume the life of a stranger.

Lena was delighted at her newfound opportunity to explore the world. Ray's companionship was an unexpected bonus. He was like a curious child, discovering the world for the first time. Many everyday experiences were new to him, even if previously sampled via virtual reality. And when they traveled together, all of his senses were fully engaged.

"Lena, come look!" he'd exclaim, gazing over a grove of olive trees or holding out a palmful of multicolored sand.

"Taste this," he'd urge her, popping a morsel from a street vendor into her mouth.

Lena was never happier, though, than when she was working. She loved meeting and interviewing creative people, then lovingly crafting verbal portraits of what made them beautiful to her. Now that Ray no longer depended upon her presence to feel secure, she was free to resume her work and develop her craft.

"I have a new assignment, Ray," she said one day upon returning home, "and I want you to come with me this time."

Ray was intrigued. Lena had never before invited him for a glimpse of her personal world. This was new territory in their relationship.

"Why now?" he asked. "What's so special about this one?"

"She's an artist," Lena replied, "no, more than just an artist. She has some very special talents. For one thing, she's a synesthetic."

"You mean her senses bleed together?"

"Yes. She visualizes sounds and she hears what she sees. Even the textures of things she touches transform into music and pictures. She's an extraordinary talent. I'd like you to meet her."

When Ray and Lena arrived at the artist's studio the next afternoon, it was like walking into a fantasy world. They were completely immersed in color and sound, which seemed to blend so synchronously that it was impossible to know where one ended and the other began. Even the boundaries of their bodies melted into the surrounding space.

The artist led them outside into a lush garden where their senses were sufficiently freed to permit a dialogue.

"Ray, meet Haley Sellica," Lena said. "Haley, this is my husband Ray."

"Delighted to meet you," said Haley, extending her hand and making eye contact. Her hand was soft and warm, but her handshake was firm and assertive.

Haley was pleasing to the eye, but not beautiful in the conventional sense. She looked in her mid-thirties. Her skin was clear and smooth, her hair somewhere between sandy and brown, pulled tightly back in a ponytail and secured by a plastic clip. She was dressed plainly in a white, men's button-down shirt, at least a size too big and hanging over khaki twill pants that looked as though they'd been washed a few too many times. Both garments, speckled with multi-colored paints, hid a body that was trim and healthy, but as nondescript as her dated clothes. Her whole appearance seemed incongruous for someone so attuned to creating beauty.

Haley read the question in Ray's eyes. "You'll have to forgive my appearance," she said, passing a hand down the front of her body and smiling. "I try not to upstage my work."

Ray listened intently as Lena conducted her interview. He hadn't heard her work since they'd first met and he'd been her subject. He was as fascinated to hear how her technique had evolved as to learn about the woman they'd come to see.

Haley had long been aware of her special gift, but she didn't always know that everyone else experienced the world differently. When she'd created her first painting, everyone around her knew right away that she'd be capable of transforming the world of art with a unique vision. When she'd composed her first sonata, they realized that her talent was multi-layered and her potential limitless. She was given every possible tool to nurture that talent.

When the interview was done, Haley led them back into her home for a more detailed tour of its contents. This time, the first thing Ray noticed went beyond the sights and sounds. As he walked through the rooms, he became attuned to their aromas, which he inhaled deeply, arousing a medley of emotions evoked by his sense of smell. The aromas flowed and shifted with the visual images and the music, reproducing with remarkable fidelity the artist's synesthetic perceptions.

Across one wall was an expanse of shimmering butter yellow canvas, accompanied by the subtle hum of a sweltering afternoon, and the smell of fresh sweat mixed with honeysuckle blossoms. Standing before it, Ray felt a deep sense of longing for something that felt like a lost memory, but had never been part of his actual youth. Crossing the threshold into another room, he found himself looking at swirls of black, accompanied by a deep base cadence, and the smell of charred flesh. Ray felt a flash of the horror that he'd experienced on the day of the fire, but it vanished as soon as he'd moved on to the next image. None of the emotions evoked by the pieces lingered beyond the physical boundaries of the work.

Even in the vast database of Ray's MELD chip, he'd never experienced anything with the evocative power of Haley Sellica's art. He was grateful to Lena for allowing him to accompany her to the interview and understood why she'd chosen to do so.

"She's amazing," Ray said when they were on their way home. "The genius of a savant without any of the deficits. Warm, witty, emotionally complete."

"I told you it'd be worth coming to meet her. It's something you have to see for yourself to believe."

"She's a perfect example of why SPUDs will never be like us," Ray said.

"Huh? That was out of left field, Ray. What the hell do you mean by that?"

"Just look at what she's done. Creating art requires an appreciation of the senses. And art that speaks to people like hers does requires an understanding of human emotions and experience. No machine could ever produce that kind of work."

'Perhaps you're right, Ray," Lena said. "Would you like to come back with me for the followup interview?"

"Wouldn't miss it."

Lena's first interview had focused on the artist's work. When they next returned to her studio, Lena's focus shifted to her personal life.

"Tell me," Lena asked, "who is important in your life."

"Why, you are for this moment...and your husband. You have my undivided attention for as long as you remain in my home."

Lena was thrown by this odd response and rephrased her query.

"Is there anyone more permanent in your life? Have you ever been in love?"

"Oh, no," answered Haley. "I'm completely devoted to my work...and of course to my Creator."

"So you're religious?"

"Religious? No, not really. I'm not even sure what that means."

"It means belief in a higher power, a supreme being that created us and the world."

"So you believe you were created, too?" answered Haley, wrinkling her brow. "What is your Creator's name?"

"Why God, of course."

"Mine's Gideon," said Haley without looking up. "He's only made a few of us."

Ray and Lena looked at each other, each searching the other for clarity. Ray spoke next.

"How many of you are there?" he asked.

"Five altogether. I have two sisters and two brothers. I'm the youngest."

"And how old are you?"

"Six hundred seventy-two days, twenty-two hours, and seventeen minutes."

"So Gideon is a person and you're..."

"An artificial intelligence. What you people would call a SPUD," replied Haley. "Didn't you know? How many humans can do what I do?"

Lena grinned. Ray's logic had been turned on its head. The reddening of his face and neck betrayed that he'd come to the same conclusion.

On the way home, Lena couldn't help but rub it in. "So SPUDs can't be as creative as people. Do you still believe that?"

"OK, Lena. I get it," Ray said. "I'm going to have to rethink a lot of what I believe. Be patient with me. I'm still a work in progress." He flashed her a grin. She smiled back. "So what are you planning to write?"

"Her story is remarkable even if she weren't a SPUD," answered Lena. "She's not secretive about it, but I think that people will appreciate the magic more if they think she's human. It's like she said. She doesn't want to upstage her work. Neither do I."

Ray was grateful to be sharing this part of Lena's life. They were at ease together for the first time in years, possibly for the first time ever. Intimacy, both emotional and physical, was seeping into their still fragile relationship. As they walked together hand in hand, he realized that Lena's walks in the park had stopped months ago. Whatever needs her friend had fulfilled Ray was now satisfying, and at least for now he was enough.

21

RAY OPENED HIS EYES and saw the mountainside streaking past on the left and the open expanse of water far below the road's edge to his right. He heard the roar of the engine that was propelling him forward on wheels that picked up the irregularities of the road's surface and made his body vibrate and his teeth chatter. His right foot was pressing on a pedal that made the sound of the engine louder and the vibrations more intense.

He instinctively let up the pressure and shifted his foot to the brake pedal, but the car continued to career with increasing speed along a curving path with nothing between him and a precipitous drop to the sea below. Most gasoline powered vehicles like this one from the early 21st century were now in museums and the fuel that powered them was scarce. He hadn't driven a car like this for nearly two decades and had no idea how he came to be behind the wheel of this one.

He gripped the wheel tightly, concentrating on the turns, as he searched for a way to stop the car. He reached momentarily to turn off the ignition, but was terrified that it would disable the steering. He resumed his death grip on the wheel as he heard the pulse in his ears ramp up to a pace that seemed to track the vehicle's speed.

Years before, he'd once found himself driving on a deserted road miles from home after taking a sleeping pill before going to bed and had no idea how he'd gotten there. But at least then he was on level ground and driving at an ordinary pace. And he'd heard of others having similar experiences with the same drug. That was the last time he'd ever used a sedative. And back then, he lived alone. There was nobody around that night to stop him and nobody to help him retrace his steps.

How had he been able to leave his fortress of a home with the alarm system fully armed and Lena sleeping by his side? Could one of his many enemies have breached his defenses and put him in this fix?

The sound in his ears intensified as the car sped closer and closer to the cliff's edge with each turn. His hands were frozen to the wheel, but no longer seemed to be controlling the wheels of the car. And then he was airborne. He felt a crushing sensation across his chest. The beating in his ears made a last crescendo, then sputtered randomly and went quiet.

The next sounds Ray heard were cheers. He was standing on a platform looking out upon a sea of faces, both arms raised above his head. And the sensations that fed back the position of the muscles in his face told him that he was smiling. The crowd was still cheering and clapping as he felt an arm encircle his shoulders.

"Incredible speech," came a familiar voice from behind him. "Listen to how they adore you."

He was still trying to place the voice when a tall, regal woman strode to the podium, threw her arms around his neck, and kissed him on the mouth. The kiss was brief, but soft, conveying as much tenderness and affection as was seemly for a public display. The roar of the crowd rose again and the woman turned forward, holding his hand in hers and raising them in a victory sign.

She looked into his eyes. "You were wonderful, darling," she mouthed silently. Her face was a perfect oval with features so sculpted and refined that her bald head set them off to breathtaking advantage.

The identity of the first voice now came to him. It was the President's. He'd heard it many times before, but never in person.

Ray struggled to orient himself as the cheering subsided and the crowd began to disperse. As tall as the woman was who stood beside him, he was half a head taller than she was. He stretched out his arms and looked at his hands. They were large and powerful and covered tightly with smooth, flawless, and hairless skin. He passed his right hand over the top of his head, which was as bald as hers. She was leading him down from the podium by the hand.

"You were spectacular tonight," she said, this time aloud. "Now it's time to get you home."

"Marcus," the president's voice again came from behind them. Ray turned to face him. "We'll meet tomorrow morning at ten in the Oval Office. We've got a lot of work still to do."

"Sure, Mr. President. I'll be there."

"Zachary, Marcus, Zachary. Why so formal?" The president clasped his shoulders with both hands.

"We're still in public. Seemed proper," Ray covered.

So I died in the car, after all," thought Ray, "and the exchange happened exactly as Terra said it would. But I'm not prepared. I have no idea how to be him."

Ray and Corinne reached the limousine. The Secret Service man opened the door. They got in and were whisked away. How was he going to pull this off? How could she miss the differences in his gestures and speech and in the ways he would touch her, aside from how limited his knowledge was of their lives together? As the vehicle slid silently and frictionlessly over the roadway that encircled the city, Corinne's eyes closed and Ray was grateful for some time to think.

While the totality of Ray's knowledge and experience accompanied him in the exchange, Marcus's body was still implanted with the MELD chip that had been his conduit of knowledge and training. Ray focused his attention on joining his consciousness with the device that would give him access to Marcus's world. He felt the channel open and sensed the flow of data as it poured into his awareness.

His surroundings became increasingly familiar and he began to anticipate what would appear around the next bend. He could envision their mansion, their kitchen, and their bedroom. And visions began to form of moments together, starting from the present and stretching increasingly back toward the past.

The words of the speech that he'd just delivered that evening came to him first. It was about freedom and equality and stressed the rights of SPUDs to participate as equals in the affairs of state. Not a position that Ray readily embraced, even in the light of his recent encounter with Haley Sellica. That could be a problem.

Then he was back home in the bedroom with Corinne, getting dressed for their appearance. He was watching her slip the french blue dress over her head and down over her long, sleek, hairless body until it hugged the tight curves of her breasts and hips. As he felt the stirring of movement between his legs, he wondered whether these feelings of arousal belonged to him or to Marcus.

When they reached the house, it was dark except for some light in the kitchen window toward the rear of the house. The driver let them out of the car and led them to the door. Ray willed the lights to go on in the foyer and the hallways and the house lit up. He was getting the hang of running Marcus's programs, many of which were similar to his.

As they entered the house, another woman approached them in the hall, appearing somewhat younger than Corinne. Her skin was lustrous, almost polished in texture, a shade or two lighter than Corinne's, and perfect except for a splash of freckles scattered evenly over the bridge of her nose. Like Corinne, her body was hairless, but a tight spray of straight black hair sprouted from the top of her head and covered it to just behind her ears. Shiny lavender pants and a white pullover top clung snugly to a body that was as shapely as Corinne's but somehow lacked its sensuality.

"It's all ready for you, Corinne," she said as she passed them. "Good evening, Mr. Takana."

"Good evening, Photina," Ray said, pulling her image from his new database, "and thank you."

"You're both welcome," Photina said as she moved into the cold night air, seeming oblivious to the chill.

"Photina was kind enough to make dinner for us tonight," said Corinne as she led him toward the back of the house. "She's made all your favorite things. I thought we'd celebrate after your speech."

"Mushroom and squash risotto?" Ray lied. His favorite meal was filet mignon and he'd resumed his meat-eating ways once the grazing lands were restored and cattle farming had come roaring back to life. But Marcus and Corinne had remained vegetarians, just as they'd continued other aspects of their lifestyle from the days when water and agronomic products had been scarce.

"Yes, to begin with," she said, "and I've planned a very special dessert."

"Where's Nat?" asked Ray, drawing again upon his new database.

"She's at a sleepover with a friend. And Photina won't be back until morning. I thought it would be nice if we could be alone tonight."

The dining room lights were dim and candles lit the table, their reflections dancing on the surface of the goblets, each filled halfway with ruby red wine. The vineyards had only begun over the past several years to recover sufficiently to produce palatable wines. A few wineries had managed to age their last few vintages enough to create exceptional wines reminiscent of the days before the scourge. One such bottle graced their table.

"Make yourself comfortable and sip some wine," she said, sitting him down and kissing him softly on the back of the neck. "I'll be back in just a bit."

Ray breathed deeply and lifted the goblet to his lips. He swirled the liquid in the glass, watching the reflection of the candlelight in the moving liquid and inhaling deeply. The aroma was rich and earthy. He took a sip and let it linger on his tongue. It was round and mellow. He took a longer swallow. "At least in wines," he thought, "Marcus's taste agrees with mine."

When Corinne returned to the room, she took his breath away. In place of the tight blue dress was a flowing translucent gown that reached all the way to the floor. In the candlelight, Ray could make out the outlines of her body through the material as she stood framed by the doorway. The exposed skin of her forearms, hands and face shined with the glossiness left by the surfactant wash that Corinne and Marcus had continued to use even after the water shortage eased. The satiny texture that it left on the skin had a luscious sensuality that had become both familiar and exciting.

Corinne took her place at the table and lifted her wine glass. The candlelight playing on her face through the liquid made her face look like a Gothic ivory masterpiece. In this light, the slickness of her head seemed a particularly fitting enhancement to her exotic features. At closer quarters, he could see the curve of her breasts through the gauzy material and could make out the outlines of her nipples. The wine was beginning to relax him, but he was also starting to become light-headed. Intense and conflicting emotions swirled in his head, each leaving trails like the wine swirling in his glass.

"To us." She held her glass toward him until he touched it with his own, making both glasses ring.

"To us," he repeated, struggling to make sense of his role in this duet. Before him was one of the most exquisite women he'd ever laid eyes upon. And she was his for the taking. But was she? She'd been Marcus's wife and lover. Could she possibly love the new entity residing in her husband's body? His face flushed warmly in response to a combination of the wine, the excitement, and a nagging sense of embarrassment. Soon he'd make love to another man's wife. Or was she? Marcus no longer existed. So how could this be betrayal? And could taking Marcus's wife be any more of a betrayal than taking his body?

And what of Lena? He'd thought little about her in the flurry of events that led to this moment, but now he wondered whether he owed her fidelity from the other side of this divide. What effect would his death have upon her? Did she even know by now that he was dead, or had he simply gone missing? And what happened to her that night? Was she left safe and sound in their bed when he was spirited away on his fatal ride or had whoever was responsible taken her as well?

As they ate, Ray let the wine numb his senses and erode the sharp edges of his compunction. When they'd finished the last morsel of dark chocolate soufflé, Corinne rose from her seat, took him by the hand and led him into the bedroom. He smelled the sweet scent of jasmine on her body. She placed both hands on the back of his head and pulled his face to hers. He felt their lips melting together, then just an instant of hesitation on her part that made his heart skip and she was back, exploring his mouth with her tongue and undressing him.

The wine was doing its job. Ray felt the rigidity spreading into his penis. He could feel the throbbing of his pulse between his legs and the pulsations also rose in his ears, for a moment reminding him of the sensation that had accompanied the terror of his death only hours before. But the passion of the moment prevailed as they fell together on the bed in deep embrace. He closed his eyes and felt himself sink into the moist, warm cleft between her thighs.

22

MARCUS FELT a tight band around his chest as the car sailed silently over the void. The silence was broken by a loud thump that seemed to come simultaneously from the pit of his stomach and his ears. At the same time, the tightness released like a broken rubber band and he drew a deep breath. He had no idea how he'd gotten there, but the acceleration of the plunging vehicle reminded him of the thrill of the daredevil days he left behind when he'd accepted his Faustian bargain.

Through the windshield he saw the water's surface rapidly approaching and braced himself for the impact. He had no idea from what height his fall had begun.

The nose of the car broke the water's surface and he was surrounded by churning surf, but the vehicle bobbed back toward the surface, buoyed by the air still trapped within the cabin and the air in the tires. The roof and half the windshield cleared the surface before the car started to sink back toward the depths. Marcus groped for the window controls and managed to trigger them, but the windows lowered just a few inches before the electrical system cut out.

He released his seat belt and scanned the passenger compartment for something he could use to break a window. His eyes went to the knob on the gearshift. He tried to unscrew it, but it wouldn't budge. His hands were clumsy and weak. When he held one of them before his eyes, it was soft and pudgy. He brushed a hand across his face and it was rough with stubble. His head was covered with thickly matted hair. And when he looked into the rearview mirror, there was the ridged and mottled face of a stranger.

He fought back panic as the possibilities began running through his mind. The last thing he remembered before this nightmare began was the rise of applause at the end of his speech in front of the Capitol steps. Corinne had been walking toward him to join him on the dais and in the next instant he was plunging from a height in an antiquated car within an aging body. He'd been in lots of tight spots before, some worse than this one, and had always managed to prevail, but something unfathomable was now occurring that reeked of doom.

Water was beginning to seep over the edges of the cracked open windows and the passenger compartment was starting to fill. Marcus braced his arms against the passenger side door and kicked his left foot back against the driver's side window at its front edge where it should have been weakest. It didn't give. He kicked back with his right foot against the window's rear edge, but still it wouldn't break. He'd performed this maneuver before and had managed to handily smash similar windows. He could usually press hundreds of pounds with his legs, but now it felt as though all the strength was drained from his body.

He pushed against the driver's side door, but the water pressure was too strong. The door wouldn't budge. The front of the car was nosing down as it continued to sink. He climbed into the back seat to get to the small pocket of air that remained only there and slowed his breathing to conserve the remaining oxygen. And as he waited for the car to take him to the ocean floor, it dawned on him that he must be there because he was already dead. The exchange had occurred. The owner of the contract must have died in the plunging car and was now in possession of Marcus's body. And he was in this body to conclude its death and fulfill his destiny. His awareness that death was inevitable brought with it an unexpected calm. Time seemed to stop as the rest of the cabin filled and the car glided soundlessly to the bottom.

Marcus held his breath and waited for the thud of the impact. His survival instinct prevailed. As soon as the car was at rest, he pushed on the rear door, which now gave way easily, placed one foot on the threshold and thrust himself toward the surface. This time, the pudgy body that he now commanded provided an advantage, buoying him easily to the top. Once at the surface, he drew a few gasping breaths, flipped onto his back, and floated until his breathing slowed to normal.

His whole body ached. Clearly, his alter ego hadn't been taking care of his body as well as Marcus had taken care of his and wasn't accustomed to the kind of exertion to which it had just been subjected. Nonetheless, he seemed to be alive, at least for now. If he managed to survive, Marcus now wondered, would he be destined to live out the remainder of his days in this alien and pathetic incarnation? And who the hell was this guy, anyway?

His body began to chill in the frigid water. If he were to survive, he would have to choose between the insulating effect of the clothing that clung loosely to his body and the superior speed of an unencumbered form. Shoes were a no brainer and he kicked them off first. He next stripped off the waterlogged trousers, but kept on the briefs and t-shirt. He surveyed his surroundings and could see in the distance the shoreline where the sea abutted the base of the cliffs.

When Marcus rolled onto his stomach and began to swim, he was pleasantly surprised to discover that his new body seemed up to the task. Perhaps it was the strength of his will together with his experience and skill that enabled him to muster the strength. He was just grateful to have found it.

Halfway to shore, Marcus spotted a boat a few hundred yards away and parallel to the shore. Should he make for the beach or turn and swim for the boat, which was closer? He was tiring fast and headed for the boat. As he got closer, it appeared to be some sort of patrol boat. For the first time, it seemed that he might survive this strange ordeal, whatever that would mean.

As he got within hailing distance of the boat, he noticed the gun mounted to the bow. Suddenly there were bursts of gunfire. Bullets chopped at the water surrounding his body. He dove and turned, but when he broke the surface, the boat was bearing down on him and the bullets kept coming. He felt a bullet rip through his right shoulder, burning along its track. Another tore through the back of his left thigh and exited at his groin. And he felt three more in rapid succession tear a hole through the middle of his back and explode through the front of his chest. The water surrounding his inert form turned crimson as blood pumped for an instant, then oozed to blanket the sea around him. The boat swung around and sped away, leaving his body to the sharks.

23

CORINNE FELT Marcus's body rising and falling rhythmically to penetrate her depths as she straddled him. He was moving more slowly and driving more forcefully than she was accustomed to and she found herself responding to the novel cadence with a level of arousal reminiscent of their first time together. His expression was intent, seeming to trace her face with his eyes as if he were trying to memorize it. She met his gaze and bent down for a lingering kiss.

She rose again astride him. Their pace quickened and her arousal peaked and hung just at the edge of climax when something else remarkable happened. The muscles in Marcus's face contorted into a grimace that bespoke more agony than ecstasy. His upper body lurched sharply forward, then dropped back to the bed. She felt the contractions as he ejaculated, but the disturbance had rattled her and interrupted her momentum, preventing her from coming, too. By the time she rolled off him, he was sound asleep, tears streaming down his face.

Corinne opened her eyes as daylight began filtering through the shuttered windows. She saw Marcus standing naked in front of the full-length mirror staring at his own reflection, touching his face, and running his hands over the prominent muscles of his abdomen and thighs. The bull's image glowed faintly on his chest, then faded away. His hands formed tight fists, relaxed, and clenched again. He shook his head. Then she saw his body shake ever so slightly. He was laughing.

*****

As Ray peered into the bedroom mirror, he was oblivious that anyone else was in the room. A cauldron of conflicting emotions washed over him: relief, exultation, disappointment, sadness, elation again. What was clearest to him was that he had never felt so intensely, had never been so alive. He reached up to his face and ran a hand over the crown of his head.

"Honey..." came the tentative voice behind him.

He turned toward the voice and saw in Lena's face the same boldface question mark that had punctuated every one of his thoughts since he'd awakened that morning. He looked down at the strands of black and gray hair on his fingers, then back at Lena. She looked as exhausted as he felt. She hesitated another moment to be sure she had his attention before speaking again.

"There's a woman here to see you, Ray...a very young and very attractive woman. She insists on talking with you right away...says it's urgent." Every statement bore another question mark. Her voice was imploring. "Ray, who is she?"

He threw on some clothes and descended the stairs to find a familiar redhead waiting in the foyer. He'd not seen her in a decade and a half, but she looked exactly as he remembered her. Unlike him and Lena, she'd not aged a day.

"Hello, Terra," Ray said.

"Hello, Ray." she replied. "As you are surely already aware, there's been a terrible accident. We must talk." She glanced toward Lena, reminding Ray wordlessly that what they had to say to each other had to be private.

"It's OK, honey. This is business and it's urgent. I'll explain later." He had no idea what he would tell her later. He would assure her that his relationship with Terra wasn't romantic, but it would be all the harder to be convincing having made passionate love to another ravishing woman just hours before.

Lena was already running Terra's image through the Universal Data Base and came up empty. Terra was a ghost on the grid.

"I know this was awkward," Terra apologized once they were alone outside, "but given what's happened, I figured I owed you an explanation face to face."

"Explain away, Terra. I've probably got lots more questions than you have answers."

"Nothing like this has ever happened before in the history of the program. We have so many safeguards and we're constantly upgrading our security." She hesitated, searching for words. Ray didn't offer any help.

"Someone hacked into our system. They found a vulnerability, accessed several of our clients through their MELD chips, and corrupted their perceptual fields with virtual scripts. When it first came to our attention, we could only monitor the scripts. It took a while before we found a way to terminate them. We stopped yours just in time. Another few seconds and we wouldn't have gotten you back."

"What were they after?"

"It's not clear. But in each case, they created a scenario that was so terrifying that the subject's heart stopped, triggering the exchange. When the...surrogates took over, the programmed scripts maintained their hold and the scenes played out. Until we regained control, we were unable to abort the exchange."

"It was that close?"

"You were one of the lucky ones. We lost two other clients. Their surrogates were terminated virtually before we could get back in and their hearts stopped permanently."

"So they were trying to kill us all?"

"We're not sure. They may have been after one target and attacked the others as a diversion to keep us off balance. Any one of you could have been the primary target, or the program itself. Our technology is priceless. We have competitors hot on our trail."

"What happened to my surrogate after the exchange?"

"His survival skills were strong. He managed to escape from the car after it sunk to the ocean floor, but he was shot while trying to swim to safety and was barely alive when we interrupted the script."

"And reversed the exchange?"

"Yes, he's back in his own body, at least for now. He'll remember for a time what happened, but then it should fade and seem like a dream."

"What about the ones that didn't make it?" asked Ray.

"The exchanges had taken place, so our clients assumed their new lives when their surrogates...perished."

"So who were really the lucky ones?" wondered Ray. He'd tasted youth, power, perfection and the joy of an exceptionally sensual and energetic sexual partner. And he'd momentarily gone from being one of the most despised men on the planet to standing before an adoring throng. Did he really want to be back in an aging body leading a plodding life?

"We are so very sorry this happened," Terra continued. "We understand that what you've been through has been traumatic and...confusing. You've seen things that you weren't supposed to see or know yet. And now you can't unknow those things or forget where you've been."

"And if I want to go back?"

"You know the rules. You're not allowed to do anything to hasten your demise or the contract becomes void." Terra moved a step closer and looked directly into his eyes. "And I'm sure that when you've had some time to think about it, it's for the best that you've returned. It wasn't yet your time...or his."

"You mean Marcus...Marcus Takana. That's who I was...he is. That's whose life I have to look forward to."

"You'd do best to forget that for now. Nothing good can come of dwelling on it," said Terra. "Now I must go. I have lots of damage control to attend to."

When Ray returned to the house, Lena was sitting and waiting for him. She looked small and fragile in the oversized chair. He scoured her face, but her mouth formed a straight line without any hint of curvature that would signify either pleasure or displeasure. Her eyes were clear and followed him into the room. Her hands rested softly on the arms of the chair.

"It's not what you think," he began.

"I haven't any idea what to think," Lena replied, her voice as even as the line of her mouth. "Nothing's made any sense since the morning began and I found you examining yourself in the mirror like a cadaver on a dissecting table."

Ray was almost relieved to hear the faint tremor in the last few words that hinted at the rage that she was struggling to contain.

"Who the hell is she, Ray?" Lena exploded before he could get a word in. "Where did she come from? She's not even in the UDB."

"Terra deals in...final arrangements. What happens after I die." Ray stayed within the broad outlines of truth.

"She doesn't look like a funeral director," Lena said. "More like a spy. Since when do funeral planners have emergencies?"

"It's not about my body," Ray began straying from the truth. "She handles the future. You know our lives are complicated."

"You mean the money?"

"That's part of it. It's important to plan ahead." He had no idea where to go from there. It suddenly occurred to him that he should have bought a contract for Lena, too. He wondered what it would be like for them to reunite in youthful bodies. Would any tension that remained between them persist in their new incarnations or would the cynicism of age yield to the promise of youth and permit them a fresh start? More likely, they'd never meet in their new lives. And then there was Corinne...

*****

"Marcus?" Corinne said softly behind him. He turned to face her.

"What are you doing? You're acting so strangely. You haven't been yourself since last night."

Marcus flushed from head to toe. He'd been unaware that she'd been watching him while his thoughts were in another world.

"It's a beautiful morning, sweetheart. It just feels good to be alive."

"No, Marcus. Things started getting weird last night...in bed." Corinne scanned his body with her eyes, lingering a moment at his genitals. "You were so incredibly passionate," she continued, "it was like we were making love for the first time." She took a long breath. "But for just a moment I had the odd feeling that you were a stranger."

Marcus held his breath and felt his heart skip a beat. He was focused intently on her words.

"And then, just before you came, your face screwed up like you were in excruciating pain and your whole body convulsed. It looked like you'd just been shot. After that you were gone, like I wasn't even there anymore. You left me high and dry."

Marcus opened his mouth to begin an apology. Corinne placed a finger on his lips before any words could come out.

"I was angry last night," she said, "but this morning I'm just worried. I want my husband back. I need you to be OK." For the second time in a matter of weeks, she feared she was losing him.

Marcus's thoughts returned to the night before. While he'd been lost in someone else's nightmare, they'd been living his dream and making love to his wife. And she'd apparently enjoyed it. He felt the muscles tense in his temples and neck. Damn! It wasn't supposed to be like that. Not just his body, but his life and everything he held dear. He'd always believed that Corinne was faithful. Now she'd been screwed by another man and she felt it even if she didn't know it.

That afternoon while he was on his daily run in the park, a woman ran up beside him and kept pace. It was unusual for anyone to keep up with him. She was barely breaking a sweat when he caught his first look at her.

"Hello, Terra," Marcus said. "I was expecting you'd show up, given what happened."

"Hello, Marcus," said Terra. "You've been next on my list."

"I want out," blurted Marcus before she could say anything else. "I'll give back the money. I just want my life back." By now they'd stopped running and were standing by the side of the trail facing each other.

"Which life, Marcus? The pathetic one you had when I found you or the one you've been enjoying for these past fifteen years?" She waited for her words to sink in. The corners of his mouth were twitching and tears welled in his eyes.

"The money wasn't a loan, Marcus. It was an investment in everything that's changed in your life since the contract began. We...he owns you. You can't turn back the clock and make it go away. If you could, there would be no knowledge, no fame or fortune, and definitely no Corinne. Your body would be slowly deteriorating in an inexorable crawl toward death. And the planet would probably still be overrun with HibernaTurf, growing hotter and more barren by the day."

Marcus's shoulders fell. For that moment, his body felt as decrepit as Terra's description and it seemed like he was carrying the whole weight of the world with no way to shrug it off.

"Isn't there any way out?"

"The contract is irrevocable. You can't go back. And the secrecy of our operation is of paramount importance to us. If you tried to escape from your agreement, we'd be forced to terminate your identity." The glow in Terra's emerald eyes and her fiery red hair made her look almost demonic. Marcus had had no idea what forces were set in play when he'd first agreed to the arrangement.

"You mean you'd have to kill me?"

"Not kill, Marcus, not your body, anyway. We would just wipe out those parts of your memory that are essential to who you've become since the Conversion. You'd continue to live, but your memory would pick up where you left off when we first met. You'd have no knowledge of your accomplishments, of the position you've attained, of me, or of Corinne. And we would amend the Universal Data Base so that the world would forget you, too."

"That's impossible!"

"You wouldn't believe the power we wield," Terra's voice resounded. "Our capabilities can work for you or against you. It's up to you."

"Will you at least explain what just happened to me?"

"Let's just say there was a glitch in the system. It's been patched and we're pretty sure it won't happen again." She blinked and the glare was gone from her eyes. She put a hand on his forearm. "Look, we're...I'm very sorry about what you had to go through. It was never supposed to happen. Go back to your life. Try to forget it. With any luck, you'll live another 30 or 40 years without ever having to think about us again."

"Yeah, right. You're asking me to just forget that I nearly died while my wife spent the night with some son of a bitch that she'll eventually spend the rest of her life with. How the hell am I supposed to forget something like that?"

"That's your problem, Marcus." She pulled back her hand. "Either you make peace with it or it'll take over your life a lot sooner than the transfer will. There's nothing else I can do." She turned, began running back down the trail, and was soon out of sight.

24

THE HEADLINE caught Lena's attention as she lay in bed and scanned through the database updates for the day: "Man disappears. Wife claims imposter."

Lena opened her eyes and sat up. What was it about this story that seemed to resonate with her? She closed her eyes again and let the full content of the story flow into her consciousness.

The missing man, now in his mid-thirties, had been a world class competitive skier in his early twenties when he'd come into a small fortune, apparently an inheritance from a long lost relative. Around the same time, he'd abandoned skiing and begun satisfying his appetite for rigorous competition by training for triathlons, a less risky endeavor. Much of his time and the majority of his fortune was invested in a foundation devoted to the pursuit of life extension.

His wife told the authorities that she'd noticed changes in him a couple of months earlier that left her wondering whether he could be an imposter. It had been hard for her to put her finger on it, but there were subtle changes in his mannerisms and behavior. She was sufficiently disturbed to see a psychiatrist, who suggested that she was suffering from a delusional syndrome and recommended medication. She refused treatment and didn't go back.

The detail that most grabbed Lena, though, was a visitor who'd come to their home the day before the man disappeared. The man's wife described a striking redhead with piercing green eyes. She'd been certain that her husband had been having an affair with this woman and guessed that he'd probably run off with her. But when she'd scanned the UDB for facial recognition, the search had come up blank. A redheaded ghost. Could this be the same ghost that had visited Ray?

Lena was on the vacuum tube transport to Phoenix that afternoon to interview the missing man's wife. She introduced herself ahead of time as a journalist with a special interest in missing persons.

"I'm Katrina," said the woman greeting her at the door. "Please come in." She seemed surprisingly calm, given her husband's recent, abrupt disappearance.

"Thank you. I'm Lena. I'm sorry for what you must be going through."

"The worst part is everyone thinks I'm crazy. Even my closest friends. It's a relief to talk to someone who might take me seriously."

"You told the reporter that something had changed about your husband a couple of months ago. Can you tell me more about that?"

"It's hard to put your finger on what defines someone's identity. On the surface, he said and did all the right things. He had an extensive knowledge of our lives and treated all our friends as familiar." Katrina shook her head. "Even his body was identical, right down to birthmarks and scars. But something told me he was someone else. He wasn't my Jorge."

"What was the first thing you noticed?"

"It was when we were making love. It felt different." Katrina blushed. "Better...like we were doing it for the first time."

"What else?"

"The way he touched me was...just different. You get to know a lover's touch. It's not something you can describe. You just know it. This man was a stranger." She'd been looking away and now looked Lena straight in the eye.

"You probably think I'm crazy, too."

"Not at all." Lena reached out her hand and touched Katrina on the arm. "I wondered, though, since you seemed to think he'd been having an affair, if his behavior could have changed because he'd been with someone else?"

"I thought of that after the redhead came to our home. I thought back and tried to figure out if that's what it was, but it was more than that. After that first odd lovemaking session, I began observing him and making mental notes. There were other things."

"Like what?"

"Like the way he ate, the way he held his fork, the order in which he ate things, and what he seemed to like. He always kept a stash of chocolate, a favorite type of dark chocolate that he ate every day. I noticed that he hadn't touched it for weeks."

"What else?"

"We were at our favorite restaurant where he always orders the same wine. He asked for one he'd never ordered before."

"Maybe he was just up for a change."

"You have to understand, Jorge was a creature of habit. When he liked something, that's all he wanted. He didn't need variety." Katrina sighed deeply and blew the breath all the way out. "Except perhaps in women."

"Tell me about the woman...the redhead."

"She just showed up out of the blue. I'd never seen her before, but Jorge seemed to know her."

"What did she look like?"

"Her flowing red hair was her most distinctive feature. Her skin was white, she had a flawless complexion, and her green eyes sparkled from across the room. She was almost too perfect to be human."

Katrina's description fit precisely with Lena's picture of the woman who'd visited Ray. And the woman's visit had followed shortly after the morning that Ray's behavior had seemed so odd and foreign. This couldn't be just a coincidence. And it was increasingly clear that the visits had nothing to do with sex.

"Did you hear anything that they talked about? Did you catch a name?"

"No, the woman insisted they go outside and they talked in whispers. Jorge seemed very upset by the time she left. I asked him what she was doing there and he just got mad. He wouldn't talk about it. He went to bed without saying another word. When I awoke the next morning, he was gone. No note. Nothing."

"You're not crazy, Katrina," Lena said. After a long pause she added, "I've seen her, too."

"Oh my God!" Katrina was in tears and threw her arms around Lena. "Then you know who she is."

"Unfortunately, no. She's just as much a mystery to me as she is to you, but I can tell you that I don't think she's been having an affair with either of our husbands. And her appearance probably has a lot to do with their sudden odd behavior and with Jorge's disappearance."

"Their behavior? So your husband changed, too?'

"Not in quite the same way," said Lena. "His quirks were temporary, just a few minutes or an hour. Then he was back to himself. But something strange had definitely occurred. And the woman showed up later that day."

Lena's head was swimming with questions when she finally left Katrina's home and headed back to San Francisco on the tube. Who was the mysterious woman without an identity? What did Ray and Jorge have in common?' And what was responsible for Jorge's metamorphosis and Ray's less enduring singularity?

One possible explanation came to mind, but it seemed too outrageous to give serious consideration. Lena had been following the developing science of life extension for years and was impressed with the progress of the technology. The most striking public accomplishment was the Ambrosia Conversion, a genetic process that extended the life of cells indefinitely, enabling the body to stop aging. The Conversion only worked, however, in the first three decades of life while the body's cells were still relatively intact. It was still very expensive and created a whole new potential divide between the haves and the have nots. There was a popular movement to outlaw it entirely rather than make it available to a privileged few.

At the fringes of this technology was a small group of enthusiasts who were pursuing ways to upload mental contents to cybernetic hosts that might function as avatars for people's consciousness after their bodies had died. There were many ethical conundrums about how such a technology would be implemented. But even further beyond the boundaries of responsible scientific pursuit was the possibility of moving consciousness from person to person. In Lena's study of the field, she'd stumbled across rumors that a secret organization, perhaps within the government, had brought this body hopping technology to fruition.

The rumors went on to suggest that the secret agency was now trafficking in bodies, providing wealthy older people the opportunity to move their consciousness to healthy young bodies that had undergone the Conversion. Perhaps, suggested one source, such transfers had already occurred and mind-body hybrids walked among us.

"That's really crazy," Lena thought as the capsule slowed to a halt and she prepared to disembark. "It couldn't possibly be."

And yet the pieces seemed to fit. Lena did have a name for the redheaded visitor: "Terra." And Ray had told her that Terra dealt in final arrangements. Maybe that was his version of not lying to her.

*****

"Where have you been?" asked Ray when Lena walked in the door. It was after midnight.

"Phoenix."

"What the hell were you doing in Phoenix?"

"I was following a story." Lena paused and drew in a breath. "I met a woman, Ray," she continued, "a woman who's met Terra."

171

Ray fell silent. Whatever this meant, it couldn't be good. How much did Lena know?

"Talk to me Ray. You need to tell me who Terra is and what business you have with her, because whatever the truth is can't possibly be as outrageous as what I imagine."

"I'd tell you if I could, Lena," Ray said, "God knows I've wanted to tell you. But I can't. I'm sworn to secrecy. If I told you, I'm afraid it would endanger us both."

"This woman's husband disappeared right after a visit from Terra. But it gets worse. She told me that for the past couple of months, he'd been replaced by an imposter...someone else living in his body."

"What are you getting at?" Ray asked, but he already knew exactly what Lena was implying. His wife was extremely bright and intuitive, which made her an outstanding investigator. She'd figured it out, at least in its broad outlines. She might not know, though, quite how deep he'd waded into this mess.

"When you said Terra deals in final arrangements, did you mean she arranges for life after death?"

"I told you. We can't talk about this. It's too dangerous. She's too dangerous. I don't want to put you in her crosshairs."

"If you can't trust me with your secrets, I'm not sure what kind of future our marriage holds. And if you're planning what I think your planning, then I have no idea how to understand what our marriage means. This gives 'til death do we part' a whole new twist. Do you even know who you'll become? And what will become of the person whose body you wind up in?"

"Do you know how crazy all this sounds?" Ray exploded. "Your imagination's running wild. What you're implying isn't even possible. You have to let this go."

"Isn't it, Ray? I may have to believe it until you come up with a more plausible explanation. I'll let you off the hook for tonight, but we'll keep coming back to it until you tell me something I can believe. You know how I can be when my mind is made up. I'll get the truth one way or another."

25

RAY AWOKE suddenly from a sound sleep and sat bolt upright with a piercing scream. Both hands pressed against the sides of his head.

"Ray! Ray! What's wrong?" asked Lena.

"Pain!" Ray answered. "Pain! Pain!" He searched for other words, but could find none. The pain in his head was searing, worse than any he'd ever experienced. Terror pierced the fog that was settling over his consciousness. Was this the event that would end his life as he knew it forever?

"I'll call for an ambulance," said Lena.

"No...ambumens," Ray stuttered, grabbing her arm. "No...popsicles." Aside from his usual terror of hospitals, Ray knew that going to a hospital risked exposing the network of nanoparticles in his brain and the microprocessor in his neck. Even in his confused state, Terra's prohibition against seeking medical care held sway.

Lena pulled away, but before she could call for help, there was a pounding on the door. She ran to open it. In rushed a team of five, all in surgical costume, wheeling in a long, closet like structure. Bringing up the rear was the mysterious redhead who'd visited Ray. Once inside, the structure unfolded into a fully equipped operating room.

"We've got this," said Terra to Lena while the team moved Ray to the operating table.

"But how...?" Lena began.

"Doesn't matter," Terra interrupted. "We'll take care of him."

The team swarmed over Ray. One injection and the pain subsided. His body relaxed. They placed a transparent bubble over his head. As an arc of light moved around the perimeter of the bubble, a high-resolution picture of his brain appeared on a screen mounted on a wall of the enclosure.

"Here's the bleed," said one of the attendants, pointing at a place on a side view around halfway down. "It's in the superior gyrus of the left temporal lobe."

"Lucky it's not in the brainstem," said another. "We can probably save him."

The team stepped away from the table. A transparent dome descended over Ray's entire body, its edges mating with a groove that ran around the perimeter of the table. It sealed with a hiss. Six mechanical arms dangled from the top of the dome, each holding a surgical instrument. One held a long coiled catheter, its leading end free and the other anchored to a machine through a tiny opening in the dome.

"Lower the temperature to fifty-five degrees," commanded the team leader. "And fill the chamber with oxygen."

Between the effects of the stroke and the haze of the pain medication, Ray's consciousness was suspended somewhere between trance and sleep. Both pain and fear had seeped away. His body was sufficiently immobile to undergo a procedure.

Three of the team members now donned metallic gloves adorned with glowing lights on each of the fingers and surrounded the dome. They each held their arms flexed at the elbows, palms pointed toward Ray's body. The leader of the surgical team began moving his fingers. Two of the mechanical arms reached down, coordinating their instruments at the surface of Ray's left groin. As the others began moving their fingers, all six of the arms joined in a dance of exquisite precision.

A quick incision and the catheter shot into the femoral artery. Its progress up the iliac artery and through the aorta appeared on one of several screens on the walls of the operating theatre, its position tracked digitally by its coordinates. As it snaked its way up the carotid artery into the brain, it appeared on the scanner's image that now refreshed every five seconds. A doctor closely monitored its progress.

"We're there," she said at last, and the catheter froze in place, its tip alongside a tiny opening in the blood vessel. A pocket of extruded blood sat just outside the opening. The tip tilted slightly until it filled the opening in the vessel. "Now or never."

A faint hiss and the blotch adjacent to the artery shrank and vanished. A few clicks and the catheter tip withdrew from the opening in the vessel, which now appeared sealed.

In a time long past aneurysms were plugged with tiny wire coils. Now the defects were fused instantaneously via catheter with a stem cell impregnated mesh that adhered to their edges. A few weeks and all traces of either the aneurysm or the bleed would be gone.

"It's holding," said the doctor at the screen. "Time to finish."

"What about the other ones?" asked another member of the team, pointing on the screen to a scattering of tiny bubbles on blood vessels throughout the brain.

"There are way too many to fix," said the first doctor. "We'll just have to leave them and hope that they hold."

Within less than a minute, the catheter was withdrawn completely and the surgical wound was closed. Ray still lay quietly within the dome. His breathing was slow and regular.

Twenty minutes later, Ray was back in his own bed, asleep. The mobile operating room had been packed up and moved out. The team vanished as swiftly and mysteriously as it had arrived. Terra was the last to leave.

"What do I do now?" asked Lena, grabbing Terra by the wrist.

"You wait," said Terra, "and be patient. It may take a while for him to wake up, but he should recover fully." Before Lena could articulate her next question, Terra was gone.

Lena sat vigil at Ray's bedside until daybreak. As the sky began to light up with the crimson glow from the rising sun, Ray's eyes fluttered open.

"Thank God," said Lena, embracing him, tears streaming down her cheeks onto his chest.

I'm...still me," said Ray, taking a long, deep breath, his eyes scrunched and the creases in his face exaggerated with bewilderment. "I didn't...die."

"What an odd way of putting it," thought Lena.

"What happened to me?" Ray asked.

"You seem to have had a stroke," said Lena. "An aneurysm burst in your brain. And your mysterious redhead showed up for a house call with a team of doctors and a portable operating suite. I've never seen anything like it."

"Terra," said Ray. "She came to save me."

"Whoever Terra is, you must be very important to her. I'll let you rest for now. But we're long overdue for a talk."

26

CORINNE TAKANA haunted Ray's thoughts. He awoke every morning to the image of her face while his eyes were still closed. He traced its oval outline, ran his gaze along the fine straight ridge of her nose, lingered a moment on the moisture between her slightly parted lips, and came to rest on her bottomless, ebony eyes, dilated with arousal. Her ivory skin was flawless, flowing smoothly over her forehead and the crown of her head. How sweetly sensual he found the barrenness of her skin. He would wait as long as possible before opening his eyes and allowing his surroundings to swallow his dream.

She returned to him each night when he closed his eyes and lingered in the twilight stage of sleep. Now he saw the outline of her body beneath the diaphanous nightgown and allowed himself to reach out and draw her body close to his. As he slid his hands past the material, he felt the luxurious silkiness of her skin, embellished with its surfactant film. And his body was no longer old and soft. His muscles were firm and his skin as slick and bare as hers as their bodies glided seamlessly together until sleep overtook him.

Against the backdrop of his fantasies, Ray's days became tortured. From the moment he looked in the mirror at his age-lined face, straggly graying hair, and pudgy belly, he felt disgust at who he was. He'd once considered himself a decent looking man, but the soft hairy image before him paled in comparison to the sleek, youthful perfection of the body he'd fleetingly inhabited.

It wasn't just his body that disgusted him. His life was tainted with failure. He'd become a pariah, responsible for one of the worst disasters that had befallen civilization. The revulsion with which the world regarded him for the rampage of HibernaTurf had only been partially mitigated by the reversal of its devastation by Takana Grass. Marcus Takana was now enjoying the adulation to which Ray had once aspired and had briefly attained.

Even more than Ray longed to be with Corinne, he longed to be Marcus Takana.

But Terra had made clear that he didn't have the power to choose when that might occur. Suicide was against the rules of the contract and out of the question. He was sure that Terra would terminate him if he deliberately killed himself. And as jealous as Ray was of Marcus Takana, he understood that suicide would be tantamount to murdering an innocent man. Even Ray had limits of what moral lines he was willing to cross to get his way.

He became obsessed with finding a solution. He was a resourceful man. There had to be a way. He considered what had happened with the hack. His brain had been tricked into perceiving that he'd died in order to trigger the switch. If he could only find another way to flirt with death without it becoming final, then perhaps he could go back to being Marcus, while Marcus would get to live out his life as Ray. Not exactly fair, but at least not suicide and not murder. Maybe Terra would let him live.

He considered ways to slow his biological functions sufficiently to simulate death. Stimulating the vagus nerve was one way to slow heart rate, sometimes drastically. There were a number of natural ways to trigger the vasovagal reflex that would slow the pulse, but the duration and degree of such slowing would be hard to modulate. On the other hand, heart rate and respiration could be controlled more precisely via the modulating functions of his MELD chip. Even so, getting to the cusp of death and maintaining his vital signs there long enough to trigger the switch without damaging his brain would be close to impossible by this means alone.

Hypothermia was another means by which biological functions could grind nearly to a halt without compromising brain tissue. This had been used to protect surgical patients from irreversible brain damage during cardiac surgery early in the century. It would be both difficult and painful to self-administer and still might not achieve the degree and duration of suspended animation to convince the implanted transducer behind his ear that he was dead.

There were also chemical means of slowing metabolism while protecting the body and brain from oxygen deprivation. One approach involved a combination of adenosine, lidocaine, and magnesium, powerful regulators of heart rate and rhythm. But even with all the resources of the UDB, finding just the right combination of doses to create a near death experience would be daunting.

Perhaps, though, combining each of these three imprecise approaches could provide sufficient protection to balance him on the razor's edge of death just long enough for the transfer of consciousness to occur. If he failed to get close enough to his target state, then nothing would happen and nothing would be lost. If he failed to limit the duration of his intervention, then Marcus would certainly die and his fate would be up to Terra. In Ray's flawed moral calculus, it wouldn't be murder if he didn't intend for Marcus to die. He was willing to take that chance.

Ray scanned the UDB for a suitable setting in which to execute his plan. He found an abandoned warehouse that had once belonged to a charity that distributed food to the poor. It was still equipped with an aging refrigeration unit and a laminar flow device for circulating cold air throughout the containment room in which fresh produce had been stored. It was capable of maintaining the temperature as low as 38 degrees F, perfectly suited to his purpose.

When he surveyed the warehouse and walked inside the 8X10 ft windowless storeroom enclosed by slick white surfaces, he smiled.

"This will be perfect," Ray thought, "and remote enough to work in secrecy."

The next step was to acquire the pharmaceutical agents. That was a snap. They were all common and readily available. The only remaining question would be the route of administration. He'd have to give himself precise doses of each drug simultaneously, so that they would act immediately, then dissipate within minutes. An intravenous line could get the drugs in quickly, but it would take too long for them to become inactivated.

Ray settled on a transdermal injector invented in the early thirties. Its unique capability was that it could extract drugs back through the skin once their action was no longer needed or desirable. The duration of action could be dialed in prior to injection.

It took Ray five weeks to prepare all the components of his system for the experiment. He tested the cooling system in the storeroom. It worked amazingly well, considering its age and years of disuse. He tested the transdermal device with a fast-acting sedative, setting the duration of action to five minutes. When he applied the perforated round head of the delivery device to his forearm, it attached by suction, resembling a leech and releasing only after its payload had been extracted. He became briefly drowsy, but was fully alert within ten minutes.

Lena might have noticed something amiss about Ray's behavior had she not been preoccupied with a project of her own following the appearance of the mysterious redhead. Ray wondered how long Marcus would be able to escape her detection once the exchange was completed.

Ray woke early on the morning of the experiment. He lingered on Corinne's image, anticipating seeing her in the flesh hours later. It took most of the day to prepare the room and was nearly dusk when he finally closed the door and locked it behind him with the biosensing lock that he'd installed. He climbed naked onto to the table in the middle of the room, lying supine on its pliable surface, and turned on the motor that sent waves of fluid coursing down the length of his body to prevent pressure from damaging his frigid skin.

Then he engaged the laminar cooling system with his MELD chip and set it for 40 degrees. The transdermal gun was poised for action in his right hand, already loaded with its near lethal concoction.

As his body began to cool, he drew slow deep breaths and willed his heart to slow. His pulse dropped to fifty, then forty, thirty-five, thirty. He shivered, then willed his body to be still so that its temperature could continue to fall. When his pulse hit twenty, he felt lightheaded. The cold made him drowsy. He struggled to stay conscious as long as possible, then applied the injector to his forearm and pulled the trigger.

The lights went out.

27

MARCUS'S BODY SHOOK violently. He lay naked on a pliable surface that moved in waves beneath his body. Frigid air flowed across his body and face. He opened his eyes to darkness.

"Where am I?" he wondered, "and how did I get here?" But for the moment, all he could think about was the bone-chilling cold.

Then the moving air stopped. The room began gradually to warm as his shivering body labored to warm him from the inside.

He lay still, allowing time for his body to restore its equilibrium. It was difficult to think with his chilled brain. He could hear the slow bounding pulse in his neck and counted the beats. Thirty. His oxygen deprived brain struggled to make sense. Thirty-five...forty...forty-five. His thoughts began to clear.

He brought his right hand to his face to rub his eyes. It brushed his right cheek. Prickly. Stubble? He slid it over the top of his head. Strands of hair. His pulse now rose more rapidly with the rising panic.

He moved both hands over his chest and belly. More hair. Soft flesh. When he pushed on his belly, the flesh gave easily beneath the tips of his fingers. He couldn't feel the underlying ridges of muscle that he'd worked so long and hard to define.

As he explored the contours of his body, it began to feel familiar. Not his body, but he'd been here before. He swallowed hard, nearly choking on his dry tongue. The last time he'd occupied this body, he'd nearly drowned and was shot. How did he get back here? And what was in store for him this time?

As his eyes adjusted to the dark, the scant light seeping under the only door in the room enabled him to see the shadows of objects. Tilting his head, he could see his protruding belly with its hairy swirls around his navel and his toes beyond it. He moved his hands away from his sides until they dropped off the edges of the surface. He was on an elevated platform of undetermined height.

He sat up on the edge of the platform. A gun-like object lay on the floor. In the corner of the room was a pile of neatly folded clothes. The door had no visible handle or lock.

Sensation was gradually returning to his body. His hands and feet went from numb to pins and needles. It seemed to take forever for the tingling to go away and the normal sensation to return. Then he felt the pressure in his bladder rapidly building until he was desperate to pee. The pain concentrated in his prostate at the base of his bladder. He stood and piled the clothes on top of the platform before relieving himself on the floor in the corner. As badly as he had to go, it took several minutes before he could start his stream, which finished weakly in a series of dribbles. The smell of the freshly voided urine assaulted his senses within the otherwise sterile enclosure.

He slipped on the clothes: boxer shorts, jeans, a collarless button-down shirt, socks and running shoes. They all fit well, tailored precisely to the irregular shape of his badly flawed body. It felt good to be covered and warmer. He looked around for something that might cast his reflection. There was nothing.

It was time to find his way out of this prison. He stood in front of the door and ran his hands around its edges. Around halfway up just to its right was a barely perceptible heat gradient, defining a rectangle of wall surface about the size of his hand. Placing his palm flush against the wall within the outline of the rectangle opened a small portal just above it with what looked like a camera lens. He looked into it and the door slid open. Beyond it the dark of night was broken by the faint light of a sliver of moon. Then the sky slowly filled with a canopy of stars.

There were no other buildings, no vehicle, no road, no landmarks. He still had no way of knowing where or even who he was. He'd need to find some way to navigate back to civilization. But what would happen to him when he got there? Would anyone have missed him? Was he a fugitive? Would whoever was responsible for his predicament try to finish the job?

"Not likely," thought Marcus. "Whoever did this did it to himself. And now I'm him and he's me." He considered the implications of this conclusion.

A whirring sound broke the silence around him. He looked up to see an object hovering fifty yards or so away and approaching fast. As it got closer, he could make out a human form suspended from a small aircraft, a personal passenger drone. It stopped ten feet in front of him. Its passenger unhooked the harness and stepped free. Marcus could make out the silhouette of a woman.

"Hello, Marcus," said the visitor. Her voice was unmistakable.

"Terra," replied Marcus. "What the hell is going on?" The sound of his own voice startled him. It was low pitched and gravelly, the voice of an older man.

"I'm afraid we've both been double crossed," said Terra. "Your partner in this contract is both resourceful and greedy. He found a way to game our system and has reclaimed your life."

"Then you can switch us back like you did before?"

"I'm afraid it's not that easy. The last time, all we had to do was interrupt a rogue script in the program. Your experience in his body then was virtual, playing in his brain as his body slept. When the script ended short of death, you switched back. This time was different."

"How?"

"The exchange was completed before we detected it. He simulated death long enough to convince the system it was final. It's too late to undo it."

"There must be something you can do."

"No, at least not now," said Terra. "Even if we had a way to reverse the exchange, we have no idea what the effect of multiple exchanges would be. It's too dangerous."

"What happens now?"

"You live each other's lives. The Director is very angry with your counterpart, but he has reasons to let him live, so your body will survive, even if you may never get it back. And if you want to stay alive, you'll both have to continue to obey the rules."

"Which rules?"

"Mainly secrecy," answered Terra. "You will have to fit into his life and never let anyone know what happened. This project has a lot at stake if it were to be exposed."

"Fit into his life," echoed Marcus. "Whose life? Who am I supposed to be?"

Terra held a small mirror in front of his face. The face in the mirror was familiar. He watched it turn white at the moment of recognition.

"This can't be possible," he exclaimed.

"I'm afraid it is," said Terra. "Welcome to your new life, Raymond Mettler."

28

THE CHILL was gone. Ray felt the snuggly warmth of the wool afghan wrapped around his shoulders and the living creature nestled in his lap. He glanced down at the smooth-shaven head of a child of seven or eight and inhaled its sweet, freshly bathed scent.

"Don't stop, Daddy," said the child, looking up at him. "Keep reading."

He could see now that the child was a girl, an exquisite looking child, clearly feminine despite her bald head. And he became aware of the open book in his hands propped across her lap. Her name popped into his mind from his last visit to Marcus's life.

"Of course, Natasha," he replied. "My mind wandered for a moment, honey. Where did I leave off?"

"Dumbledore's pocket watch, with the planets all around," said Natasha, smiling.

It was her bedtime and they were reading *Harry Potter and the Sorcerer's Stone*, a classic fantasy from the end of the last century. Ray knew Natasha to be a precocious child, who was fully capable of reading on her own. So this must have been a bedtime ritual that Marcus shared with her. Her body was still, a blend of attention and contentment.

Ray read to her for a few minutes, then invited her to pick a stopping point, but her eyes were already heavy as sleep overtook her. Only then did he notice Corinne standing in the doorway, watching them. He blushed at the sight of her. She was every bit as stunning as he'd remembered. And his rising erection with the child still on his lap added to his unease.

"Time to put her to bed," said Corinne. "She's had a busy day, but she always looks forward to your time together."

Ray rose carefully from the chair, cradling Natasha in his arms, and let Corinne lead the way to her room. The charade was on. He'd plunged into the middle of it with no time to prepare for this encounter.

Once they'd tucked the child in bed and tiptoed out of her room, Ray felt Corinne's hand brush his shoulder and turned to face her, inhaling the sweet jasmine that emanated from her body. She brushed his lips with hers, turned and led him by the hand to their bedroom.

It was all happening so fast. As much as he'd fantasized about this moment, he was unprepared for it. He'd played this scene before and gotten away without detection, or so, at least he thought. But this time, he was there to stay. He was Marcus Takana, for better or for worse, and he would have to keep playing the role, perhaps forever.

Her hands cradled his erection, but it began to soften in her grasp.

"What's wrong?" she asked, releasing her hold.

"Sorry," answered Ray. "I'm just tired. Working out issues at work. It's been a very long day. You know how politics can be."

"Do you want to talk about it?"

"Not tonight. I think I have a handle on it now. I just need to sleep."

"Must have been a really hard day if you have nothing left for me." She smiled. "That's not at all like you, Marcus."

He smiled back, then kissed her gently on the cheek, went into the bathroom, and closed the door.

He surveyed the room. It barely resembled the bathroom he'd left behind. In the middle of the room was a circular glass pod barely large enough to contain him. The walls of the pod were studded with tiny nozzles all around and ranging the length of his body. But when he touched the controls by the door, there was no flow of water, just hissing bursts.

He stripped off his clothes, stepped into the pod and touched the controls again. He felt bursts of air striking every inch of his body, strong enough to be invigorating, but not painful. The bursts abruptly stopped. Then a ring of nozzles that had been hidden in the ceiling appeared and drenched him with a slick solution. More air bursts blew the liquid away, leaving his skin with a silky coating that felt luxurious.

He'd heard of the water sparing cleansing pods that many young people used during the peak of the drought, but had never experienced one. From his privileged position, he'd had little compunction about exceeding his share of resources, particularly since he'd set out to solve the water shortage with HibernaTurf.

Back in the bedroom, he looked for night clothes, but found none. Concluding that Marcus must sleep in the nude, he slipped between the sheets, exhausted.

"She has no idea how stressful my day has been," he thought, then drifted off to sleep.

The next morning, he faced a whole new challenge. He headed for work at the Ministry of Discovery, where Marcus was in charge of the division. He would face coworkers and subordinates and might even have meetings with Presidential aides or the President himself. He'd covered his change of identity during his brief earlier encounter with the President, but now would undergo more extended scrutiny.

As the limo pulled up to the front door, he anticipated the first challenge would be his driver. What was his name? He'd have to pull it from the UDB when he saw his face. The door opened. He slid into the back seat. When he looked at the driver, his breath stopped short.

The flaming red hair was all too familiar.

"Hello, Ray," said Terra, as the limo moved forward. "Looks like we need to talk."

"How did you know?" said Ray.

"We are always watching," said Terra. "And you've double crossed us. The Director is very, very upset with you."

"So what happens now? Are you here to send me back or to kill me?"

"Neither, at least for now. We don't know if it's even possible to send you back. The system was designed for a single transfer. You've now undergone three switches of identity. We have no idea what the effect might be of multiple switches. There could be cognitive degradation. Or another transfer might just vaporize you both."

"Then you're going to kill me?"

"You're a very lucky man, Ray. The Director is very resourceful and sees an opportunity arising out of your disobedience. If you cooperate with us, you will get to live."

"Cooperate...how?"

"First, you must not remove your transducer. It's how we keep track of you. And if we ever decide to switch you back, we'll need both of you to have them. It's also the way the network of nanoparticles in your brain stays organized. Without it, your personality could disintegrate."

"Is that all?"

"No. As you are aware, Marcus has become a very important, and potentially powerful man. He could even become President someday. The Director is very happy to have someone in that position who would answer to us. And now we have you."

"So you want me to be an agent?" exclaimed Ray. "I don't even know who you are or what you're trying to do? What good would I possibly be to you?"

"Your role will evolve, and you will learn just as much as you need to know at every step to carry out your mission."

"And if I refuse?"

"Then we'll expose you. Everyone, including Corinne, will know that you're an imposter. And we'll let them deal with you. It won't be pretty. You could die or live the rest of your very long life in captivity. So we have a deal?"

The car slowed as it pulled up to the Ministry of Discovery. The passenger door opened. Ray got out without a word. He would have to pull himself together before meeting his next challenge. The stakes just got higher.

29

AS RADICALLY different as Ray Mettler was from Marcus Takana, they had at least one thing in common. They both possessed a MELD chip, linking their brains to the vast data trove of the UDB. Marcus had no difficulty engaging the interface with Ray's chip, providing him access to the minutest details of Ray's life.

Terra airlifted him by drone to the edge of the city by the waterfront. It was still dark when she disappeared back into the sky. Marcus could hear water lapping against the seawall and a cacophony of barking sounds.

"Seals." His MELD chip fed its sound recognition result directly to his thoughts. He'd encountered seals on the Oregon coast during his childhood in the Willamette Valley. The memories blended seamlessly with the data from the MELD chip so that he was unsure whether his recognition came from memory or the UDB. He wondered, too, whether all his memories had traversed the void between his own body and this one.

Learning to navigate his new life challenged Marcus and distracted him for the time being from his panic and grief. He would need to survive and blend in long enough to figure out a way, if there was one, to get back home. Meanwhile, home would be a penthouse atop a tower at the corner of Powell and Sacramento in San Francisco. His first test awaited him there when he was to meet Ray Mettler's wife Lena.

He arrived at the penthouse in the middle of the night. Lena was at the door as soon as he'd engaged the lock.

"Ray! Thank God you're OK. Where the hell have you been?"

Marcus could barely conceal his surprise. Lena Mettler was actually Lena Holbrook, the journalist who had visited his home to write his story. She'd never let on that she was married to the man who had created HibernaTurf. And now she was to be his wife.

"Sorry, Lena. I was working on a project and got carried away. The time just slipped by me." It could have been worse. Marcus and Corinne both liked Lena Holbrook. She was someone who could be trusted, perhaps even with a secret as potentially lethal as the one he now bore.

"I was worried sick, Ray. With all the strange things happening, you could have been dead."

"Strange things?" said Marcus.

"Like the visit from the mysterious redhead who you claimed was there about final arrangements," answered Lena, "and then, of course, there was the stroke and the mobile surgical suite and the redhead again." Tears now ran down her cheeks. "I thought you'd had another stroke and that you were lying somewhere all alone, helpless or dead."

"Stroke?" thought Marcus. "Terra never said anything about a stroke."

While the UDB had provided considerable detail about Ray Mettler, his relationships, and his life history, he had no memory at all of a stroke. Either it had failed to upload to his MELD chip or had somehow been deleted from it. And if Ray remembered the event, his memory of it had traveled across the void and now resided with him in Marcus's body.

Marcus put his arms around Lena to comfort her. She stiffened for a moment as if the gesture was either unexpected or unwelcome, then relaxed and returned the embrace. Her hug felt warm and safe.

"Your face is so cold," Lena said as their cheeks met. "How did you get so chilled?"

"It was really blustery out there, tonight. You know how windy it can get at night on our hilly streets."

Lena moved back a couple of steps and scrutinized his face. She furrowed her brow momentarily, apparently doubting his word. Marcus felt his head jerk almost imperceptibly to the left, accompanied by a twinge of pain in the right side of his neck. Then Lena relaxed and smiled.

"Can we expect another visit from the redhead?" she asked, but didn't wait for an answer.

"I'm just glad that you're safe and home," she added. "Now we both need to get some sleep."

"Stroke," thought Marcus as he lay in bed next to Lena. "That can't be good."

He searched the UDB for a record of the event, but there was none. Terra and her team had done a good job scrubbing it from the historical record. She had reasons to keep it secret from the world, but she was also keeping it secret from him. Did Ray know what had happened to him? Could it have been part of what led to him simulating his death? And what was to keep it from happening again, a ticking time bomb in his head just waiting to go off?

Marcus awoke at daybreak the next morning to the early rays of the sun streaming through the huge windows of the penthouse. He stripped naked and stood before the full-length mirror in the bedroom, studying the image before him. He ran his fingers through his hair, then slid his hands the length of his torso before coming to rest at his genitals. This penis was thicker than his and the skin more wrinkled. The testicles hung lower and looser. And everything was surrounded in a tangle of coarse dark hair.

He felt a moment of revulsion as he clutched himself in both hands, then noticed Lena's reflection behind him, watching, her face a mixture of confusion and concern.

"What's going on, Ray?" she asked. "This is the second time I've seen you examining yourself as if you were seeing a stranger or a ghost. Maybe it's time to see Dr. Jensen again. You're not yourself. Maybe the stroke…"

"The stroke is a blur," said Marcus, seizing an opportunity. "I can hardly remember it. Could you walk me through what happened?"

"You awoke with excruciating pain in your head. Then your speech became jumbled and you couldn't find words," Lena began. "When I said I was calling for an ambulance, you became agitated and forbade me to call for help. It was as if you were hiding something." She sighed deeply.

"Then she arrived out of the blue…the redhead, along with an entourage of medical personnel and an entire operating suite. After imaging your brain, they threaded a catheter from an artery in your groin to your brain and stopped the bleeding."

"Did they say what caused the bleed?" asked Marcus.

"They said it was an aneurysm that had burst. They patched the blood vessel and repaired the damage to your brain. They assured us you'd be OK. Then they dismantled the operating suite and were gone." Lena looked as though she had something else to say, then screwed up her mouth and looked away.

"Is there something else," asked Marcus, holding his breath, "anything you haven't told me?"

"I wasn't going to say anything, but maybe now it's time you knew." said Lena, hesitating. "When they were examining the images of your brain, I thought I overheard them referring to the aneurysm in the plural. Not just the one, but others. Possibly many others. I was scared, but I didn't want you to worry. I didn't want to stress you right after such a major trauma. I was afraid the stress could kill you. But with this odd behavior, perhaps we need to find out."

It was even worse than he thought. Not one ticking time bomb, but many. And Terra was the only one that held the key.

"Let's get you to a hospital. They can do studies and give us answers."

"No, Lena, no hospitals. No studies. If it can't be fixed, I'd rather not know. Let's just keep all this between us."

"Between us," said Lena. "You mean between us and the redhead...Terra. That's what you call her. We never had that talk. I think it's time."

Marcus wanted desperately to tell Lena everything. She was a journalist, accustomed to keeping other people's secrets. And he was sure that she could be trusted. But even if she believed such an outlandish story, her reaction would be unpredictable. And the knowledge could place her in lethal danger.

"I wish I could tell you, Lena," he said. "I really do. But for your own protection, this needs to stay my secret. Knowing could put you at risk."

"Ray, what the hell have you gotten yourself into?" Lena's voice rose shrilly. "Are you some sort of spy? Or are you part of some crazy experiment?"

Marcus shrugged and took a long, deep breath. He was still standing naked, leaving him feeling all the more exposed and defenseless.

"Please, Lena," he begged, "for both our sakes, you have to let this go. There's nothing more I can tell you."

"All right, Ray. I'll let it go for now. But I don't know how long I can live with this...you and this mystery. You know I always get to the bottom of things. This isn't the end of it."

Marcus realized that his secret, and Ray's, hung by a thread. It was only a matter of time before Lena would figure it out. He could only hope that Terra would show mercy.

30

WHEN RAY EMERGED from the limo, he stood before a gleaming tower that seemed to reach endlessly toward the sky. Its face was metallic and smooth, unbroken by the outlines of windows or doors. It looked more like a monument than a building containing laboratories, offices and other work spaces. It was difficult to imagine human life teeming within its boundaries, busy creating the future.

A cobblestone path, reminding him of the sidewalk in front of Dr. Jensen's building, led from the limo door to the face of the structure, an odd juxtaposition of antiquated and visionary. Ray traversed the path, came to a stop, and looked all around. As he gazed up and to the right, a blue light began blinking at the surface of the wall, seeming to come from deep within it. Then a vertical crevice appeared as a section of the gleaming structure slid noiselessly aside. He crossed the threshold and the door slid closed behind him.

Before him now was a brightly lit corridor extending as far as the eye could see. He began to walk, unaware of his destination. A lone figure appeared far down the corridor, approaching him. As it got closer, he discerned a tall, slender male, with dark complexion, refined features, and piercing blue eyes. A name popped into his thoughts.

"Good morning, Cisco," said Ray.

"Good morning, Marcus. I'm glad you're here. We've all been waiting for you."

"What's going on?"

"We think we've made a breakthrough in the Scotty project. We wanted you here for the final test."

"Scotty?" thought Ray. There was nothing about it in the UDB. All the research at the Ministry was top secret. Nothing had yet been published about Scotty. And if information had been uploaded to his MELD chip, it must have resided on an encrypted partition. The encryption key would have been encoded within Marcus's memories and was unavailable to Ray.

"Then let's see what you've got."

Cisco led him down the corridor until they reached an open door. Five people were huddled around a circular platform about two feet in diameter. Nothing was on it. When Ray entered the room, they greeted him with enthusiasm, then turned their attention back to the platform. Ray's curiosity brimmed, but he refrained from posing any question that would betray his ignorance. He returned the greeting and waited in silence.

His patience was rewarded. The air above the platform began to shimmer. On the surface of the platform at the base of the shimmering tube of space, a shape began to form, at first transparent, then gradually becoming solid and acquiring color. When the air above it was no longer agitated, there stood on the table an irregular round lump of a tan substance that looked glossy and wet.

Everyone in the room applauded. Then someone handed Ray a spoon. They parted to make way for him to approach the table.

Ray responded to their expectations by plunging the edge of the spoon into the middle of the mound. It yielded easily. He filled the spoon with the substance, withdrew it and held it before him. All eyes were upon him, waiting for the next step.

He took a deep breath and brought it slowly toward his mouth, then licked it. He smiled. Then everyone around him smiled.

"Ice cream," he said aloud. "Coffee ice cream."

The room burst with applause. Ray now understood the significance of the experiment and chuckled at the name of the project.

"Scotty," he thought, "a character from the videology of the last century, an engineer aboard a spacecraft in charge of teleportation."

"Beam me up, Scotty," had been a tagline for every scientist in pursuit of making teleportation a reality. The roots of the technology had begun earlier in the century with the teleportation of a single subatomic particle across space, using a principle of physics called "spooky action at a distance." Once unlimited amounts of information could be communicated over long distances and three-dimensional printing devices became sophisticated, solid objects could be reproduced instantaneously at long distances with considerable fidelity. But actual teleportation, in which the molecular structure of objects was taken apart and reassembled at a distance, remained elusive for decades.

That made the scoop of ordinary ice cream, now melting into a puddle on the table before him, the Holy Grail of applied physics. This wasn't merely a reproduction, a printed lump of matter. It was the real thing, down to its molecular structure, incorporating all of its physical properties including texture, taste, and temperature.

Someone brought out a bottle of champagne and plunged it briefly into a bucket of dry ice. Champagne had resurfaced as the celebratory libation of choice once the vineyards had recovered from the prolonged droughts and the scourge of HibernaTurf.

The cork was popped and glasses poured all around, all except for Cisco.

"Aren't you going to have some?" asked Ray.

Everyone but Cisco laughed. Ray blushed. What was he missing? His mind flashed suddenly to Haley Sellica. Like Haley, Cisco was a highly sophisticated SPUD. He was capable of complex cognitive tasks, including understanding and simulating emotions, but he was not designed to process food or drink. While it might have been possible, what would have been the point?

Ray had arrived in Marcus's life and his laboratory at an inflection point in history. Teleportation wasn't just a parlor trick. It was a tool that would enable anyone who had it to master the reaches of the universe. Soon it would be possible to transport living things and ultimately people across unlimited distances. Whoever owned this technology would have vast power over those who did not, which made Terra's words particularly ominous.

Would he be forced to turn over this technology to her and to the Director, whoever that was? Would it be used for the good of mankind or for treachery? And did they already know about it or would he be able to hide it, at least until it became public knowledge? Ray was now responsible for Marcus's discovery. For now, at least, it felt like an enormous burden.

31

IF MARCUS WAS GOING to live in this antiquated body, he would at least make it as strong and lean as possible. Nobody knew better how to do that than him after years of rigorous physical training. He'd have to find a starting point that his new body could tolerate. He may have left his strength behind, but he hoped that his skills had accompanied his consciousness across the divide.

The first day of training he ran five miles on an Endless Park in the Presidio. He was struggling for breath by the end of the run, which was just a fraction of his usual distance in his former life. As he bent forward supporting his hands on his thighs, he could hear his pulse bounding in his ears, a sign that Ray's cardiovascular system was working at its limits.

"The aneurysms," he thought. "Am I risking another blowout?" The thought was accompanied more with detachment than fear. Marcus had once thrived on risk, dancing on the precipice of death just to feel alive. He wasn't about to let the peril in his brain cripple him and keep him imprisoned in a wreck of a body.

After a week on the Endless Park, it was time to step up his game. He found a fitness center that offered many of the same virtually enhanced activities that he'd enjoyed before. The first day, he chose a bike tour. He sat on the stationary bike within the isolation booth and linked his mind to the program via his MELD chip. The walls disappeared and he was in the hills of northern France, surrounded by other cyclists all pumping furiously to lead the pack. The wind whistled past his ears. A light drizzle made the road slick, while distilling the bouquet of the surrounding fields of blooming wildflowers and wafting the sweet scent past his nostrils. He inhaled deeply as he took the lead.

In this virtual world, Marcus Takana was his own avatar. While his host's body worked to turn the pedals of the bike and benefited from the workout, Marcus got to feel like himself, at least for a while during this familiar activity. The arms and hands grasping the handlebars were sleek and sinewy. His thighs rippled with strength. There was no bulge around his middle, only taut ridges of muscle. But when the ride ended, so did the illusion, and he arose from the bike exhausted and dripping with sweat, his wet shirt drawn taut across his paunch.

"Too slow," thought Marcus. "There must be some way to speed this up."

He considered the various drugs that had been developed over the last few decades that were intended to simulate the effects of exercise, causing weight loss and muscle development. While several had proven beneficial for paraplegics and people with genetic wasting diseases, none had surpassed the benefits of vigorous exercise or had significantly accelerated those effects. And like all drugs, there were both known and unknown risks. That made them particularly dangerous for Marcus with his bionically altered brain.

"Better to go gradually," he concluded. Sudden changes would be a red flag to Lena that something essential had changed about her husband.

As his fitness improved, though, he looked for more ways to amp up his workouts. As competitive as Marcus had been in his scientific pursuits, he was equally competitive athletically. In his former life, he'd gravitated particularly to activities that pitted him directly against others. His favorite such pastime had been spherical racquetball. Through the virtual interface, he'd been able to match himself within a universe of other players with those of equivalent skill. Resuming this sport would be the best test of both the dexterity developed in his prior incarnation and the waxing strength of his current one.

Marcus stepped inside the racquetball booth. There was the familiar multiaxial cage with its three gleaming titanium rings and the harness in the center. The design had been borrowed from a 20th century NASA trainer intended to acclimate astronauts to the rigors of zero gravity activity. It maintained the user's core at the center of the structure, even as the rings rotated freely along each of the three axes of space so that the wild and often random spinning didn't induce motion sickness. While the original NASA structure attached hands and feet rigidly to the framework, this cage was modified so that each extremity was bound to a flexible band and could move freely against the resistance of the bands. These movements translated in the virtual environment as running and spinning while swinging at a moving target, all against resistance.

He strapped himself into the harness, looped the bands around his hands and feet, and engaged his MELD chip with the program. A series of avatars appeared of some of his former adversaries. He selected one of mid-level skill for his first practice session. When he started the program, a transparent sphere materialized around them, painted with a matrix of crisscrossing lines, each completing a perimeter around an axis of the sphere.

They squared off in the center. A ball appeared in the periphery. Marcus lurched forward. As his body tumbled into a spin, he swatted at the speeding object, propelling it against the sphere. It recoiled, ricocheted once from another point of contact, then was struck by his opponent's racquet. As it bounced off the sphere directly behind him, he spun around and whacked it squarely to the side. Three bounces and he'd won the point.

Marcus hadn't felt more like himself since the switch than he did in this competition. And his competitor recognized him by his avatar. At least for a while he was Marcus again, earning the respect of his opponents with his skill. Another week and he was squaring off against the top ranked players, winning as often as losing.

The fat around his middle began to melt away. His muscles gained definition, beginning with his biceps and the quadriceps of his thighs. The changes were too striking to escape Lena's notice, but it was a while before she spoke up.

"What's going on, Ray?" she asked one day when he returned from the gym. "Have you been seeing someone else?"

"What do you mean?" Marcus replied. "No, of course there's nobody else. Why do you ask?"

"You've lost so much weight. And just look at you! You're so fit. You've clearly been working out. You look at least ten years younger."

"I just got tired of looking old and fat," said Marcus. "It was time to get in shape."

"But it's happened so fast," said Lena. "You must be working out hard. I've been worried about you."

"Worried? Why?"

"After your stroke, you became even more sedentary than ever. You seemed terrified to do anything that might risk another bleed. And you haven't touched me in months, Ray. You're like a stranger." Tears welled in her eyes. She was sobbing too hard to go on.

"The stroke...changed a lot of things, Lena," said Marcus. "I didn't want to die. It paralyzed me." He paused. "But then I knew I couldn't go on like that forever. I had to reclaim my life...and my body."

"But you still haven't touched me," sobbed Lena, "so all I could think of was that this was for another woman."

Marcus took her by the shoulders and looked directly into her eyes. Her body was shaking.

"There's no other woman," he told her. "It's all been for me...and for you."

She nestled her body into his and put her arms around him. He encircled her shoulders with his arms and hugged her tightly. Her body quieted. She nuzzled his cheek so that her lips were close to his ear.

"I've missed you, Ray," she whispered. "I've missed touching you and having you touch me. It's been so lonely without you."

Marcus felt his penis engorging, becoming rigid against her body, filling him with confusion. He'd found Lena pleasantly attractive, but hadn't been drawn to her sexually. It would have been hard for her to compete with Corinne, who was both youthful and exquisitely beautiful. He'd never imagined being with anyone other than Corinne. And yet his feelings of arousal with the woman in his arms were unmistakable.

Lena brushed her lips across his, then settled in for a lingering kiss of such warmth and passion that he became lost in her embrace, suddenly in this moment in this body, oblivious to the knowledge that he didn't belong there or with this woman. Then he was lying naked behind her, sliding inside her, tenderly caressing her belly and thigh. And when they finally stopped moving, for the first time since the switch, he felt...safe.

32

OF ALL THE SURPRISES awaiting Ray in his new life, not the least was the remarkable nature of his body. One of the first things he noticed was the absence of pain. He'd long experienced pain in his neck and shoulders, a consequence of repetitive friction from his lifelong tics. It had been with him so long that he'd barely paid attention to it day to day. But the sudden absence of pain, or of any manner of discomfort, was striking. And the involuntary movements were also gone, apparently hardwired to the body he'd left behind. This new body seemed to fit seamlessly, its motion flowing smoothly in response to his will.

It felt wonderful to be young again, but the life force within him was beyond anything he'd ever experienced before, even as a child. It seemed to radiate endlessly from his core, reaching beyond the boundaries of his body.

Ray remembered that the body he was eventually to inhabit would be endowed with eternal youth. What other extraordinary properties would accompany that? He'd have to put this body to the test to determine its limits.

Night was falling as he left the Ministry of Discovery. A car had come for him, but halfway home he decided to walk the rest of the way, letting himself out at the edge of Rock Creek Park. He would cut through the park to Marcus's home in Crestwood on its east side. A jogging path wound along the creek's edge toward the north. A handful of people could be seen in silhouette against the twilight sky, scattered along the trail, but moving almost in unison at a measured pace.

The sky was overcast. Once the last light of day was extinguished, it was nearly pitch dark all around him. The vintage lamps along the path were too dim to illuminate more than a few feet around the base of each, leaving the long spans between lights in shadows.

Ray picked up his pace, joining with the rhythm of the joggers while maintaining some distance from the pack. His steps were so light and his strides so smooth that he barely felt the impact. It felt almost as if he were floating.

Then rustling in the trees to his left was followed by footsteps at a sprint. His path was abruptly blocked by a tall, shadowy figure. A blade held aloft glinted in the reflection of one of the street lamps, plunging rapidly toward his face. His left hand shot up in defense, catching the blade in the center of his palm, piercing it through and through. The pain was excruciating, but he held his arm rigid, keeping the blade at bay. With his assailant momentarily off balance, he landed a blow with his right fist squarely on his jaw. The force of the blow sent his attacker sprawling, releasing the handle of the knife, the blade still imbedded in his hand.

Ray grabbed the handle with his free hand, extracting it with a sharp tug. Warm blood spurted in pulses from the wound, then suddenly stopped. His adversary sprung from a crouch to tackle him. Ray dodged the blow with unexpected agility, thrusting his foot in his attacker's path. The man stumbled, then rolled and recovered, disappearing into the woods.

Ray held his palm before his eyes. As intense as the pain had been, it had already dissipated. Blood around the wound had dried. Its edges were nearly closed, no longer leaking blood. He clenched his fist. His fingers all flexed with full strength. The tendons were intact. The puncture wound on the back of his hand was closing before his eyes.

"What an amazing body!" Ray thought. "It's practically indestructible." His body rocked with laughter. He should have been terrified, but instead was thrilled. He'd never felt so alive.

He had no idea what would have happened had the blade come down between his eyes. Perhaps he could have died. But short of a mortal wound, this body was incredibly resilient. It was capable of pain, but only as long as the damage lasted. And it was astonishingly strong and quick.

While his response to the attack answered many of Ray's questions about Marcus's body, it raised new questions about his life. Random muggings in the park hadn't occurred for decades. Nobody carried anything worth stealing anymore. Transactions of value all occurred over the UDB and there were sufficient safeguards to prevent people from entering transactions in response to threat.

"So this wasn't a random attack," Ray thought. "Someone must want Marcus dead." He accessed his MELD chip and replayed the action, noticing particularly the force that was returned through the blade of the knife in his hand as he held it off. It had been well-matched to his own strength.

"And that was no ordinary man," he concluded. "Strong and resilient like me. Another immortal? Perhaps." The only thing of which Ray could be sure was that the assassin, whoever he was, would be back.

When Ray turned the corner onto his street, the front of the house was illuminated with flashing lights. Through the wrought iron fence he could see Corinne pacing in the yard, while uniformed personnel swarmed around the premises. When she saw him come through the gate, she came running toward him and threw her arms around him. He returned her embrace.

"Thank God you're home," she said breathlessly. "I was so worried. You weren't answering any of my calls."

"What's going on?" In the midst of his altercation in the park, Ray had been aware of a signal in the periphery of his consciousness, but his linkage to Marcus's MELD chip was too new to identify the source. By the time the fight was over, the signal had stopped and he never retrieved Corinne's messages.

"Someone has been watching us," she said. "I noticed a car circling the block a few times. Then it parked across the street. I didn't think much about it until a man got out just after dusk and was looking through the fence. He was holding something and pointing it through the posts."

"A gun?"

"I don't know. Maybe a gun. Maybe a camera. But when I saw the red dot on the window, I called for help." Corinne was sobbing. "You've never ignored my calls. When you didn't answer, all I could think of was that you were dead."

Ray considered telling her about the attack, but thought better of it. He held her closer until her breathing slowed to a regular pace. From his first encounter with Corinne, he'd been impressed with her composure. She was not a woman he expected would be easily rattled.

"When you took the position with the Ministry, I wish you'd accepted their offer of protection. I hope you'll reconsider," she paused, looking into his eyes, "for Natasha's sake."

Ray understood why Marcus might have rejected a Secret Service detail. He had secrets to protect, secrets perhaps more dangerous than any enemy. Too many eyes and those secrets could be blown, with perhaps fatal consequences for his family. And now Ray had inherited Marcus's secrets along with his life. And the secrets he brought with him to this life were even more perilous than Marcus could have imagined.

33

RAY METTLER'S AGING body, as challenging as it was to Marcus Takana, was the least of the problems that came with living his life. The scourge of HibernaTurf had left an indelible scar on the population and indelible memories of the damage done to individual lives. Marcus still despised him for the havoc it wreaked on his family's farm and on his parents. He'd yearned for vengeance for his father's death.

Ray had led a reclusive life, occasionally venturing outside his home at Lena's beseeching and usually only in her company. People had tended to be respectful of her presence and seldom became aggressive toward Ray when she was around.

Marcus couldn't tolerate such confinement. His excursions to the fitness center were discreet and his workouts private within the virtual reality booths. He avoided the exposure of the locker room. But Ray and Lena's condo made him stir crazy. When he looked out over the city from the huge glass window, he longed to be walking its streets, climbing its hills, and enjoying the aromas of its ethnic cuisine.

When he finally couldn't stand it any longer, he discovered the intensity of the hatred that had rained down upon Ray in the aftermath of HibernaTurf. Walking down the street for the first time, he was bumped so roughly by a passing stranger that he nearly lost his balance. A few minutes later, he felt a splash of something wet on his cheek and when he turned around was greeted with an obscene gesture. Several people stopped him forcefully, regaling him with their stories of how he'd ruined their lives. And when he emerged from his building on another day, a soft impact between his eyes, accompanied by a crunching sound was followed by slimy egg dripping down his nose and face. There was no anonymity for a villain as well-known as Raymond Mettler. No peace was to be found in these outings.

Marcus hoped that as he changed the shape of his body, he would become less recognizable. He grew a full beard and tried dressing like a vagrant, but his disguises were easily defeated by the augmented reality through which most people perceived their world. The beard irritated his face and the grubby clothes felt like sandpaper on his body. When he finally shaved the beard and his head, the slickness of his face and scalp were soothing, making him feel more like himself. But with all the drastic changes, Lena became alarmed.

"What's gotten into you, Ray?" she asked. "You're behaving like a stranger. At first, I thought the weight loss was healthy, but it's become an obsession. And I figured the beard was a passing fancy. But now I'm getting worried."

"I'm tired of being a pariah, Lena," said Marcus. "No matter where I go, people treat me with contempt. I thought if I changed the way I looked, I could move around in the world without being harassed. But it's futile. Nothing I do can shake it."

"Maybe people are attacking you because you feel deep down that you deserve it. You keep taking and taking it and don't push back. So they keep dishing it out."

"And why wouldn't I deserve it?" asked Marcus. He'd wanted as much as anyone to see Ray punished. It had never occurred to him that there might be another way to look at it.

"Because you're a good man, Ray," said Lena. "That's why I've stayed with you through all this. We both know that your intentions were honorable. You were trying to combat a drought that was threatening to starve the world. And it was moving so fast that there was no time to think through every detail. I watched you work without sleep for days on end to finish the project in time to head off famine."

Marcus took in Lena's words. He'd been so enraged at Ray for the outcome of his work that he'd never considered that his intentions might have been noble or that he'd worked tirelessly toward the intended goal.

"What if Ray had never created HibernaTurf?" thought Marcus. "Would the drought have rendered the world barren and lifeless?" In that moment, the intensity of his rage subsided. Now that he was walking in Ray's shoes, he found compassion for the man he'd longed to punish, a man whose day to day existence had been punishment enough.

"Tell me, Lena," Marcus said. "Was there ever a time you thought I should give up the quest?"

"It crossed my mind," said Lena, "but you wouldn't have listened. You were laser focused on the problem and determined to solve it even if it killed you. And if you had given up…" She paused to consider the consequence. "Then Takana Grass might never have been created and the world might have been doomed."

217

"So it took both of us to fix it," Marcus thought aloud. "Without HibernaTurf there would have been no Takana Grass. And without Takana Grass, the change in climate might have rolled past the tipping point to end civilization."

"So you solved it together," said Lena. "You and Marcus Takana. It was just an accident that you took all the blame and he got the credit. In different circumstances, it might have come out the other way around."

"Little does she know that it did," thought Marcus, appreciating the irony of Lena's words. "He gets to be the hero now while I take the fall."

Marcus wished he'd had the power to rehabilitate the reputation of the man whose identity he now inhabited. HibernaTurf had been a colossal accident, the unintended consequence of a worthy endeavor.

But Ray's blamelessness was not so clear. His response to the accident, stripping his company of its assets and avoiding the consequences of his creation's effects settled his role as villain. He'd profited from something that had caused innumerable others harm. And the public had no idea that he'd used his ill-gotten gains to rob Marcus Takana of his identity and his life.

34

When Ray awoke the next morning, Corinne and Natasha were sitting in the kitchen over breakfast. Corinne was talking and smiling at Natasha, who was nodding and smiling back. Ray felt the corners of his mouth spreading up and out along with an unexpected wave of warmth washing over his body. Corinne turned her face to him and returned his smile. As odd as these feelings felt to Ray, Corinne seemed to find his reaction a matter of course.

"Good morning, Marcus," said Corinne. "I was just explaining to Natasha about the people who will be watching over us for the next few weeks. The morning detail is outside the gate. She wanted to offer them breakfast." Corinne giggled at her daughter's sweet innocence.

Ray joined with her laughter, then felt another rush of warmth. He looked at Natasha, who grinned at him. As extraordinary as the prior night's events and his discovery of the unusual powers of his body had been, he was even more unsettled by the unfamiliar feelings of pleasure that this sweet child's face aroused. Not his child, but yet an odd sense of connection, of belonging.

"Good morning, Corinne," said Ray, grinning. "The two of you are quite a picture. I wish I could join you for breakfast, but there's lots going on at the Ministry and I need to get going."

Corinne stood and gave him a light peck on his lips. He put his arm around her waist. She raised her face again to his for a more lingering kiss, then brought her lips close to his ear.

"See you tonight," she whispered, her breath arousing his anticipation with three simple words.

He looked again at Natasha.

"See you tonight, Nat," he said.

"See you, Daddy," she replied. "I love you."

"I love you, too." Her words echoed in his head as he walked out the door.

"Daddy," he thought. The word fell gently upon him and at the same time pierced his heart more painfully than the assailant's knife had pierced his hand the night before.

At the Ministry, his research team was already hard at work on the project. The next challenge would be to teleport a living object. When Ray arrived in the lab, a small patch of green sat in the middle of the sending port. They had selected the object in his honor: a tuft of Takana Grass.

One of the technicians set the process in motion as he watched. The air above the grass shimmered and the object dissolved before his eyes. When they walked down the hall to the receiving port, the object had materialized on the platform. It was no longer green and healthy, but wilted and brown.

Ray was relieved that the experiment had failed. The value of the technology to a clandestine organization depended upon its ability to transport living things without killing them in the process. He would have a reprieve of indefinite duration before his handlers would call in his debt. And there was small satisfaction in watching a sample of his rival's creation die.

A knock on his door after lunch brought an unexpected visitor. When the door opened, he recognized the Vice President of the United Commonwealth of North America. Juliet Hauer had recently announced her candidacy for President and was considered a frontrunner. Everyone was wondering who her running mate would be.

"Please come in, Madame Vice President," said Ray, standing and extending his hand.

"Juliet, Marcus," she replied. "There's no need to be so formal. We've known each other a while, now."

"Sorry," said Ray. "Old habits die hard. What brings you here?"

"As you know, I've always trusted your judgment...and your discretion. Something very disturbing has come to my attention. As Minister of Discovery, I thought it would be important to read you in. This is a matter of utmost secrecy. So far, only the President, the head of the NSA, and I know about it. You would be the fourth."

"Of course you can trust me," said Ray. But he wondered if that were true. He'd always been fiercely loyal to his country, but now he had secrets to protect and had no idea how Terra and her organization would use that to compromise him.

"There was once an elite intelligence agency so top secret that it was known only to the President and the National Security Advisor. Even they didn't know the identities of the operatives or of the Director. It was tasked with neutralizing despots and effecting regime change in the nations that were threatening our security at the time."

"What does this have to do with the Ministry or with me?"

"They weren't only crack operatives, but also brilliant scientists. They pledged to develop innovative approaches to accomplishing their mission. Decades ago, a dictator rose to power in a small Asian nation that was developing nuclear weapons. Regime change was a complicated ask. Successors stood in line who were all as ruthless as he was. Rather than remove him by force, a plan was developed to kidnap him."

"How would that help?" asked Ray.

"So they could replace him with an imposter."

"With a double?"

"Not exactly a double. I told you they were brilliant and creative. They'd devised a way to exchange consciousness between bodies. They planned to implant someone else's identity in the dictator's body so they could take apart the regime from within."

Ray felt a knot forming in his gut. This was sounding all too familiar and he had an idea where the conversation was heading.

"So what happened?" asked Ray. "Did the plan work?"

"It did...at first," said Juliet. "If you remember the history of the early 20's, a brutal dictator had a change of heart and agreed to a treaty. He began destroying his weapons and called for elections. But before completing the job, he suddenly took back power and nearly started a nuclear war."

"I do remember that. It was a terrible double cross. He should never have been trusted." Ray tried to put the pieces together. "So does that mean that the exchange didn't work? That he was just faking the change of heart?"

"No, Marcus. The exchange worked exactly as it was supposed to. The dictator's consciousness inhabited our operative's body and he was eventually executed."

"Then what went wrong?"

"We underestimated our operative's thirst for power. Once he had all the trappings of a head of state, the temptation to consolidate his power became irresistible. He lost sight of his mission and his loyalties and became our enemy. He turned out worse than the man he'd replaced."

"Absolute power corrupts absolutely," mused Ray aloud. "So what does all this have to do with the present?"

"Have you ever heard of Ganymede?" she asked.

"No, what's Ganymede?"

"After the mission failed to accomplish its objective, the clandestine agency went rogue and went underground, rebranding themselves as Ganymede. Having developed the power to replace one person's identity with another's, they sought to use this tool for their own purposes. We believe that they've been experimenting with civilians in order to refine their technique."

Ray's heart sank. He was squarely in the middle of this struggle with no way out. He was the experiment. And he was firmly in Ganymede's grip.

"To what end?" he asked.

"To seize the reins of power, not in a foreign country, but in our own. We think they're seeking to replace someone high up in our government. And we need the Ministry to find a way to neutralize their technology."

"Wouldn't it be simpler just to find them?"

"God knows we've tried. But they're ghosts. We don't know who they are or what they look like. They could be walking among us for all we know. And the Director is the most elusive of all. It's rumored that even his own operatives have never seen his face."

They were indeed ghosts. All except for Terra. Ray and Marcus were the only people on earth who could identify one of Ganymede's agents. And there was nobody either of them could tell.

35

MARCUS WASN'T READY to forgive Ray for stealing his life, but it remained in his interest to restore his reputation so that he could move more freely in the world without fearing abuse from strangers. One possible way of doing this was to return Ray's ill-gotten gains. But return them to whom?

"I've been thinking," he said to Lena over coffee one morning. "Perhaps it's time to give the money back, the profits from HibernaTurf."

"Back?" said Lena. "To whom? Who do you think has a right to it?"

"I haven't thought it all the way through, Lena. A lot of people were hurt. But some of the people who suffered most were the ones who sued the company and were left high and dry when I dissolved it. If I'm going to make reparations, it should start with them."

"It sounds like a noble idea, Ray, but may be more complicated than it looks." She picked up her cup and paced a bit. "You never really told me. How much did the company make?"

Marcus had accessed Ray's finances soon after the switch. He extrapolated back from the present, taking into account the value of the penthouse and their MELD chips along with the $50 million he assumed that Ray had paid for his part of the contract with Terra.

"Around four and a half billion," he concluded, "give or take $100 million or so. There's around $4.3 billion left. We could give away most of that and still keep our home and our MELD chips."

"We don't really need it," Lena agreed. "It would be a weight off your mind. And we could do a lot of good. After all," she added, her eyes suddenly watering, "we have no heirs."

Lena's sadness unleashed a wave of emotion for Marcus. He, in fact, had an heir...Natasha, who was no longer part of his life. And he was aware that Ray and Lena were childless, presumably by Ray's choice. Lena had put up with so many of Ray's idiosyncrasies, including this one. But the pain of that decision lingered for her to this day.

"I'm sorry..." Marcus began, but Lena waved him off before he could finish.

"It's OK, Ray," she said. "I knew what I was getting into when I married you. And I chose to stay, even if it meant being childless."

A crazy thought struck Marcus. While he was making Ray's reparations to the world, perhaps he could also make reparations to Lena. And if he was going to be stuck in Ray's life, perhaps he could people it to his liking, including a child or two that he could love. Lena was now 45, which was once late to bear a healthy child. But with genetic engineering, women were now having children into their fifties and thriving.

"Maybe it's not too late," he blurted out. "We could still have a child."

Lena looked at him wide-eyed, then dissolved in tears.

"Don't toy with me, Ray," she sobbed. "I couldn't stand to be disappointed again."

Marcus took her in his arms and stroked her head.

"No, Lena," he said softly, "I mean it. Let's have a baby." The enormity of the idea hadn't fully dawned on him. That they would conceive a child that would be Ray's biological heir and yet Marcus's child, too. All the while that Ray was fathering Natasha and sleeping with Corinne.

"Oh, Ray. I never imagined I would ever hear those words. Not from you," she said. "Yes, let's. Let's make a baby." She was sobbing and laughing all at the same time. Her body shook in his arms. He kissed her on her forehead, then on her eyes, kissing away the tears. If he were stuck in Ray's life, he would make the best of it and bring joy to this good woman's life.

"But we can still give away the money," he said when her tears had stopped. "That hasn't changed. Our child wouldn't want blood money. We can raise it just fine without a fortune."

They spent the next several hours plotting how to allocate the money. There were the families whose livelihoods were ruined...like Marcus Takana's family. And those who were driven so deep into despair that one or more of their members wound up killing themselves.

"Again," thought Marcus, "like my father."

It was easy for Marcus to envision the most deeply aggrieved, because, after all, few had been hurt more deeply than him and his family. He'd worked hard to rise above the ruin and build a new life, only to have Ray snatch it away from him again in his prime. Now he was in a position to fix it for others, even if it was too late to save himself.

When they'd finished drafting the plan, they looked at each other with satisfaction. They were fixing the world that Ray had once broken, now putting things right, making a world into which they could in good conscience bring a child who would not suffer the sins of the father.

Lena walked behind him, draped her arms around his neck, and let her lips rest on his now shorn head. She felt waves of affection for this man, changed as he was in so many ways both physically and spiritually. If she'd stopped to think about it, the changes he'd made were so radical they defied reason. If she weren't so enthralled by the outcome, she might have come to question how a man could change so drastically within so short s span of time.

Her arms reached down inside his shirt across his newly toned and hairless chest to his now firm abdomen. He rose to embrace her, kissing her on the neck, then running his tongue around her ear, brushing his lips over her cheek, then to her lips. His powerful hands slid down over her buttocks, lifting her up, her legs wrapping around him as he carried her into the bedroom, all caution to the winds. Perhaps this would be the day they would make a baby.

36

DUSK WAS FALLING as Ray jogged alongside the creek. A gentle breeze blew and birds were singing in the trees, their disparate songs creating discordant chords. The run was primarily to clear his head and to create enough of a divide between the events of the day and home to keep his concerns from intruding upon his new family and risking exposure.

Footsteps approached from behind, gaining on him fast. Given the recent attack in the park, his guard was up. He picked up his pace, but his pursuer continued to gain ground. Abruptly he stopped and whirled.

"Hello, Ray," said a familiar voice. "We need to talk."

Ray suddenly wished that this had been a mere assailant. That would have been so much simpler.

"Hello, Terra," said Ray. "I hadn't expected to see you again so soon. To what do I owe the honor?"

"You had a visit this morning from the Vice President," said Terra. "What did she want?"

"It was just a social visit," lied Ray. "If you'll recall, she was responsible for making Marcus Minister of Discovery. She was just keeping in touch."

Terra scrutinized his face. Neither Ray nor Marcus were skilled enough liars to defeat her well-honed skills.

"No, Ray. Don't lie to me. She was there on a mission. What did she want?"

"She wanted to talk about her run for the Presidency," said Ray, taking the lie in another direction.

"And asking you to consider being her running mate?"

Ray hadn't planned the lie that far ahead, but seized on the opportunity to catch Terra off guard.

"Yes. That was it. I told her I'd think about it, but I don't think I'll accept her offer." Ray figured that this was just the situation Ganymede was hoping for.

"Good," said Terra. "We don't think you should accept it either."

"Why not?" asked Ray, trying to conceal his surprise.

"Because we have a better idea. We want you to run against her. We want you to declare your candidacy for President. You are immensely popular...or rather Marcus is. We have little doubt that you could win, especially with our help behind the scenes."

It was even worse than he'd imagined. They were going for the gold and he was now weighed down by secrets from both sides.

"But how can I do that? The Vice President would see it as a huge betrayal."

"We can't worry about her feelings. And you shouldn't either. It's just politics. People run against friends all the time."

"Can I have time to think about it? I should at least discuss it with Corinne. It will change her life, and Natasha's. They should have a voice."

"You can talk with them about it, Ray, but you don't have a choice in this. It's not a request. It's an order. We expect to see your announcement within the week." With that, she turned and jogged away before Ray could say anything more.

How would he explain this to Corinne? He would have to present it as his decision. He couldn't reveal Terra's role in suggesting it or the hold that she had over him that forced him to comply. And from what he knew about Corinne so far, he expected that she'd push back. She wasn't fond of the limelight and wouldn't want to put her family at risk.

When Ray opened the front door, Natasha ran into his arms. He embraced her.

"Hi, Daddy," she said. "Dinner's ready."

The savory aromas of Corinne's cooking washed over him. The scent of Rosemary dominated a small symphony of herbs. For just a moment, he immersed himself in the ambience of Marcus's home and forgot about Ganymede and Terra.

"And after supper, we can read together before bed," said Natasha. "I couldn't wait for you to get home."

"How could I have ever deprived Lena of this pleasure," Ray thought. This lovely child was melting his heart and unearthing deeply buried regrets. "We should have had children. It could have been wonderful. And I could have left a part of me behind."

The dining room was lit in candlelight. The flame of a candle flickered through the ruby red wine in the tall stemmed glass. A soft glow spotlit Corinne's face within the darkness that surrounded it, making her look otherworldly.

"Come sit, Marcus," she said, "and have a sip of wine. Whatever went on at work today, let it go for now."

Ray wished that it were that simple. But this was not the time to broach his candidacy with Corinne. And he couldn't let her in on any of the things that were really troubling him. Here in the bosom of the family that he'd risked everything to acquire, he now felt more alone than ever.

When he'd finished reading Natasha to sleep and emerged from her room, Corinne stood before him in a diaphanous gown, extending a filled wine glass. He took it and sipped long enough to feel the warmth rise over his face. Intoxication was a welcome relief from the secrets that weighed him down.

She led him into the bathroom. Steam rose from water in the tub, a luxury in which the Takanas had occasionally indulged once water became plentiful. A towel was warming on the rack nearby and a soft robe hung from a hook on the wall. The sound of native flutes echoed through the room. Corinne withdrew quietly and closed the door behind her.

Ray stripped off his clothes and let his body sink into the warm water. His eyes closed. He breathed deeply, inhaling the fragrant scent of frangipani as he lingered for several minutes on the edge of sleep, the image of Corinne's softly shrouded body floating across his field of vision, her angelic face capped with its slick crown, until it morphed into a cascade of red hair, arousing him from his reverie.

He arose from the tub and entered the cleansing pod, enjoying the brisk jets of liquid on his body. These new sensations brought him back to the moment, again banishing the day's travails. He ran his hands over the slickness of his body, wrapped himself in the robe, and emerged from the bathroom, leaving the flutes behind for the stirring sounds of Rachmaninoff.

There she was again in the flesh, smiling and beckoning. They had yet to reconsummate their union, although Corinne was unaware of the significance of what was about to happen. Ray immersed himself in her presence as they fell into each other's arms.

When they were at last resting side by side, their hands entwined, the events of the day were just for the moment a distant memory. He sighed deeply. Corinne mirrored his sigh.

"That was amazing, Marcus," said Corinne, breaking the silence at last. "Different."

Ray took in a breath and held it.

"Almost like the first time." she added, pausing deep in thought. "It felt like this one other time before."

"When was that?" asked Ray.

"It was the night before the mysterious redhead showed up. A magical night that ended oddly, followed by an even stranger morning." Corinne laughed. "I sure hope she doesn't show up again."

Ray shared her wish, but knew it was futile. Terra might as well already have been in the room with them. Her presence was inescapable.

37

"RAY! RAY! WAKE UP!"

Marcus opened his eyes. Lena was holding him by the shoulders, shaking him, shouting at him, her face contorted. He opened his mouth to speak, but nothing came out. His left arm reached out to her, but his right arm lay inert on the floor, as dead as a brick.

"Ray! Your face. Something's wrong with your face."

He felt saliva dribbling from the right corner of his mouth. His right eyelid obscured most of the vision in that eye.

"I'm calling for help," said Lena. "Whatever the risk, I don't want to lose you. Don't try to stop me."

There was nothing that Marcus could do. He stopped struggling and just lay on the floor while Lena broadcast the medical emergency. Within minutes, sirens could be heard in the street below. It only took seconds for the vertical pod to reach the penthouse. Three EMT's rushed into the room and quickly assessed the situation.

"CVA," said a young woman. "Right hemiparesis. Aphasia. Looks like a left frontal."

"Anticoagulants?" said another.

"Nope," said the third. "Pupil's blown. Looks like a bleed. Let's give him a bolus of steroids to reduce the swelling."

Marcus's head felt like it would explode. The intensity of the pain obscured all his other senses and his thoughts. Everything was dark. Only muffled sounds penetrated his consciousness.

One of the EMT's held a transdermal injector against his forearm and pulled the trigger, leaving a reddened disc of skin. The other two slid him onto a stretcher.

"A bleed. Yes," offered Lena. "He has aneurysms. This is his second stroke." She followed them into the pod. When they loaded him into the ambulance, she climbed in beside him.

The searing pain eased. He opened his left eye and could see Lena hovering over him, looking panicked. Voices became more distinct.

The sirens sounded and the ambulance sped off. But after a few minutes it suddenly began to swerve.

"What the hell?" exclaimed the driver. "Where'd that come from?"

The vehicle's forward motion stopped. It rocked, then rose into the air, suspended from some sort of aircraft. When it was lowered back to the ground, four hooded figures clad in sleek black wetsuits emerged from the aircraft and swarmed around the ambulance. They quickly subdued the emergency crew and extracted Marcus, leaving Lena locked inside.

"Cor...rinne!" stuttered Marcus as they pushed the doors closed behind him.

As the aircraft lifted off, one of the figures stood over him and pulled back her hood, releasing a cascade of flaming red hair.

"T...t...t," Marcus stuttered.

"Shh," said Terra, soothingly. "Try to relax. We've got this." The face that he'd only known as imperious or at best impassive, was now softened. She looked caring, almost maternal. And he was relieved to see her.

"They'll be OK," said Terra, anticipating his thoughts. "They'll wake up after a while and will find their way home. Nobody's been harmed."

A member of the team injected him with a painkiller. He felt a rush of euphoria. Then everything got blurry. He was aware of a glowing light surrounding his body. Then the only sensation was bone chilling coldness, a lot like the feeling he experienced when he first emerged into consciousness in Ray's body. Except this time, it didn't hurt. The effect of the painkiller felt as though his body was surrounded in a blanket of gauze, insulating him against any manner of suffering. He lingered on the edge of consciousness, then sank into a dreamless slumber.

When Marcus awoke, Terra was still by his side. When he opened his eyes, he saw her smile for the first time since they'd met.

"Welcome back," said Terra. "Let's take things slowly now."

He shook his head in agreement.

"Can you smile for me?" she asked.

He willed himself to smile as people did for old fashioned photos and felt both corners of his mouth go up.

"Good. Now open your eyes wide."

He opened his eyes and saw the full, unobstructed field of vision.

Terra held her index finger two feet directly in front of his nose.

"Now touch my finger with your left hand."

He touched the tip of his index finger to the tip of hers.

"Now with your right hand."

In one smooth movement, he touched her index finger with his.

"Can you tell me your name?" she asked next.

"Marcus," he replied. "Marcus Takana."

"And if anyone else were to ask?"

"Raymond," answered Marcus. "Raymond Mettler."

"Well, then," Terra smiled. "Good as new."

"Not exactly," said Marcus. "I want to go home."

"We'll get you back there shortly. Lena will be waiting for you."

"No, Terra. Home! My home with Corinne and Natasha. I don't belong here. You have to fix this."

"I'm so sorry. This isn't what you signed up for. It was never supposed to go this way. I do wish I could put things back the way they were."

"So why can't you?"

"Because I...we don't know how. This is all new territory, these multiple exchanges of identity. We don't know how much the data degrades with each exchange, or even whether another exchange is possible. If we try, you could wind up severely impaired or evaporate entirely into the ether. It's way too risky."

"So this is permanent?"

"Perhaps so," said Terra. "We'll study the situation. Do some experiments. Perhaps we can figure it out, but it will take time. And there are no guarantees. Meanwhile, I'll do my best to keep you alive."

"Both of us, Terra." He grabbed her by the arm and looked straight into her eyes. "You need to keep us both alive."

"I'll do my best, Marcus. As long as Ray doesn't screw things up again, I'll keep you both alive."

By the time Marcus got back to the penthouse, Lena had showered and was sipping coffee on the sofa, wrapped in a fluffy robe. When he entered the room, she stood wordlessly, scowling.

"Not much of a greeting, considering I almost died," said Marcus.

"Whatever you've done, Ray," Lena exploded, "it's gone way too far. You've just put me and three innocent people in harm's way."

"I'm really sorry, Lena. I'm glad you got home safely. I hope the others are OK."

"They're shocked and bewildered, but they're unharmed. I had no idea what to tell them when they came to." She paused and looked away. When she reengaged his gaze, there was fire in her eyes.

"Who the hell is Corinne, Ray?" she asked. "You called me Corinne when they took you away."

Marcus breathed deeply. In the fog of the stroke, he'd been left unguarded and had uttered the name that was most precious to him, the wife from whose side he'd been ripped by Raymond Mettler's treachery. Now was the moment of truth. He'd have to trust Lena to share his secret and hope that Terra would spare her life.

"Corinne," began Marcus, looking straight into her eyes, "is my wife." He paused long enough for the information to sink in.

"Your wife? No. I'm your wife," she protested, wide-eyed.

Marcus held her gaze. For the next few moments, he felt as if she was looking through his eyes directly into his soul. Her face relaxed. She drew a long, deep breath, whistling as she exhaled, then drew back a step.

"Who are you?" she asked. "And how did you get here?"

"My name is Marcus, Lena, Marcus Takana. And it seems your husband has stolen my life."

"Marcus...and Corinne," Lena said. "I was at your house to write your story. No wonder your eyes looked so...familiar. Not exactly Ray's, but not a stranger's either. So then it's true."

"What's true?"

"Some time ago, Ray was acting oddly. I caught him examining himself in the mirror as if he was looking at a stranger. Then a while later, she showed up."

"Who?"

"The redhead...Terra, a mystery woman. I asked him about her and he said she dealt with 'final arrangements.' He wouldn't tell me any more. Said he couldn't. It would somehow put us in danger."

"That would have been after the first exchange," said Marcus. "It was an accident and only lasted a few hours, but it gave Ray a taste of my life...and my wife. Apparently, he couldn't let it go."

"After that happened," said Lena, absorbing Marcus's words, "I found an item on the UDB that led me to a woman who swore that her husband had been replaced by an imposter before he disappeared entirely. She'd also seen a redhead whom I presumed was Terra. I tracked rumors about a secret project that involved exchanging consciousness between bodies. When I confronted Ray, he became agitated and refused to talk about it. Things got back more or less to normal for a while and I never raised it again."

"It was a condition of the contract...maintaining secrecy. We were led to believe that if we told anybody about it, they could be killed. I never breathed a word to Corinne."

"Contract...between you and Ray," mused Lena. "How did it work?"

"I was to undergo the Ambrosia Conversion to make my body immortal. Then Ray would get my body when he died. Neither of us knew the identity of the other."

"Why would you ever agree to such a thing?"

"Because I was poor and desperate, and Terra offered me an unimaginable fortune. It enabled me to acquire the knowledge to create Takana Grass and solve the scourge of HibernaTurf. Dying seemed a long way off. It seemed worth it at the time."

"Until the accident," said Lena.

"Until the accident," agreed Marcus. "And until Ray apparently decided that he couldn't wait until he died to have my life."

Lena moved closer to Marcus. She looked into his eyes and cupped his face in her hands. The edges of her robe fell open.

"I really enjoyed when you made love to me," she said. "I hope…"

"I did, too, Lena," he said. "I felt a special connection with you. As lost as I felt when I suddenly wound up in this body, I feel safe in your arms."

"So, Marcus Takana," she whispered, "it looks like you're going to share my home, and my life. I hope you'll also continue to share my bed."

38

THE NEWS STORY came over the UDB: VICE PRESIDENT HAUER CONSIDERING MINISTER OF DISCOVERY MARCUS TAKANA AS RUNNING MATE.

It was accompanied by a photo of the Minister and his family. He and Corinne flanked sweet Natasha in the middle. They were all smiling. From the background, he realized that it was an old file photo, taken before the switch.

Marcus had avoided looking at pictures of his family until then. It would have been too painful to contemplate. Now that he had stumbled across this one, grief and longing cut him to his core.

"If I could only just see them again in the flesh," he thought, "even for just a few minutes. Maybe I could find a way to say goodbye."

The thought nagged at him for days. It wasn't as if they existed in another world. They were less than an hour away on the vacuum tube transport. He could slip away from Lena for less than a day to scratch the itch that was getting harder and harder to ignore. Then perhaps he could return to Lena and immerse himself more fully in their life together.

He plotted his visit to his former life. He'd go on a Sunday morning when they were likely to be together. He wondered whether Ray was now participating in the rituals of the Church of the Double Helix. From what he knew of Ray, he wasn't a religious man. In fact, he was known to be an atheist. But then, Marcus hadn't been religious before the Church came into his life. Its special magic had transformed him. Was it possible that it had also worked its magic on Ray? Or would Ray at least have gone along with it to maintain the ruse of his identity?

Since Marcus and Lena began giving away Ray's wealth, the antipathy of the public toward Ray had substantially abated, along with its preoccupation with him, enabling him to stay more under the radar in public. His anonymity was further helped by the enormous changes he'd made in his physical appearance. As long as people weren't filtering his appearance through augmented reality, he could often blend into a crowd. And church was a setting in which most people left their technology paused for a few hours of communion with a higher power.

Marcus waited for a weekend on which Lena was traveling for a story. He slipped out shortly after midnight and made his way to the tube station. Once inside the pod with the doors closed, he felt the burst of acceleration lasting less than a minute, followed by an almost complete absence of sensation. While he could track the forward motion of the pod by the flashes of light passing rhythmically by his porthole, when he closed his eyes, he felt motionless...almost weightless. The only sound was the soothing music piped into the capsule. Before he knew it, he felt the pod decelerating at the end of its run. And then it stopped. Fifty minutes from start to finish and he was on the East Coast in the DC station.

Marcus parked the leased hovercar down the street from the brownstone mansion, waited and watched. Dawn had just broken on a clear Sunday morning. The streets were still empty, even in one of the capital's most densely populated bedroom communities. In this neighborhood, though, the houses were surrounded by generous tracts of land and many were fortified with tall iron fences or stone walls. The Takana home was notable for the lush foliage that completely hid the lower level from view behind the black wrought iron fence.

His patience paid off. After several hours, a steel gray vehicle glided through the gate onto the road. Ray activated his vehicle and felt it silently lift off the surface beneath it before moving forward. He maintained a respectful distance as the two vehicles left the neighborhood and navigated onto the elevated ringway. The third exit took them to the familiar country road that led to the church.

The gray vehicle came to a stop in front of the building. Ray, Corinne, and Natasha emerged and entered the church. Marcus parked his car around the side, entered through the front and ascended the stairs to the balcony. From the front row, he watched the pews fill up on the ground floor and spotted the Takana family sitting together in the middle of the third row.

As the people filed into the Church of the Double Helix, the music of the pipe organ wafted through the building. It sounded viscous as honey and sweeter as it poured out of the organ pipes, the notes fed straight into the instrument from the patterns in the Coded Word, stirring his memories of the happier times spent within these hallowed walls, sitting with his family just a few rows from the preacher.

The Takanas were now surrounded by a sea of heads, mostly as bald and shiny as theirs. Even embedded within this throng of peers, Ray and Corinne's regal bearing set them apart. Eight-year-old Natasha stood straight and tall, carrying herself as someone destined for nobility.

The preacher entered from the side of the stage and ascended the pulpit, resplendent in a silver robe embellished with holographic images that sparkled in the laser light that bathed the pulpit. She raised his arms and the assemblage rose to their feet. The scene was at the same time both palpably familiar and oddly distant.

The preacher held her arms out in front of her and gestured for the congregation to be seated. Huge holographic images of double helixes flanked her as the service unfolded, with readings from the source code interspersed with musical interludes choreographing the rotation of the helixes. As they turned, segments lit up sequentially in seemingly random order, signifying portions of the code that bore the scriptures. During some of these interludes the congregation vocalized in unison sustained tones that emanated from the core of their bodies and together filled the entire volume of the church with commanding resonance.

It was during the sermon that Marcus noticed a man at the other end of the balcony who also seemed focused on something other than the preacher's words. Like Marcus, he was dressed very differently from most of the congregation, an apparent outsider. He not only had a full head of reddish brown hair, but also a closely cropped beard covering his face. As Marcus observed him more closely, his gaze seemed to be directed toward the same section of the congregation in which his family were sitting. When the organ music resumed at the end of the service and people began filing out, the man maintained his focus until Ray and his family stood and moved into the aisle. Then he hastened toward the balcony door and bounded down the steps.

Marcus followed and upon reaching the ground floor found the bearded man and four or five other people obstructing the space between him and the Takanas. He'd hoped for an opportunity to get a better look at them close up, to see Corinne's radiant face again and hear Natasha's voice. He'd even imagined that if he could get close enough, he would smell the jasmine emanating from Corinne's body.

As soon as his family emerged from the church, the gray hovercar pulled up to the door and the driver let them in. Right behind the gray car a white vehicle pulled up. The intruder entered on the passenger side and the car sped away in the same direction. By the time Marcus got to his car, both other vehicles were long gone. He assumed that they were headed home and sped toward their house on a shortcut.

As he pulled into his street, he watched the gray car disappear behind the gate. The white vehicle had pulled over on the opposite side of the street several houses back. Marcus drove past the entry gate and parked around the corner. From his position at the side of the house, he could barely make out Ray and Corinne through the underbrush getting out of the car. Natasha was no longer with them, perhaps dropped off on the way at the home of a friend. Once they were inside, Marcus peered around the corner just in time to see the driver's side door of the white car open.

The driver, a rugged looking young man with wavy blond hair crossed the street and moved swiftly down the sidewalk in front of the house. Marcus flashed back with alarm to the same man watching Natasha from across the corral. He held a cylindrical object in his right hand that he flung over the fence with inhuman force. It soared across the yard and landed just in front of the entry door, rolling the last few feet across the stoop.

The explosion knocked Marcus off his feet and blasted open the front gates. A fireball enveloped the house. Marcus got to his feet just in time to see the white car speed away. His heart was pounding and he felt himself scream, but no sound came out. In fact, his whole world had fallen silent following the blast, a fitting accompaniment to the hollowness that gnawed at his gut.

Marcus ran across the fallen gate toward the front door, but the flames spitting from the opening forced him back. He ran around the back of the house to find the kitchen door blown out. Smoke billowed from the opening. He pulled off his shirt, wrapped the fireproof fabric around his face, and plowed into the house through the smoke. The kitchen was empty. He ran into the hallway and stumbled over a body.

Corinne lay unconscious at his feet, while Ray lay motionless just a few paces away, barely discernible in the smoke. The fire had entered the long hallway at the front of the house and was moving quickly toward them. Marcus could feel the intensity of the heat on his bare chest. He could only save one of them.

If Ray perished, the possibility of Marcus ever having his life restored would be gone forever. And if he tried to save either one of them, he would risk his very survival. But there at his feet was the woman he adored and had been yearning to be with ever since his life was stolen.

With a burst of strength reminiscent of his former body, Marcus scooped up Corinne's limp form and carried her out through the kitchen and the smoke. He ran another fifty feet beyond the house before collapsing to the ground with Corinne still in his arms. Another fireball shot flames toward them through the door and the framework of the house began to crumble.

When he laid Corinne's body on the ground, he brought his face close to hers and couldn't feel her breath. He pinched her nose tightly shut, sealed his lips over hers, and expelled a mighty breath to fill her lungs. She coughed, then drew a deep breath of her own. Marcus brought his lips back to hers and kissed her softly.

Marcus didn't hear the sirens approaching in his still soundless world. He rolled onto his back to see the rescue personnel in their reflective suits sweep Corinne's body onto a stretcher and roll her away. By the time they came back for him, he was gone. The rented car was barricaded by the rescue vehicles and he fled on foot. How would he ever explain what he was doing there when the house was firebombed? With the white car long gone, he'd become the prime suspect.

He longed to know whether his sacrifice paid off, but had no way to know for sure whether Corinne would survive. Now he had a more immediate problem. The police would identify him from the rented hovercar and would soon be looking for him. Where could he hide in this too transparent world? And how could he ever clear his name?

Marcus navigated to the edge of the neighborhood via side streets and alleys until he reached a more densely populated section and emerged onto a busy thoroughfare. His flight had continued in silence until then. Now sounds were beginning to filter back into his awareness. Footsteps galloped toward him from the distance to his right and he took off in the opposite direction.

His pursuer gained on him fast. He glanced behind him just long enough to see a shock of blond hair. Marcus was breathing hard as the pursuer closed in. With his last burst of energy, he swerved into the street and saw the red hovercar barreling toward him just as he felt the palm of a large hand land on his back. If only he were back in his own body with powerful legs propelling him forward. Instead, his leaden limbs rooted him to the pavement in a killer's grasp.

39

SUNDAY MORNING. Ray was awake at the crack of dawn. He was lingering over a second cup of coffee and catching up on the news of the day when Corinne and Natasha came to breakfast.

"Ready for church?" asked Corinne.

"Wouldn't miss it," said Ray.

He'd accompanied them to the Church of the Double Helix every Sunday since the switch. The first time, he was reluctant, being a confirmed atheist, and had anticipated being bored to tears. It had turned out to be an uplifting experience. The music and the liturgy were hypnotic. And when he heard the story of the Coded Word that had been discovered in human DNA, he was intrigued. By the third visit he was looking forward to it, finding an odd sense of peace within the walls of the church.

The hovercar traversed the winding country road to the stone-faced chapel, pulled up to the entrance, and let them out. The weathering of the stone and the style of the steeple bore witness to a century or more of homage within its walls. Above the massive wooden doors was a tall iron post encircled by a double helix in multicolored crystal.

"Holiness sticks to places," mused Ray, recalling archaeological digs in his database from the Holy Land with mosques built over churches built over temples built over the ruins of ancient shrines.

Walking down the aisle toward the pulpit, the music from the pipe organ filled Ray's head and resonated within his chest. As they filed into their pews, he smiled down at Natasha taking her place between them. Within the magic of this place and with his family by his side, there was just for a while no Terra and no Ganymede, no secret projects and no politics. When the congregation joined with the music, his voice rose from the depths of his lungs, blending melodically with the others. In his former life, he'd never been able to carry a tune, but his new body was a magnificent instrument.

Partway through the service, though, he had an uneasy feeling that he was being watched. When it came time to file out of the church, he turned and looked up to the balcony, where he spotted two strangers. One appeared in his twenties, had a reddish beard, and was wearing a cap with curly hair sticking out from the edges. The other, at the opposite end of the balcony, appeared middle aged and was smooth shaven and bald like him. Something was oddly familiar about this man. Had he not been trim and fit, he might have been a ringer for his old self.

Both men were looking in his direction before disappearing from the balcony. And he caught another glimpse of them as he left the church. Once the car was underway, he breathed deeply and let the disturbing images go. He was just being hypervigilant, he reasoned, because of all the intrigue in his life.

They took a detour through a neighboring community and let Natasha out at a friend's house for the day. He was looking forward to a quiet day at home with Corinne. He didn't notice the white car parking down the street as they passed through the gates to the house.

Photina greeted them at the door and informed them that lunch was ready. Ray washed up in the foyer bathroom and was heading down the hallway toward the back of the house when the front door blew out and a fireball shot toward him, bathing him in searing heat and knocking him flat. He saw Corinne go down around ten feet in front of him while Photina crashed against a wall, landing with a sickening thud and becoming motionless. Then silence enveloped him.

He struggled to move, but even his extraordinary body had been immobilized by the force of the explosion. Corinne lay well out of reach. There was nothing he could do to save her. Then through the smoke a shadow moved swiftly from the back of the house toward Corinne and swept her up and out of the house. He wondered whether she was being rescued or abducted, but the only thing that mattered was that she would get out alive. He was not likely to be as fortunate.

As Ray struggled to maintain consciousness, he was flooded with images of another fire from long ago, a house consumed in flames, and a charred body being wheeled out of the rubble. Then his mother was framed in the light coming from the end of the hallway, beckoning to him, smiling gently. It had been hubris to think that he could cheat death. Perhaps death wouldn't be so awful, after all.

*****

Photina opened her eyes and assessed her surroundings. The blast had knocked her against a wall and triggered a reboot of her system. She was now fully up and running. The hallway was filled with smoke and she could feel the heat of the fire moving toward her from behind, but her body could withstand temperatures far beyond the tolerance of a human and she didn't need to breathe oxygen to survive. Fire rescue personnel had been almost entirely replaced by SPUDs like her because of their superior physical strength and relative invulnerability.

251

Just before the blast, Corinne and Ray, whom she knew only as Marcus, had been walking toward the kitchen. Now Ray lay by her feet and two life forms just beyond him were moving toward the house's rear entrance. The standing figure was unknown to her. She identified the limp life form in his arms as Corinne and determined that she was alive.

Photina bent over Ray's inert form and hesitated a moment. Marcus had been good to her and she was almost certain Corinne would want her to save him. Corinne and Marcus had usually seemed happy to see one another, greeting each other with friendly looking gestures, including a form of embrace they called "hugs." Sometimes they would touch their mouths together and commingle their microbes.

But there had been one time very early in her education when she'd returned late to the house with a question for Corinne about the day's lessons. The front door was unlocked. She'd let herself in and wandered through the house until she heard voices coming from the bedroom. Corinne's voice came at first in almost a whisper, but soon became louder and higher pitched, similar to the distressful utterances that she'd tutored her about days before. She peeked into the room. Corinne was lying on the bed and Marcus appeared to be holding her down and hurting her. The utterances increased in tempo and pitch while they moved rhythmically together in an apparent struggle. She didn't know what to do and was about to rush into the room to save Corinne when it all suddenly stopped and they became quiet. Corinne had her arms around Marcus with her left hand cradling the back of his head and was whispering again. Photina had backed away from the door as softly as she could, walked to the front door and run all the way home.

The heat at her back intensified. When the second fireball swept through the corridor, Photina threw herself upon Ray, absorbing the brunt of the heat. Once the explosion was over, she threw him over her shoulder and ran to the front of the house where the fire was already starving for fuel. He was no longer breathing by the time they got outside, but the rescue team arrived in time to resuscitate him. Photina sat a few feet away and watched as he began to come around.

"That's good," she thought, while dimly aware that an alternate scenario in which she would have had Corinne all to herself might have been even better for her.

40

MARCUS DOVE for the embankment beyond the car's path and heard the dull thump of the impact behind him as he landed and rolled. He watched the body land behind the now stationary car and bounce once before coming to rest on the pavement.

"Get in," came the command from the two-seater that had pulled up beside him with the passenger door flung open. Without a moment's thought he propelled himself through the opening and pulled the door shut as the car sped away.

The first thing Marcus noticed once inside the hovercar was the driver's flowing red hair. He exhaled slowly and let his body settle into the seat, which conformed instantly to the shape of his body. In the rearview mirror he saw the blond man on his feet in pursuit of the car, but the figure soon faded into the distance.

"For a brilliant scientist, you're pretty brainless," chastised Terra. "What could you possibly have been thinking by coming here?"

"Good thing I did," replied Marcus, "or Corinne wouldn't have had a prayer." He would have gladly traded his life for hers.

"Perhaps, but that was serendipity. You put yourself and our project in jeopardy, along with the possibility of ever getting your old life back. And now look what a mess you're in."

"I guess it doesn't matter anymore now that Ray is dead."

"You're an amazingly lucky man, Marcus," said Terra. "Ray is alive. He was rescued by the SPUD who stays with them. She shielded him from the fire and pulled him out."

"Photina," Marcus thought. "I always wondered if she liked me or would have preferred to have Corinne all to herself." He drew a deep, luxurious breath that cleared the last of the smoke from his lungs. Ray had grabbed his shot at immortality by stealing Marcus's body, but even the Ambrosia Conversion was no guarantee against accidental death...or murder.

"What are you doing here, Terra? How did you find me?"

"Don't think I came here just to rescue you. I came to stop you once we'd tracked you to the capital." Terra's voice was quiet, but her disapproving tone came through loud and clear. "You were breaking all our rules. We wanted to keep you from doing something that you were sure to regret."

"All I wanted to do was to see them again," Marcus said, "my wife and daughter. Stealing them from me was even crueler than stealing my identity."

"Look, Marcus. It's not fair. I get that. But you have to play the hand you've been dealt. Your life is with Lena, now. You belong with her. And Ray, despite the devious way he managed to get here, now belongs here with Corinne...and Natasha."

"I could just stay," said Marcus, "and you could send him back to San Francisco."

"That can't happen," said Terra. "My superiors wouldn't permit it. Ray set things in motion by his impulsivity that you can't imagine and that can't be undone. Exposing your exchange of identities would expose secrets that are crucial to the future of our organization and of the Commonwealth. If we interfered, they would likely kill you both and probably me, too. Even if I wanted to, I couldn't help you now."

"Or ever?" asked Marcus. "Does this mean you won't ever find a way to switch us back?"

Terra looked straight ahead, avoiding his gaze, which was enough to give him her answer. The possibility that she might ever reverse the exchange had been an empty promise either to soften the blow or to keep him in line.

The car veered sharply from the road and within minutes was in a long tunnel that descended at a steep angle into the earth. When it finally leveled out, the car slid into a brightly lit underground chamber and abruptly stopped. Terra switched off the power and the vehicle settled softly to the ground.

"You can get out now," she said.

"Where the hell are we?"

"We're in a project safe haven. We have a number of them throughout the world. This chamber is completely shielded from airborne communication signals. Here we're completely off the grid."

"So the authorities can't track me?"

"The authorities are the least of your problems. Your impulsive actions have placed you right in the crosshairs of The Tribe of 23."

"You mean the hate group?" Marcus and Corinne had long been targeted by them because of Corinne's zealous advocacy of SPUD rights, a cause with which Marcus had joined. His rise to power as Minister of Discovery had cast their advocacy into the limelight. His security detail had protected them from a prior attack, but it was only a matter of time before they struck again.

"The same. They were behind the firebomb. And the man that was just chasing you is Samson."

"Fast as hell," said Marcus, "and the collision barely slowed him down."

"He's a SPUD, of course," said Terra. "He's their poster boy for the threat of SPUDs against humanity. They also use him to do their dirty work."

"So what happens now?"

"We lay low while our collaborators cover your tracks. By now they've removed the car from the scene. They're preparing an upload to your MELD chip that will place you back home at the time of the fire. It will load as soon as we're back outside."

"So my MELD chip won't function here?"

"No, nor, for that matter, mine," answered Terra. "If we want to find out anything, we'll have to do it the old-fashioned way." She pointed to a laptop computer sitting on a marble platform. It bore a logo in the shape of an apple.

Marcus had seen one like it, stashed in a drawer in Ray's apartment. He stumbled upon it soon after Lena discovered his true identity. She'd explained that it was a keepsake. Ray had used it in the early days of his work on HibernaTurf. It was the last of its kind, the final model before computer hardware became obsolete forever.

"We fortunately have powerful friends," Terra continued. "As far as the authorities are concerned, you were never here. The Tribe of 23 is another story altogether. Samson got close enough to analyze your DNA. They know who you are."

"Lena!" exclaimed Marcus. Terra saw him flinch, his eyes darting around like a rabbit exposed to the hunt. The intensity of his alarm took him by surprise. As much as he adored Corinne, his time with Lena had formed a bond between them. He'd come to love her, too. And he wasn't prepared to lose them both.

"Operatives have been dispatched to protect her," Terra assured him. "They should already have her under surveillance."

"Who the hell are you, Terra?" Marcus asked with simultaneous relief and indignation. He hadn't given a lot of thought to the nature of his benefactors when Terra had first approached him with her proposition of wealth and power. Now it was becoming apparent that there was more to her organization than the service they provided. They seemed to have the kind of power that was usually available only to the stealthy arms of governments.

"You don't need to know," Terra replied. "Just be glad we're on your side."

*****

Ray and Corinne arrived in separate ambulances at the hospital, where they were both swarmed by security personnel. Corinne was still unconscious, but her vital signs were strong and she was breathing on her own. Ray had begun to regain consciousness at the site of the fire. His extreme fitness had served him well. Within an hour, he was awake and alert. His last conscious images had been of the blast and the fire.

"Corinne! Where is she?" were his first words.

"She's here in the Emergency Pod," said the nurse. "She hasn't woken up yet, but they expect her to recover."

"And Natasha?"

"Safe at her friend's home where you left her. We've dispatched people to protect her," said one of the guards by the door.

Ray felt a wave of relief. He'd underestimated the depth of feelings that had flourished in his heart for this child.

Photina was at Corinne's side, holding her hand, when Ray arrived at her cubicle. He smiled at the gesture of concern and affection that was becoming commonplace for Photina and many others like her. Before he'd met Haley Sellica, he'd considered SPUDs inanimate contraptions. His respect for Photina had grown rapidly since his arrival in Marcus's home. How could anyone regard her as anything but a fully sentient, feeling being? She looked up and smiled when she saw him.

"They tell me you saved my life," he said extending his hand to her. "Thank you."

"You're welcome."

"And Corinne? You got her out, too?"

"No. There was a stranger...a man. I don't know where he came from. He pulled her out before I could get to either of you." She hesitated a moment. "If he hadn't been there, I would have rescued her instead of you."

"And that's exactly what I would have wanted you to do." Ray smiled and squeezed her hand. "Now...tell me about this stranger."

41

MARCUS CLIMBED into the front pod of the six-pod cylinder and took a last look at Terra standing on the loading dock before the hatch was shut. After coming so close to Corinne and Natasha, it was painful for him to leave. But there was nothing more that he could do for them. And he felt responsible for Lena and for the danger in which he'd placed her. He'd at least managed to keep from Terra that Lena had discovered his secret. It was time to return to her side.

As the cylinder entered the vacuum tube and accelerated on its frictionless path to thousands of miles per hour, Marcus recalled the history of this mode of transportation, which had begun around the time of his birth and was well-established by the time he was a teenager. Before he was old enough to remember, vacuum tubes were used to transport money and documents between customers and tellers at banks.

A bright entrepreneur had realized that the technology could be scaled to move people over great distances at lightning speeds that surpassed air travel for a fraction of the energy cost. Soon networks grew like giant spider webs, crisscrossing continents, and vacuum tube transport became the dominant form of mass transit.

Marcus smiled as the transparent capsule glided soundlessly past the landscape at nearly four thousand miles per hour. Had he been born a little earlier, he might have invented this technology. It had taken him a while to become accustomed to the landscape passing across his field of vision so quickly and so close at hand. The perception of speed with air travel was blunted considerably by the distance between the aircraft and the ground. Marcus found tube transport, in contrast, dizzying until his body accommodated to the sense of speed. What he found most remarkable was that the feeling of being in a speeding vehicle came almost entirely from the visual realm. After he closed his eyes for a few seconds, it felt as if he were motionless, so smooth was the course of the capsule and so constant the speed.

With a whoosh, the cylinder came to a stop without even a quiver. The hatch opened automatically and Marcus stepped onto the underground platform. The whole trip had taken less than an hour, a fraction of the time it took to fly cross country in his youth. He navigated the underground walkways until he reached a pod that said "Powell" and got in. The pod whisked him silently to the station.

When he emerged onto the street, he headed for the corner of Powell and Sacramento and the building where Ray and Lena had lived for a decade. Once inside, he stepped within the force field of the unwalled elevator and was on the twentieth floor within seconds.

In front of the entrance to his condo stood a black clad woman with dark glasses, armed with an ultrasonic sidearm. She performed a retinal screen as he approached and stood aside to let him pass. Marcus stood in front of the body scanner and the door slid open. He stepped inside and heard it latch behind him.

"Lena," Marcus called as he moved through the front hall to the great room in the center of the unit. There was no response. He entered the huge central room with the twin support pillars. Still no Lena. He went next to the bedroom, but there was no sign of her. He began running from room to room. She was nowhere to be found. He ran back to the front door to find the guard, but the door was locked from the outside. He beat on it with his fists to get the guard's attention and tried over and over to open it, but it was sealed shut. He moved back to the great room and, standing in the middle, tried to think.

Then he heard a faint hiss, turned and spotted the end of the canister peeking from behind the sofa just beyond its edge. His heart pumped double time and sweat poured down his forehead, clouding his vision. His thoughts became too scrambled to find an escape, even with all the knowledge available to him through his MELD chip.

He ran to the periphery of the building as far from the canister as he could get. The outer walls were floor to ceiling glass, but there were no windows that opened, and the glass was designed to withstand earthquakes and high winds. It was virtually unbreakable. He grabbed a marble sculpture and flung it against a window with all his strength. It just bounced off.

He lay on the floor, pressing up against the glass, and pulled his shirt up over his face, breathing as shallowly as possible. The dizziness swept over him all at once. His vision dimmed like a shade coming down over his eyes. A faint scent of almonds wafted past his nose at the same time he heard a high-pitched whine. Calm set in just before the last wisp of light was extinguished.

42

"**THERE WAS SO MUCH** smoke," began Photina, "I could barely see the man who saved Corinne."

"Think hard, Photina. What did you notice?" asked Ray.

"He wasn't as tall as you. A little heavier around the middle, but burly and fit, and a good bit older."

"What else?"

"I couldn't see his face, but there was something very familiar about him." She closed her eyes to visualize the data streams.

"Familiar? How? You mean you've seen him before?"

"Yes...and no," she replied. "I don't think I've ever seen his body. But the way he moved. That was familiar. I know I've seen someone move the same way."

"When?"

"I don't know. My memory traces are contaminated. There was an anomaly as a result of the explosion."

"Anything else?" asked Marcus.

"Yes. One other thing. The way he moved through the house. It was like he'd been here before. He knew the house. That's how he was able to get to Corinne so quickly."

Ray considered the implications of what she'd told him. A stranger had rescued Corinne from the fire, someone who'd been in the house before, but whom no one had seen there. Photina had somehow encountered someone with a matching kinetic pattern, but it wasn't the same man. Why would he have been there in the first place? And why would he risk his life to save Corinne's?

"Where did they put Corinne's clothes?" he asked next.

"I don't know. They were pretty badly burned. They might have disposed of them."

"Let's find out. If we can recover the clothes, there would be DNA traces on them from the stranger. You'd be able to analyze them. Wouldn't you?"

"Yes. That is among the capabilities in my programming. I'll ask about the clothes." She left the room.

One possible solution to the mystery crossed Ray's mind, but it seemed too outlandish to be true. He shook his head. Corinne was beginning to stir. He turned his attention to her, touching her cheek with his hand. She moaned. Her eyes opened. Her lips parted as if to speak, but no words came out. Instead, she began coughing and choking.

"Shh," he said, raising a straw with some water to her lips. "Take a few breaths. Then have a sip." The coughing stopped. She breathed deeply, then sipped on the straw.

"Thank God you're OK," he said, reaching down to kiss her forehead. For the first time since they'd met, he noticed the signs of aging that had gradually crept over her face, the deepening folds around her mouth and the tiny lines fanning out from the corners of her eyes. She wore reading glasses to enjoy her books. They'd been hard to come by since the digital media most people used automatically corrected for vision. Ray liked seeing her in them, peering at him from above the half lenses. He wondered if she'd ever noticed she was leaving Marcus behind. And he realized with a twinge of regret that she'd continue to age without him and he'd eventually lose her.

"Thank God you're OK," she mouthed silently and smiled. Tears welled in the corners of her eyes.

The doctor appeared in the doorway to the cubicle. "I see we're awake," he said cheerfully.

"She just woke up," answered Ray. "She still seems to be suffering the effects of the smoke."

"That's to be expected," said the doctor, turning to Corinne. "It may be awhile before you can speak. Just be patient. Don't strain your vocal cords. You'll be talking soon enough."

Corinne moved her hand in the air as though she was writing on a tablet and looked at the doctor.

"Sure," he said, understanding her gesture, "I can get you a pad and a pen. Better yet, how about a keyboard?"

She shook her head and repeated the writing gesture. Corinne liked things simple and leaned toward low tech whenever possible. A nurse arrived shortly with the requested implements.

"I love you," was the first thing she wrote.

"I know," Ray replied. "I love you, too." The words sounded strange as he uttered them, but they felt true.

"Natasha?" she wrote next.

"Safe where we left her." Corinne smiled and paused a few moments before she wrote again.

"Our house?"

"Gone. Burned to the ground." He shook his head.

"My books? Gone, too?" She already knew the answer. Tears filled her eyes, dripping onto the paper as she wrote, smearing the ink. She looked away for a moment to pull herself together.

"You're going to think I'm crazy," she wrote next. "I saw the man who saved me before I passed out."

"And...?"

"He was a stranger," she wrote. "I've never seen him before."

"So what's the crazy part?"

"When he touched me, just before he picked me up, it was like I knew him. His touch felt so familiar." Her mouth and eyes crinkled in a silent laugh. "I told you you'd think I was crazy."

"Not at all," Ray said. He was looking straight at her, but his thoughts were now a million miles away. It was crazy, but the pieces were starting to fit together. And he had no idea how he felt about what they meant. If Marcus had come to their house that day, was it to stalk them or just to have a last glimpse of his former life? God knows he had a right to be there, but he'd risked exposing both their identities and putting both their families in danger.

But if he hadn't been there, Corinne would almost certainly have died. For that Ray was grateful. And Marcus didn't share Ray's terror of fire. Had it been Ray on the outside, he wasn't sure he would have been brave enough to rush in.

When Ray left Corinne's room, Photina met him in the hallway.

"They had the clothes in a plastic bag," she said. "They were about to incinerate them, but I got there just in time. There was DNA residue that wasn't Corinne's. I got a sample. I'll have the genome read in an hour and compare it with the Universal Data Base."

"Thanks, Photina. We owe you a lot for what you've done for us today."

Photina looked into his eyes and looked as though she had something else to say. She held back.

"Photina," Ray coaxed, "Was there something else?"

"Mr. Marcus," she said, looking flustered, "the way the stranger moved...looked a lot like you."

43

THE EXPLODING charge of the drone as it struck the corner of the window shattered it into millions of beads that sprayed across Marcus's inert body. Fresh air rushed into the room and filled his lungs. On the other side of the condo, Terra's confederates stormed the door and raced to his side. They zipped him into the hyperbaric suit and loaded him onto the copter that now hovered by the opening.

As the craft veered around and headed over the bay, Marcus began to regain consciousness and for a moment wasn't sure whose body he was in. As his mind cleared, reality set in. He was still trapped in Ray's body, but felt grateful he'd survived at all. He was still struggling to breathe and the anxiety was returning.

"Odd," he thought, "how powerful is the drive to survive. As drastically as my life has changed, I still cling to it, just like people who've been crippled or disfigured." And having saved Corinne, he now had other unfinished business: to find Lena. He prayed that she was alive.

Within minutes, the aircraft was far out to sea with no land in sight. Then it stopped all forward motion and began to descend rapidly and apparently randomly toward the water. Just before impact, the water beneath it began to swirl, creating a void in the center that swallowed them up. They descended into the funnel as Marcus watched the spot of light from the sky getting smaller and smaller, finally slowing to a soft landing on solid ground. With a whirring sound, something slid across the opening overhead and they were in total darkness. The copter's motor silenced.

Suddenly the space around them was flooded with light. They were in an underwater chamber the size of an airplane hangar. He was quickly removed from the aircraft and placed inside a clear enclosure. Once the hatch of the container was sealed tight, it began filling with gas. Marcus felt pressure surrounding his body. As the pressure increased it became easier and easier for him to breathe. The hyperbaric chamber was providing oxygen to flush the remaining poison from his system. The panic that had overtaken him as he suffocated in the apartment and had returned as he regained consciousness now began to recede and was replaced by calm.

Through the canopy of the enclosure Marcus saw a flash of fire red hair, then a familiar face peering down at him. A brief crackling sound and he could hear sound from around the enclosure coming through a speaker.

"Hello again, Marcus." Terra's voice echoed in the space around him. "We've definitely got to stop meeting like this." Her face was somber despite the humor in her words.

"Where the hell are we this time, Terra?"

"It doesn't really matter. Your antics have created an enormous mess for us. You're turning into quite a liability."

"I've created a mess for you? What about me? I was supposed to live for decades in an ageless body. And look at me."

"Our deal didn't include babysitting you for the rest of your life and rescuing you over and over from your impulsive blunders. Make no mistake, Marcus. Ray is still of value to us, but you're expendable. Don't expect another rescue." The distortion of Terra's amplified voice within the hyperbaric chamber underscored her threat with an ominous tone.

"Lena!" Marcus exclaimed. "What happened to Lena?"

"They took her. We don't know where." replied Terra. "She's gone dark."

"Who took her? Is she alive?"

"The Tribe of 23. I told you they'd come after you. We don't know whether Lena's alive, but I'd guess she is. They're likely to use her to get to you."

"What do they want?"

"They want you dead. And they still want Ray and Corinne dead, too.

"What happens now?"

"Now we wait," said Terra. "Our people on the outside will watch for signs of Lena's whereabouts and wait for any communication from The Tribe. I expect that we'll hear from them soon."

The canopy of the hyperbaric chamber began to open. His treatment was complete. Marcus was surprised at how well he felt. He had more energy than usual, almost like his old self. His blood was still supersaturated with oxygen and all the poison was gone. He stepped out of the chamber and looked around the space.

The helicopter took up half the room. The other half was buzzing with activity. There were around a dozen people beside him and Terra. Most were at workstations staring intently at the blank spaces in front of them. They were watching encrypted holographic images visible only to them.

"What are they monitoring?" asked Marcus.

"You don't need to know. This station wasn't put here just for your convenience."

One of the people who wasn't watching a monitor approached him. She passed an instrument over his body from head to toe while looking at the space just above her eye level.

"He checks out," she said. "The body scan is normal. He's in pretty good shape for a man his age."

One of the people at the workstations looked in their direction and waved Terra over. Marcus watched their animated whispered conversation until Terra shook her head and headed back his way.

"As I expected," she said, "The Tribe of 23 has Lena and they've made their demand."

"What do they want? Ransom?"

"They couldn't care less about money. They want you. They're offering an exchange. And it's no mystery what they'll do with you when they get you. Either Lena dies or you do. That's what you've gotten you both into."

44

THE THREATS were mounting fast in Ray Mettler's new life. Someone had tried to kill him twice and had nearly succeeded. From what he knew of Marcus Takana's life, he'd made a lot of enemies for an otherwise beloved public figure. As Minister of Discovery, he'd been instrumental in initiating some controversial programs. And even as the creator of Takana Grass, he was despised by extremists who opposed some of the consequences of his discovery. The revival of farming animals for meat production brought animal rights groups out of the woodwork that opposed raising animals for food. He'd received threats from members of several of these groups. And despite the many benefits that Takana Grass bestowed on humanity, there were still those who opposed genetically engineering any living things.

Marcus's role as a vocal advocate of SPUD rights had probably earned him the most vicious enemies. The Tribe of 23 was the largest and most vocal anti-SPUD organization. Their rhetoric and tactics were reminiscent of the Ku Klux Klan that terrorized African Americans in the last two centuries. One difference is that they didn't wear hoods or otherwise hide their identities. They were sufficiently self-righteous that they felt no need to be secretive and skated very close to the edge of the law, sometimes sliding across it. There were stories of assassinations both of SPUDs and of some of the people who stood up for them. The firebombing had the earmarks of their style.

If that weren't enough, Ray now had an enemy of his own: Ganymede. Its Director had demanded that Ray run for President as a way of gaining control over the government of the Commonwealth. If he complied, they would control him with the compromising information they had on him, much like the Russians had controlled an American President decades before with *kompromat* and had almost succeeded in bringing the nation to its knees. Ray would become a traitor, having sold out his country for the promise of immortality. How could he have been so vain or so arrogant?

What were his options? He could go underground, but that would leave Corinne and Natasha vulnerable and they could be used to draw him back out. He could confide in Vice President Hauer or in the President, but Ganymede would be almost certain to find out and punish him for his disobedience.

"What if I reached out to Marcus?" he thought. "Perhaps between us and with his knowledge of the government, we could figure out a solution." It was an audacious idea. For one thing, Marcus must despise him. Why would he even consider helping him get out of this jam? But on the other hand, Corinne's and Natasha's safety also depended on finding a way out. Marcus would do it for them, even if it helped his enemy.

He would have to announce his candidacy for President. Terra had left him no choice. It would thrust him even more into the limelight, but he and his family would have the enhanced level of Secret Service protection afforded to Presidents.

And he'd have to find a way to get to Marcus. It would have to be in person. Any other form of communication would be too vulnerable to intrusion. And if he got to San Francisco, he might also have a chance to see Lena. Even in Corinne's bewitching presence, he'd begun to miss her deeply, another reason that triggering the exchange had begun to feel like a disastrous mistake.

273

Photina was back in an hour as promised. She stood beside Ray and projected a huge holographic image of a nest of twenty-three chromosome pairs in front of them. As often as Ray had seen such images of the human genome, he retained his childish delight at its elegance and beauty. In front of him now was the blueprint of the man who'd saved Corinne. And he already had a good idea to whom it belonged.

"So were you able to identify him?" Ray asked.

"Yes, I was," She replied. "His was a well-known genome, given his identity. His name is Raymond Mettler. He was the inventor of HibernaTurf."

"Have you told Corinne?" he asked.

"Not yet," said Photina.

"Then please keep this between us for now. It would be safer for her if she didn't know."

"I don't understand. I've never kept secrets from Corinne."

"Sometimes secrets are dangerous, Photina," said Ray. "People who don't want their secrets to be known might kill to protect them. Corinne is safer not knowing this one. You're just going to have to trust me."

Photina stared hard at his face. Corinne's lessons about reading emotional faces had included training in lie detection. Photina's expertise in this area had developed beyond the skills of most humans. Finally, she nodded assent.

When Ray returned to the Ministry of Discovery, he scanned the UDB for scientific events near San Francisco. An Artificial Cognition Conference was scheduled to meet that weekend at the Four Seasons Hotel right in the heart of the city. He contacted the conference organizer and asked whether he could be squeezed into the program as a speaker.

"I'm planning an important announcement," Ray said as an incentive. As long as he was going to have to declare his candidacy for President, he figured he'd kill two birds with one stone and do it at the conference. That would keep Ganymede at bay for a while. Running for President wouldn't turn him into a traitor. Only winning would. And it suddenly occurred to him that perhaps he could find a way to lose.

The Minister of Discovery was a solid draw for any scientific conference. The teased announcement sealed the deal and he was included in the program. He'd find an opportunity to meet with Marcus. It shouldn't be hard to find him. He was inhabiting Ray's old life, after all. And Ray would make the trip knowing that whoever tried to kill him would be watching from the shadows for another opportunity to finish the job.

45

LENA COULDN'T banish the image of the guard in the hallway, lying face up with a hole in the middle of her forehead that went clear through the back of her head, a clean, bloodless, lethal wound. The wide open, steel blue eyes stared vacantly at the ceiling.

The hood had been placed over Lena's head in the elevator. It not only rendered her blind, but also blocked her access to the Universal Data Base via her MELD chip. She had no means to navigate her position except by observing with her native senses. As a journalist, she'd developed keen observational skills that she brought to bear upon her current predicament. She counted steps and did her best to keep track of turns as they walked. She listened as best she could to the street sounds muffled by the hood. Her keenest sense was her ability to smell her surroundings through the holes left in the shroud for her to breathe.

Just as the pungent scent of Asian food wafted its way to her nostrils, a hand pushed her head down from behind and shoved her into a vehicle. Her step count was no longer relevant as the vehicle sped away from the scene. Now she attended to the motion of the vehicle, which descended steeply before leveling out for most of its course. By the time it came to a stop and she was roughly pulled to her feet, she could smell salt air.

She was led a short way on pavement and then onto softer ground. A creaking sound erupted a few dozen feet ahead of her, reaching a crescendo as she approached. As she moved forward, the air around her began to feel damp and the ground under her feet became slippery and boggy. The creaking sound was now behind her, ending with a clank.

She sniffed the air. The muddy organicity had the kind of familiarity that resonates with long forgotten feelings and sharpens faded memories from long ago. Lena felt herself smile, ever so briefly, despite her peril. She knew this place and perhaps could use her knowledge in some way to her advantage.

Lena was born in the fall of 2008, the day after the investment company Bear Stearns suddenly went broke, which became part of the folklore of her family. Her father was an investment broker with another firm, but failed to escape the ripples that went through the financial world and left her parents destitute just as they were building their family. While many Wall Street executives continued to make high salaries and collect bonuses, her father had been too low in the hierarchy to merit such protected status. When he was unemployed, her mother went to work as an office manager for a medical practice while he stayed home and tried to care for their infant daughter.

When her mother came home unexpectedly early one afternoon, she'd found her father in the bedroom with a gun to his head. There was a note by the bedside telling her that Lena was at a neighbor's house and that he was sorry he couldn't handle things better. She convinced him to put the gun away and he was admitted to a hospital for treatment. Over the next year, he was in and out of the hospital until he finally renounced the possibility of killing himself and committed to rebuilding his life.

With the hospital bills on top of their other debts, her mother was unable to keep up with the financial demands from her modest salary. They wound up homeless until Lena was four. It took another five years for them to work their way out of poverty on the combination of her mother's salary and her father's modest income teaching economics at a community college.

For most of the first decade of her life, Lena had either lived on the streets or spent her time scrounging on the streets along with a gang of similarly impoverished kids. They entertained themselves by exploring the nooks and crannies of the city, from the basements of the neighborhood businesses to the buildings and wharves along the waterfront. One day, they stumbled upon a pair of massive and mysterious iron doors. At the top of the doors was a space large enough to crawl through, but too high for them to reach.

The children returned a few days later with hooks and rope. Using the door hinges as braces, they scaled the doors and descended into the darkness armed with flashlights. Once they became accustomed to the company of the rodents and raccoons that inhabited the space, it became their secret hideout where they spent hours playing and carving their names into the rock. With time they became nimble at scaling the barriers to enter the tunnel in just a few minutes. The dank atmosphere of the tunnel grew familiar and welcoming. Now Lena imagined herself surrounded again by her childhood gang.

"If we finish her here, we could just leave her body for the rats." The voice of one of her captors shocked her back to the reality of her present danger. The image of the dead guard in the corridor reminded her that the people who held her didn't hesitate to kill. She felt something hard thrust against her left temple. She drew a short breath and held it, as if not breathing might somehow make her invisible.

"First we need confirmation that Mettler's dead," came another voice. "Otherwise we'll still need a hostage." The pressure against Lena's head subsided.

"Can't imagine him surviving the cyanide. We already got word that he was in the apartment. Our sentry locked him in tight. She should be here any minute."

Now Lena's breath came in short gasps and her chest felt like it was going to burst. Her relationship with Ray had long been ambivalent. But Marcus was another story. Despite the unfairness of him being ripped away from Corinne and Natasha, she was falling in love with him. The exchange had become a guilty pleasure and she desperately wanted to keep him. If he died, a good man's life would be cruelly cut short and neither of them would have him. Sobs bubbled to the surface and threatened to strangle her within the hood.

"If you're going to kill me, anyway, could you at least take this off?" Lena pleaded, her words coming in choking fragments.

"Guess there's no harm in that," said another one of her captors. "The tunnel walls are thick enough to keep her off the grid." She felt the ties around her neck loosen and the hood came off. Her eyes were already used to the dark, so things around her came quickly into focus.

Her assessment of her location was immediately confirmed. Light filtered through high arched spaces from both ends of the quarter mile long tunnel. She could see familiar niches in the contours of the walls where she and her friends had hidden various mementoes and toys. She now counted three human figures, corresponding to the three distinct voices that she'd heard through the shroud. Her sobs subsided as her attention turned to integrating the new information she now had about her surroundings.

One of her captors took pity and freed her hands so she could wipe away her tears with her sleeve. They had nothing to lose. The tunnel was secure and she was defenseless.

Lena tried to connect her MELD chip to the UDB, but the kidnappers had been right. There was no access to the cloud from the tunnel. Which meant that her captors were also cut off. That explained why they weren't still in communication with their accomplice on the outside.

The creaking sound suddenly rose behind her. She turned to see one of the huge iron doors slowly moving outward as the aging hinges squealed and groaned. A female figure appeared silhouetted against the sky and pulled the door shut again with apparent ease.

"He got away." she shouted from the entrance once the door was closed. Lena's heart skipped with the hope conveyed by those words. Marcus was alive, after all, and she'd likely at least bought some time.

"How in the world did that happen?"

"They blew up the window with a drone and extracted him," replied the woman, now standing directly before Lena, who recoiled in shock at her appearance. There before her was the face of the woman on the floor with the steel blue eyes, identical in all respects absent the hole in the middle of her forehead.

Once the shock had worn off, it all began to come together. This was not the guard that had been posted outside her door. She was an identical replacement. The wound had been bloodless because no blood had ever flowed in either woman's body. They were SPUDs and had been manufactured at the same time in the same version. Somehow, whoever had abducted Lena had been able to replace the one who had been posted to guard her with this one. Lena wondered whether this SPUD had been the one that destroyed her double and what, if anything, she might have felt when she did it.

"Who the hell are these people?" thought Lena. And who, for that matter, were the people who'd tried to protect her? They'd just shown up at the penthouse without any explanation. Now that she knew about the exchange and Terra's role in it, she guessed that Terra was likely behind the security detail. But her captors were a mystery. Did they have anything to do with Terra's scheme or were they among the many people who still despised Ray for HibernaTurf?

The four abductors moved a short distance away and conversed in whispers. Then one of them approached her.

"You're a lucky woman," he said. "We'll need you alive a while longer, at least, to help us get to your husband. Enyo will keep an eye on you here," he added, nodding at the woman in black with the steely eyes. "I wouldn't try anything stupid. She has five times your speed and ten times your strength. She can crush you like an insect and without a moment's pause. You must have seen what she did to her twin back there."

The three remaining captors gathered up their things and left through the iron doors that faced the sea. She watched the huge door swing shut, this time with a resounding ringing sound, and heard the sound of the lock closing to fasten the enormous chain that held the doors together. Enyo stood a few feet behind her, arms folded, locking her into focus with a piercing gaze.

Lena struggled to remember what she'd learned about SPUDs that could help her gain the upper hand. While the latest models incorporated massive data bases and advanced logic algorithms, they still acquired their intelligence by learning, just like people, and started their existences intellectually, and especially emotionally, as children. Learning from experience turned out to be the most efficient way to maximize their potential. So like children, they were programmed to be curious and to enjoy mastering new skills.

She scanned her memory for anything in the tunnel that might be useful in defeating her android captor. She and her friends had secreted many things within the tunnel that they used in their play. Some of their games involved intricate skills that they'd honed over time. Her thoughts wandered to an item that she'd left decades before in a niche in the wall not fifty feet from where she sat. She wondered how many of her toys were still where she and her friends had left them. She walked casually toward one of the walls and ambled along its perimeter.

"Look what I found," said Lena, holding out an object she plucked from one of the crevices.

"What is it?" asked Enyo.

"It's called a yo-yo. It's a toy. It must have been left here by some children."

"What does it do?" Enyo's gaze was now glued to the curious object.

"Let me show you," replied Lena, winding the string around the spool. As she began to throw the yo-yo toward the ground, Enyo recoiled momentarily, then stared as it stopped and rolled back up into Lena's hand. The feel of the yo-yo was familiar, and she proceeded to 'walk the dog' along with other tricks that had once been second nature.

"Let me try," said Enyo, her hand shooting out for the toy. Lena removed the loop from her own index finger and fastened the slip knot over Enyo's.

Enyo's first few tries were clumsy and Lena helped her wind the string back onto the spool. By the time she got it to return to her hand, the yo-yo was occupying most of her attention, leaving Lena free to wander a bit further down the wall. She felt along the wall at what would have been a child's shoulder height until she reached another chink in the stone.

When she reached into the crevice with her right hand, her fingers found a sturdy forked stick. At the open end of the Y, she felt the small patch of suede that was attached to the ends of the stick by two heavy rubber cords. She prayed that the rubber hadn't dried and cracked. Her heart skipped a few beats as she ran her fingers over the cords. They were still supple to her touch and her heart resumed its normal rhythm. Within the crevice was also a small pile of smooth stones, each around an inch in diameter. She drew two of the stones from their hiding place and put them in a pocket. Then she carefully drew out the slingshot and tucked it in the waistband of her pants behind her back. As she turned back toward Enyo, who was now trying some of the tricks that Lena had shown her, she scoured her memory for more data.

Every SPUD had a central processing device, the anatomical location of which varied, depending upon model. And every one had some way to deactivate it. Many of the earlier generation models used a combination of remote controls and manual switches, and many of these had the switches conveniently located in the small of their backs behind a cover. Lena visualized the woman with the hole in the middle of her forehead and concluded that her CPD, and Enyo's, lay somewhere in the path of the hole.

Enyo glanced at her as she started back in her direction, but saw nothing amiss and returned to her play. Lena was just a few feet away when Enyo turned toward her again. She drew back on the slingshot with all her strength and the missile found its mark in the center of Enyo's forehead. The force of the blow was apparently sufficient to disrupt her CPD and she crashed to the ground, limbs askew, haphazardly twitching. Lena sprang to her side, swept her hand over the android's spine, and located the hidden compartment. She flipped the switch. Enyo's body stilled.

Lena was now aware of her own breathing, coming in gasps from her burst of activity. She paused long enough for it to settle back into a regular rhythm, then took several long, deep breaths. She felt the sweat running down her face and the wetness under her arms, contrasting with the smooth dry skin she'd felt in the small of Enyo's back.

Tucking her trusty slingshot back in her waistband, she returned to the crevice and scooped a handful of stones into her pockets. Approaching the gates that faced the bay, she remembered the hooks and ropes that she'd used as a child to climb over them. They weren't in the cave. But she was now taller and, thanks to an ambitious exercise regimen, stronger than she was back then, even at forty-five, capable of using the hinges as hand and footholds to scale the gate. In just a few minutes she was under the open sky and had full command of her MELD, which was broadcasting her location. She could only hope that the rescuers would get to her first.

46

AS CORINNE RECOVERED, questions began to form that nagged at her attention. The memory of her rescuer's touch remained vivid. When had she felt it before, and where? The answer was almost palpable like a word balancing just at the tip of the tongue, but not quite articulated. She tried discussing it with Photina, but on this subject Photina was uncharacteristically evasive and provided no clues.

Another recent surreal experience floated around the edges of Corinne's awareness. She suspected that they were somehow connected, but had no idea how: Marcus's odd behavior the morning after the speech with the President...and the familiarity of the rescuer's touch. None of it seemed to make sense. And yet, there was a symmetry to it all that was compelling.

As her memory cleared, Corinne kept returning to the scene of the fire for any missing clues. It was hard to distinguish the dreamlike images of her delirium from the real events of that morning. Right after the explosion, she felt suddenly at peace, standing in a dark tunnel, bathed in silence, looking at a dazzling light at the end of the tunnel. The radiance coming from the light felt like love and she found herself moving toward it without hesitation.

Then it felt like something shoved her back. Her chest filled with pressure. The tunnel vanished and she could see the sky above her. A shadow blocked out the sky and soft lips touched hers in a tender, fleeting kiss...Marcus's lips...Marcus's kiss. The next thing she remembered was awakening in the hospital. Had she imagined the kiss? Was it part of a dream? It had felt so real, so loving and safe. But she'd left Marcus behind in the burning house.

When Corinne got to their temporary home the next morning, the first thing she did was shower off the remaining traces of soot and the smell of the hospital. The apartment's shower was the conventional type, not the water sparing type to which she'd been accustomed and which left her body slick and dry. She stepped out of the shower and reached for a towel. Once dry, she stood naked before the full-length mirror.

As she assessed the scorches on her body, she noticed again the subtle signs that her body was aging. The creases under her breasts were now a little more pronounced as were the indentations from her nose to the corners of her mouth. The delicate lines around the corners of her eyes seemed to have sprouted more branches.

She didn't hear Ray walk into the room until he gently touched her shoulder. She turned to face him. He was smiling.

"Good morning," he said. "I'm glad you're home."

"Good Morning, Marc. It's good to be home."

He was still smiling. But he had neither fine lines at the corners of his eyes nor deepening creases around his mouth like hers. In fact, she still saw no signs at all of the passage of time on his face or body. She was continuing to age and leaving him behind. Another piece of the puzzle.

Ray leaned over to kiss her. She instinctively turned her face away. She felt a wrenching sensation in the pit of her stomach.

"Not now, Marcus," she said. "I'm still a little shaken from the fire."

Ray looked into her eyes as if searching for her thoughts.

"I have to go to work," he said. "Then I might have to go on a trip."

"A trip? So soon after the...accident?" But as she said the words, she realized that she would be relieved for him to leave. She needed time to think, to find more pieces and solve the puzzle. It was becoming clearer. The redhead, Terra, was part of the puzzle. And the Ambrosia Conversion...the arguments they'd had years ago about them both undergoing it. She'd steadfastly refused. But Marcus had apparently already had it and had been lying to her about it the whole time.

"And Natasha," Corinne thought. "She has half his genes. No wonder she healed so quickly from a broken arm. Who knows what her future holds? How could he have been so rash and so selfish?"

But the Conversion was just part of the picture that was forming before her. It was the background, the edges and corners of the puzzle. What was starting to take shape in its center was even more astonishing and alarming. The man whose bed she'd shared for who knows how long looked like her husband, but might, in fact, be a total stranger. And the man in a stranger's body who'd rescued her from the fire might be her husband Marcus.

"Photina!" Corinne called after Ray had left. "Please come here now. We need to talk."

Photina appeared in the doorway.

"Is there something you're keeping from me?" asked Corinne.

"Yes," answered Photina. Parts of her program still functioned literally. She answered questions sparsely, like a skilled trial witness.

"What is it?" asked Corinne.

287

"Mr. Marcus told me not to tell you. He said it would put you in danger."

"I'll take that chance, Photina. I have to know what secret you've been told to keep."

"It was the identity of the stranger who saved your life," said Photina. "His name is Raymond Mettler."

Corinne felt like she'd been struck in the chest.

"Raymond Mettler...the inventor of HibernaTurf?"

"Yes. That is correct."

"Do you have any idea what he'd have been doing here?"

"No, not exactly, but there was something I noticed about him, an odd anomaly."

"What was that?"

"It was his kinetic pattern. He moved exactly like Mr. Marcus. If he was taller and thinner, it could have been him."

The last piece of the puzzle had dropped into place. If Corinne was ever going to see Marcus again, the real Marcus, she'd have to find Raymond Mettler. And she had no idea what she'd do when she found him.

47

NO SOONER HAD LENA switched on her MELD chip than she spotted the hovercraft swooping toward her over the water. She ducked behind cover and instinctively switched her chip back off. As the craft approached, she saw a woman at the helm that bore a remarkable resemblance to the SPUD she'd just left behind in the tunnel. The only difference was a small round bandage applied to the middle of her forehead. Lena concluded that she was looking at Enyo's double, the original guard who'd been posted outside her door back home, now refurbished and hopefully an ally. But was she?

All Lena really knew was that these two forces seemed to be fighting over her. When Terra's security detail had first approached her at the apartment, she'd taken their word that they were there to protect her, but they never explained from whom or why they were there. Maybe there weren't any good guys in this strange battle that seemed to be raging over her. And she had no idea whether Ray or Marcus was the main prize. There was no way to know who could be trusted. As the craft approached land, Lena slipped into the shadows of the waterfront buildings and disappeared.

Where to next? It would be risky to return home, but for the same reason, her pursuers would hardly expect her to go there. She might find clues about what happened to Marcus. Perhaps he'd even return to the apartment once he recovered from the cyanide. It was her only chance for them to meet up without revealing her location to everyone.

Lena wound her way among the still familiar array of buildings near the waterfront, navigating her way back toward the heart of the city. When she reached the corner of Powell and Sacramento, there was nobody near the entrance to the building. She disappeared inside. As the elevator glided upward, the pulsations in her ears reminded her of the uncertainty of what she would face when she reached the top. Her left hand found the slingshot that was still in her pocket and the fingers of her right hand closed over a round stone the size of a large marble. The elevator reached her floor and the force field containing her dissolved. She stepped out.

An imposingly tall figure in a hooded sweatshirt stood at the door of the apartment with its back to her. The door had been damaged in the rescue, but was now shut tight against the intruder. She placed the stone in the web of the slingshot and took aim. The hooded figure whirled around. Lena caught herself just in time, lowered her weapon, and stared open-mouthed at the intruder.

"Ray!" Lena exclaimed, "What are you doing here?"

"Lena," Ray replied, stunned. "How did you know?"

"You abandoned me Ray," she said. "You have a hell of a nerve coming back now."

"I should have known you'd figure it out. You've always had a knack for solving mysteries."

"He had another stroke and nearly died. He was having trouble speaking and called me 'Corinne.' When he recovered and I confronted him, he came clean."

"It's good to see you, Lena," said Ray. "I've missed you."

"And yet, it's hard to believe that that's why you're here." She fixed her gaze on his clear blue eyes. "It isn't. Is it?" she challenged.

"No, it isn't," Ray replied. It would have been useless to try to lie to Lena. She could always tell just by looking at him. "I came to see Marcus. I have to talk with him. Do you know where he is?"

"I have no idea," said Lena. "I was kidnapped and got away. When Marcus came home, they tried to poison him with cyanide, but he was rescued. I don't know by whom or where they took him. Why would you want to talk with him? If I were him, I'd want to kill you for what you did to him."

A long silence filled the space between them before Ray could respond.

"That's a very long story, Lena," he said at last. "Can we go inside?"

Lena stood before the body scanner and the battered door creaked open. They slipped inside. The door closed behind them. They could hear the wind whistling through the shattered glass wall in the next room. Upon entering the great room, the first thing to strike them was the precipitous drop at the edge of the space. Lena felt lightheaded watching Ray walk close to the brink. There were still beads of glass scattered about the room, making his footing all the more treacherous. As angry as she was at Ray, she wasn't prepared to watch him die.

"Please be careful," she said. "Come back inside. You're making me nervous."

When he turned around, Lena was sitting on the sofa on the opposite wall to the gaping opening. He came back inside and took a seat next to her.

"I'm pregnant, Ray," she blurted out. "I just found out. He doesn't know, yet." She wanted to hurt him. But his eyes betrayed more sorrow than anger.

He reached out and took both her hands in his. She didn't resist.

"I'm really sorry, Lena," he said. "There's so many ways I've let you down."

"I'm glad you're here," she said at last, her mouth wavering between smiles and sobs. "I've been so scared and so alone."

"What happened to you?" Ray asked, looking at the bruises on her arms and her torn and soiled clothes.

Lena told him about the guard detail at the apartment, her abduction, the attempt on Marcus's life, and her escape from the Amazon-like SPUD who'd been left to guard her.

"Someone firebombed our home," Ray said, "and Marcus was there. He pulled Corinne out of the fire and saved her life."

"So all this is about that?" she concluded. "The people who tried to kill you and Corinne are after us, too?"

"It would seem so," replied Ray. "They think it was The Tribe of 23. Someone saw the man who threw the firebomb and he's been identified as Samson, a SPUD under their control. They were after us because of Corinne and Marcus's advocacy for SPUD rights. I'm pretty sure Samson saw him and now they're after him for interfering with their hit."

Ray watched as Lena's wheels turned. Her forefinger lay across her mouth and her thumb against her jaw for nearly half a minute before she looked at him again.

"So who's been trying to protect us?" she asked next. "They seem awfully invested in keeping Marcus alive. I'm guessing this has something to do with the redhead...with Terra."

"You're right," admitted Ray.

"Then she's on our side?" asked Lena. "She's the good guy?"

"I wish it was that simple," said Ray. "Terra and her people have an agenda, which is why I need Marcus's help."

The sound of the elevator stopping at their floor was barely audible in the pause between their words. Footsteps approached the door to the apartment. The door had been broken in when Marcus was rescued, leaving it compromised and visibly damaged. Would it still hold? Lena and Ray slipped behind the door to the bedroom and fell silent. With a resounding blow, the front door burst open. Then Samson was standing in the middle of the great room just a few feet away, looking all around the room. They held their breath as long as possible.

As soon as Lena exhaled, Samson whirled and headed straight for them. Ray gambled that Samson was looking for him and would think he was alone. In one motion, he shoved Lena away from the opening and leapt out at Samson. The SPUD had superhuman strength, but Ray was exceptionally strong for a human, having the advantage of Marcus's lifelong training and of the Conversion. He was also considerably taller than Samson.

The struggle went on for minutes before Samson prevailed. He dragged Ray to the edge of the room and pulled him roughly to his feet by his armpits, preparing to throw him over the edge. Ray got a second wind and clamped his huge hands onto Samson's shoulders. The two teetered on the edge of the precipice, locked in combat. Ray's back faced Lena, his body obscuring Samson's face.

Lena pulled the round stone from one pocket and the slingshot from another, placed the stone in the webbing, took aim, and prayed for an opening.

48

BY THE TIME the hovercraft pulled up to the pier, Lena was long gone. The SPUD at the helm stepped out of the boat first, followed by Marcus, Terra, and two other members of Terra's team. They'd traced Lena's trajectory when she was captured before she went dark and had concluded that she was being held somewhere along that section of the waterfront.

Marcus had insisted on going along on the search. Terra objected at first, but he argued that his presence could be valuable if Lena activated her MELD and tried to contact him.

It didn't take long for them to locate the tunnel. Once inside the massive gate, they saw footprints tracking in both directions across the muddy ground. The SPUD was the first to spot her clone lying inert in the shadows. She kneeled down beside her, touched her hand to her twin's right cheek in an apparent gesture of tenderness, then ripped her face off and stomped on her head. Marcus was horrified to see such an act of naked aggression perpetrated by a SPUD no matter whose side she was on.

There was no sign of Lena or of her other captors. If they took her with them, who was responsible for disabling the SPUD? So Lena may have escaped, but she would still be in danger from The Tribe of 23 unless they got to her first. Marcus drew hope from the possibility that she'd managed to flee.

A more immediate problem faced them. Voices were coming from just beyond the gate. Lena's other three captors had returned for her. Marcus and his companions were trapped like ducks in an ancient shooting gallery. They all hit the ground, rolled to the edges of the tunnel and waited.

The huge gate creaked open. The three men were silhouetted against the sky. Terra's team now had the advantage of darkness and surprise. The half-crazed SPUD moved first, rushing the intruders at full speed, her arms spread like wings. She took out two of them before the third, a man with reddish brown hair and beard, fired his weapon at point blank range and finished the job they'd started back at the apartment. He was able to flee before Terra's team was upon him, and he was lost among the buildings that had earlier concealed Lena.

Terra and her team fanned out in pursuit of Hector Lasko. Marcus took the opportunity to disappear and was long gone before Terra returned.

Once clear of the waterfront, Marcus flagged down a taxi and headed for Sacramento and Powell on the outside chance that Lena had had the same idea. He wanted to go dark, but that would have prevented Lena from being able to contact him, so he counted on his head start to buy him time.

When Marcus arrived at his building, he had the driver stop halfway down the block on the side where the window of the apartment had been blown out. They got there just in time to see two figures teetering on the edge of the opening. They were too far away to identify either. Marcus could only see that one of them was bald and very tall and the other had a shock of ash blonde hair.

Marcus watched one body fall from the window, arms and legs askew. Then a drone hovering below the window rose in place, scooped the falling body from the air, and sped away.

Another car, a sleek silver limo, drove up the street, pulled up in front of the entrance, and waited. Marcus decided to bide his time before risking entering the building. A few minutes later, Lena and Ray, his hood covering his face, emerged, headed straight for the limo, and got in. The car pulled away and Marcus followed until it stopped in front of the Four Seasons Hotel. Lena and Ray got out, accompanied by a man who looked like a Secret Service agent. As Ray turned, Marcus caught enough of a glimpse of his face to confirm his suspicion before they disappeared inside.

Marcus emerged from the car and ran into the lobby just in time to see Ray and Lena board an elevator. His movement toward the bank of elevators stopped abruptly when he spotted a tall, regal looking woman at the lobby bar with her back toward him, her head wrapped in a colorful scarf. Someone got up from the seat next to her. Instinctively, he sprang to fill it.

She turned to look at the man sitting next to her and their eyes met. He drew in a breath, but held it without uttering her name.

"Hello, Marcus," said Corinne. "It seems we have a lot to talk about."

49

IT DIDN'T TAKE LONG for Corinne to figure out that Ray was headed to San Francisco and that it was probably no accident that he'd lived there before the switch of identity that landed Marcus in Rays' body and his life. Perhaps Ray had a reason to make contact with Marcus or perhaps he was hoping to have a chance to see Lena. After all, Marcus had crossed the continent presumably to see her and Natasha, even if briefly and from a distance, which was lucky for her since she'd otherwise be dead.

Corinne had scanned the UDB for events in San Francisco and had found the Artificial Cognition Conference that was scheduled to take place at the Four Seasons Hotel. It was the best fit with Marcus's, and now Ray's adopted area of expertise. She guessed that Ray would be speaking at the conference as cover for his trip west. She was in a vacuum tube pod heading west just a few hours behind him.

She wasn't sure what she'd do when she got there. Going to Raymond Mettler's home might be risky, particularly if his home was under surveillance. If she could find Ray, on the other hand, then he might lead her to Marcus. So her first stop would be the Four Seasons. She'd have to disappear into the crowd, not an easy task for a tall, striking, hairless woman.

When Corinne arrived at the hotel, she identified herself to the desk clerk as Marcus Takana's wife and begged his discretion so that she could surprise her husband, since she'd decided at the last minute to attend his lecture. She was informed that he'd checked in, but had left the hotel an hour ago and had not yet returned. She bought a headscarf in the gift shop, wrapped it artfully around her head, and parked herself in the lobby bar, from which she could see the hotel entrance.

When Ray and Lena entered the lobby, Corinne wasn't prepared to see them together and resisted the urge to confront him in front of his wife. She watched them disappear behind the elevator doors.

Then suddenly a man claimed the seat beside her with a sense of urgency. At first glance, he was a stranger, but as she looked into his eyes, she saw his flash of recognition and realized why he was there. This was the moment of truth.

"So you know," said Marcus after Corinne called him by name. "When did he tell you?"

"He didn't," said Corinne. "I figured it out for myself after the fire. You were there, weren't you?" she said.

"Yes, I was there."

"I felt your touch," she said, "and imagined you kissed me." She shook her head. "Except I didn't imagine it, did I?"

"No, you didn't imagine it."

"I was so angry when I realized that you'd let a stranger take over your life. I have no idea how or why you let that happen. And I was angry that you'd had the Conversion after knowing how I felt about it." Her brow was furrowed, her eyes intense, and her lips pressed tightly together.

"That happened long ago, before we ever met," said Marcus. "And the contract between me and Mettler was also concluded long before I met you. Once it was done, there was no turning back."

"And the redhead...Terra...was behind it all?"

"Yes, Terra arranged the contract with each of us and swore us to secrecy. If we told anyone, their lives would be in jeopardy. And until recently, neither of us knew who was on the other side of the contract."

"How could you ever have agreed to such a ludicrous scheme?"

"I grew up poor," he began, "and uneducated. I began my adult life with the deck stacked against me...until she showed up."

"The redhead...Terra."

"Yes, Terra. She came out of the blue one day while I was running on the Endless Park. She offered me wealth beyond my dreams in exchange for agreeing that another man's consciousness would take over my body when his died."

"How could any amount of money be worth giving up your life?"

"You have to understand. I had nothing. I was all alone with nothing to lose. You weren't a part of my life at that point. And if I hadn't taken the deal, we'd probably never have met."

"So you sold your future," said Corinne.

"In exchange for a chance to have a life that was worth something, that was more than just an existence. It was a fresh start and I was determined to make the most of it. I traded duration for quality. And look what I...we accomplished. We saved the world from the brink of disaster," said Marcus. "And the exchange wasn't supposed to happen for decades...not until Ray died."

"And the Conversion?"

"...was another condition. What Mettler wanted was immortality. Not only did he want to escape his own death, but he wanted the body he wound up with to live forever. That meant undergoing the Conversion. That's why I tried so hard to convince you to have it. I didn't want to stay young while you grew old."

"But what good would that have done if you were going to leave me, anyway?"

"That part seemed so far off that it didn't seem real...until last spring." His voice broke and he looked away.

"When you exchanged identities for the first time." She'd already figured that out, too. "It was the day of your speech, the one with the President. Wasn't it?"

"That's right. And I was sure my life was over," said Marcus, turning toward her again. "How did you know?"

"Because something was different about you that night. Everything, actually." She hesitated for what seemed to Marcus like an eternity. "We made love, Marcus. It was different. It felt different."

"Because it wasn't me." His voice cracked in anguish. He looked away again.

"No, it wasn't you," she answered, touching his hand. "The next morning I saw you looking in the mirror. You were acting so strangely. I knew something was terribly wrong, but had no idea what was going on at the time, but looking back..." She was angry enough now to enjoy the pain that she was causing him.

"And now he's sharing my bed again, perhaps for all eternity." She couldn't resist twisting the knife, but instantly regretted it.

Marcus's face was twisted in agony. His head was jerking repeatedly, the intensity of his emotions activating Ray's tics. Corinne reached over and placed her hand over his, rubbing it gently. His face relaxed and his head became still.

"So now what do we do?" she asked. "Is there any way to put things back the way they were?"

"Probably not," said Marcus. "Terra said she doesn't know how to reverse the exchange and that even if she tried, our identities could be severely degraded. We might both wind up dead."

Corinne sat in silence for several minutes, trying to make sense of what she was hearing.

"I've been furious since I figured it out," she said at last, "but you risked your life to save mine. Whatever drew you into this mess I'm ready to forgive. I want you back. And the man I fell in love with isn't in the body you left behind. He's right here beside me. Can't you just come home with me?"

"I wish I could," said Marcus, "but Terra's organization has a very long reach and won't permit it. They're determined to keep things as they are. I'm afraid if I defied them, we'd all be killed, even Natasha. And there's something else you need to know that might change your mind."

"What else could possibly make a difference now?"

"Ray's brain...my brain now is riddled with aneurysms," said Marcus. "I've already had a stroke and am likely to have others. One of them is likely to kill me. I'm afraid my days are numbered. You might be better off living out your life with him."

Tears streamed down Corinne's cheeks. Any words she could find were engulfed in sobs. She threw her arms around him and buried her head in his neck.

When the fount of Corinne's tears was finally exhausted and they were facing each other again, Marcus spoke first.

"Ray and Lena are both here at the hotel. I followed them here. There was some sort of scuffle at their home. The window had been broken and I watched Ray and another man struggling at the brink. Then the other man fell over the precipice and was rescued by a drone."

"Did you see who he was?" asked Corinne.

"I think he was the same man who firebombed our house. He's a SPUD. Whoever picked Ray up from their home must have brought Lena along for her safety. It would have been too dangerous to stay where they lived."

"I saw them come in together," said Corinne, "but I doubt they're staying in the same room. That could blow Ray's identity. But I did find out Ray's room number."

"Does Ray know you're here?"

"No. And he doesn't know that I figured out who he is."

"Then it's time for Ray and I to have a face to face talk," said Marcus. "And I imagine you and Lena also have a lot to talk about."

Corinne showed the desk clerk an image of Lena Holbrook and asked for her room number. She guessed that she was registered under an assumed name and told him that it was urgent that she talk with her. Corinne's face was an open book and the clerk readily complied.

When she knocked on Lena's door, her face displayed inside. Lena opened the door and let her in.

"Corinne," said Lena. "He didn't tell me you were with him."

"He doesn't know I'm here," said Corinne. "I came by myself." She paused to consider how to tell Lena what she knew.

"This is a hell of a mess," Lena jumped in first. "What I have to tell you is just too crazy to imagine."

"Then you know, too," said Corinne, sighing with relief, "about the exchange."

Lena drew in a deep breath and exhaled slowly through pursed lips. Her breath whistled for a moment toward the end.

"I'm sorry, Corinne," she said at last. "You got the short end of this exchange. Ray's a real piece of work."

"Actually," said Corinne, "he's been good to me and sweet with Natasha. He seems to genuinely care about her, not just playing a part."

"Your husband Marcus is an extraordinary man," said Lena, the shock of Corinne's words finally fading from her face, "kind and...loving. You must miss him terribly."

"I do," Corinne said, then stopped and stared at Lena, whose face had been flushed with surprise moments before but still had a rosy hue. Tears came to her eyes. She'd had enough surprises and didn't want to believe what she now intuitively knew.

"You're pregnant."

"Yes."

"And whose…?" Corinne held her breath.

"It's complicated," said Lena. "I don't understand it either."

Before she was aware of what she was doing, Corinne's arms were around Lena in a tender embrace. Aside from their shared victimhood, she felt profoundly connected with this woman by the men whose love they shared. Lena returned her embrace with a comforting hug, and just for this moment Corinne felt safe.

50

WHEN MARCUS ARRIVED at Ray's room on the top floor of the hotel, the burly guard by the door held him back. Marcus would have been an easy match for him in his own body, but in Ray's he was overpowered. When he backed off, the door cracked open.

"Let him in," said Ray from within. "I know him."

The sound of Ray's words in his own voice was surreal to Marcus. Even more surreal was the vision of the body standing before him that he'd only previously seen in mirrors.

The guard stood aside and Marcus entered the room. Ray shut the door behind him.

"I'm glad to see you," said Ray. "We need to talk."

"How can you be glad to see me after what you did to me?" said Marcus. "If I were in your shoes, I'd be terrified."

"I'm really sorry for what I did, Marcus. I understand now how selfish it was and how destructive to all our lives and wish I could undo it," said Ray. "But now we have to set our differences aside. We have a common enemy and need to join forces if we're going to prevent a disaster."

"Common enemy...You mean the Tribe of 23?"

"Them, too," said Ray, "but much more crucial is Ganymede."

"Ganymede? Who the hell are they?"

"Terra's organization. The people who created the body hopping technology and put us both in this fix. Their agenda is ambitious, and the future of the Commonwealth may be in our hands."

"Their agenda?" asked Marcus.

"...is to control the Commonwealth and the world," said Ray. "They want me to run for President, to become the President, so that they can control me with threats against our families, against Corinne and Natasha and Lena, and with the knowledge of my real identity. Part of my ruse for coming here was that I promised to announce my candidacy during my speech."

Marcus felt like the wind had been knocked out of him.

"Then what can we do?"

"I don't really know," said Ray. "Ganymede was once a clandestine arm of the government, all crack operatives whose identities were unknown even to the President. Since they've gone rogue, they've gone even further underground. I thought perhaps you'd know someone in the government we could trust to help without it getting back to them."

"Only the President," said Marcus, "and that would mean exposing our situation, which could be risky not only for us but for him. Besides, from what we know of their plan, he may already be in their grasp."

"Then there's only one other thing we can do," said Ray. "I'll do everything in my power to lose the election, but if I win, you'll have to find a way to assassinate me."

"Assassinate you?" Marcus stared at him wide-eyed. "I thought you were planning to live forever. You were even willing to take my life to make that happen."

"If I had it to do over again, I never would have taken Terra's offer. I had no idea of the consequences. I only know now that I'd rather die than betray my country."

Marcus tried to imagine what it would feel like to kill the man inhabiting his body. It would be like destroying himself. And it would end forever the possibility of ever becoming himself again. But it probably wouldn't matter, since he'd likely be killed on the spot by the Secret Service. Then Corinne and Lena would both become widows.

"We still have to deal with the man who attacked you," said Marcus. "I saw you struggling on the ledge of the apartment."

"He fell twenty stories," said Ray. "Nobody could survive that, not even a SPUD."

"I saw a drone rescue him from the fall. He's very much alive. And I'm pretty sure he was the same man who firebombed the house. He's a SPUD named Samson and he's fast as hell."

"What can we do?" asked Ray.

"Terra's seen him, so I expect she'll be on the watch for him during your talk. But I saw another man at the Church that day who was working with him. Terra and I saw him this morning, but he got away. His face was in shadows this time, so I may be the only one who can spot him in a crowd."

"Then you'll be at my talk in the morning?"

"I guess so," said Marcus. "I never imagined that I'd someday have your back."

"Lena's here in the hotel," said Ray. "Knowing her, she wouldn't miss an event like this. It's the kind of drama she loves to write about."

"Corinne's here, too," Marcus said. "I left her just before coming to see you."

"That's impossible. I left her behind with Natasha. How did she get here?"

"She came on her own," said Marcus, "to see me. She knows, Ray. She figured it out and she's been beside herself with rage and grief."

"So now they both know," said Ray. "How are we ever going to protect them from Ganymede?"

"Maybe they'll figure out how to protect themselves, as bright as they both are. If they put their heads together, they'll be a force to be reckoned with. It's no longer just up to us."

51

MARCUS TAKANA was designated the keynote speaker at the Artificial Cognition Conference at ten o'clock the next morning. His speech was entitled "How Close to Human? Sharing Our Consciousness and Our Culture." Ray had already spent enough time as Marcus with Corinne for her passion to seep into his soul.

No wonder the security was so tight around the hotel. The talk would be like a red flag to Hector Lasko and The Tribe of 23. And none of the attendees had any idea that they would be listening to an imposter or that the imposter was about to announce his candidacy for President of the Commonwealth.

As the crowd filled the veranda ballroom where Ray was to speak, Marcus melted into the crowd. He spotted Terra and her colleague Kirti, who'd assisted in the search for Lena, scanning the room and stayed out of their line of sight. The noise and bustle of the room made it easy for him to evade their notice. He spotted Lena, as expected, toward the back of the crowd in one corner of the room. In the opposite corner, he caught a glimpse of the colorful head scarf that Corinne had worn the night before.

Marcus's heart sank. He'd hoped that Corinne would have stayed out of harm's way, but the subject of Ray's talk was just too tantalizing for her to pass up. Marcus also knew that she'd been itching to confront Ray before he had another chance to slip away.

When the moderator strode to the front of the stage and raised her arms in the air to get the crowd's attention, the din gradually subsided and the sea of heads settled as the audience took their seats. Terra and Kirti, now exposed, stood toward the rear of the room near the exits while the Secret Service agent stood guard in the wings to the left of the stage. Once the room was quiet, the moderator began to speak.

"Welcome to the 15th Annual Artificial Cognition Conference," she began. "Our first speaker, Gwyneth Isaacs, will discuss advances in the life extension sciences. Please give a warm welcome to Dr. Isaacs."

The moderator backed away from the center of the stage and a diminutive woman entered from the left and took possession of the crowd's attention. When she began to speak, a resonant and commanding voice belied her small stature and wispy figure.

"We have spent the first half of this century," she began, "looking for ways to arrest the aging process and to forestall the eventuality of death." The audience was hushed, captivated by her presence.

"Despite all of our accumulated knowledge about cellular processes and genetics," she continued, "the result of our quest has been mixed." She gestured to the space to her right. A huge three-dimensional model of a chromosome appeared in the space, rotating slowly on its axis, dwarfing the speaker in its shadow. Dr. Isaacs pointed her finger at one end of the structure and a tiny segment lit up at its tail.

"Most of our attention has gone to this structure, the telomere, which we've long believed holds the key to cellular aging." She shook her head slowly. "But the little rascal's turned out to be a terrible tease." She paused while laughter rumbled through the audience.

"Our efforts to lengthen it in order to reverse cellular aging have inevitably led to the proliferation of cancerous growths and extended the life and resistance of pathogenic organisms." She waved her right hand and the image of the giant chromosome dissolved. "Even worse," she continued, "we've succeeded in finding cures for cancer, but they've all inevitably led to accelerated aging. Anything we do to address either process always seems to aggravate the other." She took a few paces back and forth across the stage.

"The one exception has been the Ambrosia Conversion. If we harvest cells from young enough subjects before the aging process has advanced in earnest, we can preserve the length of the telomeres, arrest the aging of the cells, and recolonize the body with these immortalized stem cells without the unintended consequences that occur once the aging process has already set in. For most of us, of course, it's already too late." The crowd murmured in agreement.

"The Conversion has been a boon only for those fortunate enough to be both young and wealthy. It has created a new divide in our society between those with the means to become immortal and a vast underclass of the mortal. While there are those among us who would ban it entirely in the interest of fairness, finding ways to extend it to the masses would be a far better solution."

Dr. Isaacs went on to describe the advances that would make the Conversion affordable enough to offer it to whole generations. Overcoming the age limits that defined the candidates for the process, however, would remain elusive, at least for a while. When she was finished and the applause subsided, the moderator again took the stage.

"This morning I am delighted to welcome a very special keynote speaker, a renowned inventor, icon of the environment, honored public servant, and advocate for the rights of all sentient beings to share equally as citizens of our world community. Please welcome Minister of Discovery Marcus Takana."

Ray strode to the middle of the stage amidst thundering applause. As the sound built to a crescendo, he raised his arms above his head palms forward and slowly lowered them. The applause faded away. As eager and adoring as was this audience, nobody was focused more intently on Ray than Marcus. His reputation was now in the hands of the man who'd stolen his identity. And he was astounded by the presence of this man, who had slipped into his skin and channeled his temperament and charisma.

"Dr. Isaacs has just told us about advances in the science of life extension that will help us to correct a prominent injustice in our society so that all young adults will have an equal chance for a long life," Ray began. "This morning I would like to address another injustice, the inequality between two groups of sentient beings, those of us who are carbon based and those who are silicon-based." Marcus heard the muffled sound of the bell tower next door beginning to chime the hour.

"It's time we recognized that our silicon-based brethren are imbued with life and deserve to share in all the benefits of our culture."

The sound of the bells suddenly grew louder. Marcus turned toward the sound and was the first to spot Samson entering one of the rear doors, his weapon at his side. The agent on the stage saw him next and raised his weapon, but Samson fired first and the agent fell. Then Terra was flying at lightning speed around the perimeter of the room toward Samson, distracting him long enough for Ray to hit the deck before Samson could get off another shot in his direction.

Samson fired at Terra as she drew her weapon and the shot caught her in the midsection, barely slowing her pursuit. Samson ducked through the door. The chase continued across the lobby and out onto a balcony where Terra caught up with him and they grappled hand to hand. Marcus was amazed at how strong she was, even wounded, as she held her ground in her battle with the superhuman SPUD. Then in a single, stunning movement, she ducked, grabbed him by the feet, and flipped him over the railing. Marcus heard the impact of the massive body crashing head first to the ground below.

Then from amidst the chaos, Hector Lasko emerged, racing toward the balcony.

"Terra!" Marcus shouted, but it was too late. Hector's weapon bore a hole through the back of her head and her body collapsed. Bright red blood spurted briefly from the wound, then pooled around her lifeless form. Marcus was as astonished to see the blood as he was stunned at Terra's demise. With her ageless strength and speed, he'd been sure that she was a SPUD. It now dawned on him that her powers had come from the Conversion. And it was now abundantly clear that it didn't immunize anyone against death.

Hector turned and darted back through the balcony doors into the ballroom, the crowd scattering before him. As the crowd dispersed, Marcus watched in horror as Corinne was exposed directly in Hector's path.

Kirti seemed to come out of nowhere as she bore down on Hector, but in a flash, Corinne was in his grasp, one arm around her neck and his weapon pressed firmly into her back. Kirti stopped in her tracks. Hector fired, boring a hole in her right thigh and she was down, her weapon hitting the ground and sliding out of reach.

Marcus lunged for Kirti's weapon. Hector swung his weapon toward Marcus and fired, which provided enough of a distraction for Corinne to wriggle free. Marcus felt a searing pain in his right arm where the laser bored a clean hole through his bicep. Ray bolted to sweep Corinne to safety while Hector descended upon a weakened Marcus to claim a new hostage.

52

RAY WATCHED as Hector backed toward the elevator using Marcus as a shield and resisted the temptation to charge. He couldn't risk having Marcus die in front of Corinne. Neither of them deserved that fate.

The elevator door closed behind Hector and Marcus. Ray swept the weapon from where Marcus had dropped it and sprang for the elevator bank. He dove into the first available capsule and was on the ground floor in seconds just as Hector and Marcus disappeared outside. He emerged from the lobby just in time to see the hovercar lift off and speed away.

Ray commandeered the nearest vehicle and joined pursuit. Hector's vehicle was still visible when they turned onto Market Street. As Ray began to close in, Hector left Market and wound among the streets of the city toward Nob Hill trying to lose him. With each turn Ray was just in time to see Hector and Marcus disappear around the next corner. Ray turned right from California onto Hyde and was hot on Hector's tail as he crested Russian Hill when Hector suddenly veered right.

Ray missed the turn and stopped short, causing the hovercar to hit the ground hard. He jumped out and peered over the vista toward the bay just in time to see Marcus's car miss a hairpin turn on the brick lined road, bounce off a brick wall, roll completely over and come to rest against one of the concrete barriers that lined the street. He bounded for the wreckage. By the time he reached it, he could see that the driver was dead.

Marcus was slumped in the passenger's seat wrapped in the mangled carbon fiber frame, barely conscious and unable to move. The door was ajar. Blood was running freely from a gash on his forehead and his breathing was labored. Marcus's right arm was twisted at an angle that left no doubt that it was broken, probably in more than one place. Ray put a finger on Marcus's carotid pulse, which was rapid, thready, and irregular. He struggled to free the body from the car, but it wouldn't budge. The frame of the car embraced Marcus's body snugly and would not give it up.

Ray looked down upon his former body and into the clouded eyes as the life within it ebbed. When a tear trickled from one of the dying eyes, he felt another stream down his own cheek.

He imagined Corinne's grief at losing her husband and Natasha's at losing her father. He could return to their home and continue the charade for Natasha's sake, but she'd eventually figure out that something essential had changed about her father and he couldn't bear to witness her pain and betrayal when she figured it out.

Then Marcus gasped and after a moment of darkness, Ray felt excruciating pain throughout his body and was gazing upward through a fog. He was completely paralyzed and struggling for breath. He fought to remain conscious.

*****

Marcus took a deep breath and felt the power and vitality of his own body. There was no longer any pain and the relief was exhilarating. He looked down upon Ray and into his eyes as the life within him ebbed. Ray's eyes closed, his breaths coming in clusters of ascending and descending depth, his face still twisted in agony. Then his breathing became agonal, coming in short, distantly spaced gasps.

Marcus felt tears streaming past the corners of his mouth and watched them drip onto Ray's face. Then suddenly Ray's eyes opened, looking straight into Marcus's eyes. His face relaxed into a peaceful smile and Marcus imagined just for a flash that he winked. Then he drew a last, long breath of this world's air and died.

Marcus looked down upon Ray's lifeless body, both relieved and bewildered to be alive. He drew a breath that seemed to flow throughout his body and exhaled all the way from the bottoms of his feet. It was over. The system that had linked their lives together from the beginning of the contract had worked flawlessly, just as intended, except the death of Ray's body had triggered the switch that put them back where they both belonged. He would get to live out his life.

Epilogue

CORINNE AND LENA were huddled together in the hotel lobby when Marcus returned. Corinne leaped to her feet when she saw him.

"What happened?" asked Corinne. "Where is he? Is he...?" She lingered on the last word, unable to say it.

"Ray's dead," said Marcus. "There was a crash. He didn't make it."

"Ray?" said Corinne, her eyes narrowing, mystified. "But you're..."

"Marcus, Corinne. I'm Marcus."

"But...how?"

"It all worked in the end just as it was supposed to," said Marcus. "When his body died, it triggered the switch and put us back in our own bodies. It's over, Corinne. I'm free."

"You get to live out your life," Corinne said slowly, pondering the implications, "without me."

"What do you mean?" he asked in alarm. "Are you going to leave me?"

"Not right now, Marcus," she replied, "but I'm growing older and you're not. Our lives are going to be different. And even if we're together until the end, I'm going to die."

"I've thought about that," Marcus said, looking again straight into her eyes. "I love you more than life itself. I want to grow old with you. I will grow old with you."

"How?"

"I'm going to have the Conversion reversed. Now that the contract is over, I'm free to do so. And I'll do it gladly. I was never comfortable with it knowing how you felt about it. Now we can live out our lives together...on the same terms...with no more secrets until death do we part."

*****

Lena Holbrook drove up to the Takana house, now newly rebuilt, for the second time in her life. She'd never published her story from her first interview with Marcus and Corinne. Ray was now dead nearly a year and she decided it was time to finish what she started. Now there was another chapter to the story, one of which she and Ray were a part. She wondered if she'd be able to write it.

This time, she wasn't alone. Cradled in her arms as she walked to the front door was a carefully swaddled four-month-old infant.

Corinne came to the door and greeted her with a hug. They'd bonded at the time of her first visit and again at the hotel in San Francisco. Their bond was now complexly nuanced. Corinne gazed at the child's face. Crimson curls peeked from the edges of the swaddling blanket.

"A girl," Corinne observed. "She's adorable."

"Thank you," said Lena. "She's brought sunshine back into my life."

Marcus walked up from behind Corinne. "I'm sorry for your loss," he began. Then his eyes settled first on the child, then on Lena's eyes. "She looks a lot like you...and like Ray," he said. "What's her name?"

"You'll probably laugh," Lena said. "I named her Terra."

"How did you ever wind up with Terra?" asked Corinne.

"I always thought it was a pretty name," said Lena. "It means 'earth,' you know. I want my daughter to always feel firmly grounded." She paused before going on. "And for all the damage that Terra may have done, she gave her life protecting us in the end. My daughter might never have been conceived if not for her." She gave Marcus and Corinne time to process her last statement.

"It's a good name," said Corinne, brushing back one of the child's red curls. "It fits her well."

Lena hadn't seen Marcus since the day Ray was killed. She knew only that Marcus was by his side when he died. One question still burned within her.

"Did he suffer?" she asked.

"He did, briefly," said Marcus, "but I believe he was at peace when he died."

Thank you for that," said Lena. "It was probably the only peace he ever knew."

Lena wondered at the complexity of the man with whom she'd shared her life, but hardly knew. The Takana story was now his story, too, and hers. Its arc was more sweeping and complete than the nascent version she'd buried years ago. And, Lena liked to think, telling a person's story imbued them with just a touch of immortality. She prayed that it was all Ray would ever need.

About the Author

Rick Moskovitz is a Harvard educated psychiatrist who taught psychotherapy and spent nearly four decades listening to his patients tell their stories. After leaving practice, he in turn became a storyteller, writing science fiction that explores the psychological consequences of living in a world of expanding possibilities, including even the prospect of evading death. His characters deal with enduring moral and emotional struggles against a backdrop of a near future world that is still dealing with environmental crises as it navigates the intersection of human and artificial intelligence.

CPSIA information can be obtained
at www.ICGtesting.com
Printed in the USA
LVHW010336120620
657890LV00019B/2307

9 781734 178906